House of the Spirit Levels

Nick
Revell

House of the Spirit Levels

First published in 1998
by REVIEW

An imprint of Headline Book Publishing

First published in paperback in 1999

A Headline Paperback

10 9 8 7 6 5 4 3 2 1

ISBN 0 7472 5973 9

Typeset by Palimpsest Book Production Limited,
Polmont, Stirlingshire

Printed and bound in Great Britain by
Clays Ltd, St Ives plc.

HEADLINE BOOK PUBLISHING
A division of Hodder Headline PLC
338 Euston Road
London NW1 3BH

For Muriel

ACKNOWLEDGEMENTS

Many thanks to Jonathan James Moore and Paul Schlesinger at BBC Radio Light Entertainment for their patience and support, and to all the cast and crew on the original radio serial for their excellence; also, in different ways, to Scappa, Carol, Vivienne, Tony (especially for methods of stopping nosebleeds!), Elinor, Huw, and the gang at the Eddie, especially Kevin and Nigel. Also to Laurie and Muriel once again. And, of course, to everyone at Hodder Headline for their backing and enthusiasm, and particularly my editor Doug Young, for risking it.

PART ONE

Mondongo

PROLOGUE

This afternoon, as the church bell tolled mournfully and the sun slithered wearily westwards over the volcano and into the distant ocean like an over-ripe tomato – an over-ripe tomato capable of movement that is – the Gringo was finally laid to rest beside his dear beloved; the curtain has been lowered on the final act of his strange and terrible tragedy, with all its bizarre and thrilling elements: men and women propelled helplessly by huge and awful emotions (love, hate, lust for vengeance, greed, jealousy, fear, carnal desire) – to commit awful crimes (murder, kidnapping, extortion, nuclear blackmail, fast-food); a tale of sadistic gangsters, self-destructive passionate obsession, ghosts, witchcraft, machine-gun-wielding silverback gorillas; bizarre romantic settings across three continents; sex, suspense, snake-juggling, hallucinogenic drugs, irresistibly sexually attractive *femmes fatales* and softly-spoken, self-effacing Latin American narrators (and much much more) all cramming the very first sentence to bursting point and threatening to collapse it under its own weight in a nakedly meretricious attempt to intrigue you enough to take the book to the till and buy it now.

Free!
New!
Improved!
But I digress.

It is strange to think that our siestas will never more be interrupted by the mad cacklings of Señor Tony, prancing and yodelling up there on the rim of the volcano, one hand clamped to his bottle of tequila, tempting the terrible gods Asdfghjkl and Qwertyuiop to rise from the abyss and consume him in the bottomless fire. Strange to think that, for the last time, his intoxicated rantings have chased the parrots out of the trees in an explosion of kaleidoscopic colour, as if the jungle were a student vomiting on the way home via the kebab shop after getting ratted on cheap vodka and paint. We shall miss him, for he was our friend. His story diverted us, and I like to think that by listening, we helped at least to ease the heavy pain that weighed so on his skinny little frame, even if ultimately we failed – oh so narrowly – to save him from a sad and premature demise. Yes, difficult though it is to believe, he is gone.

He was a man, and now he is dust. Or possibly a parakeet. But I run ahead.

I should perhaps explain that Tony gave us many versions of each episode of the story I now feel honour-bound to pass on, and I have made my own synthesis of all these different versions. Additionally (in my own humble way) I have attempted to piece together what must have happened in scenes where Tony himself was not present and to reconstruct dialogue by trusting in the power of my imagination. (In these latter endeavours, I must give thanks and acknowledgement to the help and expertise I received from a retired English police inspector from the West Midlands Serious Crime Squad who settled nearby a few years ago and modestly does not wish to be named.)

My only guiding rule in this endeavour is to tell the tale as simply as possible: to be succinct.

Direct, simple, laconic, concise, pithy, sparing of words, to the point, condensed, compendious, irreducible, compact, nay curt or brusque, lapidary, not beat about the bush – in a word, to be brief: or perhaps more precisely not to use many words where one would do, and at all times avoid overblown stylistic flourishes.

As the solemn funereal obsequies commenced today at the stroke of noon, a peculiar stillness seemed to descend upon us all and everything around us; it was as if Nature herself wished to mark with silence Her own distress at the unhappy tale which had just reached its climax in our sleepy little town. High, imperious storm clouds had been gathering since dawn, but only, it seemed, to force a dampening shroud of respect over the refulgence of the solar orb, and incredibly, throughout the entire duration of the service, not a single sound issued from the rain forest to challenge the authority of the passing-bell, aside from the occasional distant solemn growl of the jaguar, the periodic squeal of the peccary, the incessant howling of the monkeys, screeching of the parrots, and buzzing of the insects, all of whom carried on eating, shitting, fucking and killing each other as if nothing at all had happened. Then the storm clouds broke and it pissed down.

CHAPTER ONE

It was Father Gutierrez, of course, who had brought the Gringo to our little town of Mondongo. The commonly held view was that the priest hoped playing the Good Samaritan would perhaps to some degree compensate for the guilt he felt at his particular affliction. An affliction that most men would see as the richest of blessings. Father Gutierrez was utterly in love with his wife.

As if the state of matrimony were not itself enough of a burden for a devout cleric of the Catholic Church to bear, the wife of Father Ramón Gutierrez was not only a woman, but also a voodoo priestess. In our part of the world, the two religious traditions co-exist, battling it out for superiority like the plants in the rainforest who fight for the light and grow side by side in an uneasy symbiosis; for people hereabouts have always been shrewd enough to spread their bets across the whole gamut of whichever various all-powerful Gods might be active in the area at any given time. While the organised persecution systems of the early Christian missionaries dictated a certain ostensible deference to the cult of the Saviour of Souls and Advocate of Brotherly Love, they could never entirely eradicate the dark seclusion of the forest and the opportunity this provided for clandestine acknowledgement of the Old Gods, especially as the Old Gods tend to be a lot less heavy on fornication and the consumption of hallucinogenic drugs. Thus it was that Messalina de las Manitas de Oro could continue to celebrate rituals and rites that would not have seemed out of place in a Ken Russell movie while the Christian priest absolved her followers in the confessional next day.

Our priest is a long-suffering, broad-minded man, and realistic enough to know that while he could offer spiritual salvation and the promise of eternal bliss in the after-life, Messalina provided more attractive short-term benefits: love potions, good-luck charms, protective amulets, auguries, and a free chicken dinner – if eccentrically prepared – at most midnight rituals. The people bought her wares in the same way they bought a lottery ticket, knowing that the odds were against them, but hoping, nonetheless, that from time to time maybe their number would come up.

Thus, however much he might disapprove, Father Ramón Gutierrez decided that provided Messalina conducted herself with discretion, he was prepared to live and let live.

Father Gutierrez has always attended assiduously to his flock, from the most pious to those who have strayed furthest out along the precipice of damnation. Most of both groups spend a fair amount of their time in my humble cantina, especially whenever an attractive football match is being broadcast over the huge satellite TV screen in the main bar. Selflessly the priest will walk among the sinners on such occasions, greeting them by name, with a smile and a handshake, gently pointing out to them how long it has been since their last attendance at Mass and accepting for his troubles only one drink for every four or five he is offered. He has the common touch, mixing his pastoral agenda with shrewd and witty observations on the match in progress, and invariably has my customers in hysterics with his parodies of the stunted idiolect of the sports commentator, roaring with laughter at his satirical demolition of the ludicrous adverts for the various trappings of machismo – beer, cars, penis enlargers – which fill the commercial breaks, and most hilariously of all, has us falling about with his uncanny impersonations of lumbering, ungainly English central defenders – the cruel accuracy of his mockery greatly helped by his own huge, uncoordinated frame and the fact that one of his legs is considerably shorter than the other. Such was his concern for the spiritual salvation of my customers that he even altered the time of his morning service when English Premier League games started to be broadcast regularly. His friendliness was not an act, but merely reflected his genuine good nature. Indeed, the minor earth tremors that periodically ripple through our town are commonly ascribed to the long-buried nuns in the cemetery of the ruined convent of Our Lady of the Unspared Rod rolling in their graves in lamentation at the presence of a representative of the Church with neither a malicious bone in his body nor the slightest capacity for the gratuitous acts of petty spite and sadism which have made the Holy Catholic Church the great institution it is and to which they selflessly devoted their lives.

*   *   *

It was one fateful night, during a meaningless, nonde-script midweek goalless draw from the Bundesliga, that the destinies of Father Ramón Gutierrez and Messalina de las Manitas de Oro became inextricably and eternally entwined. Was it Destiny or Chance? Had the televised match that evening been more important than a mid-table end-of-season clash between Karslruhe and FC Bocum, my bar would have been busier, and had it been busier, the regular clientèle would have been less easy-going when the hen-night arrived, hell-bent on intoxication and noisy merriment with no regard for televised football whatsoever, and instead of tolerating the gibbering, whooping gaggle of drunken young women with a wry resignation, would have no doubt encouraged me to eject them. Instead the hen-night stayed and drank and gibbered and whooped with more and more abandon as the evening went on.

The bride-to-be was one of the village girls, for whom one of Messalina's love potions had been a complete success. Initially the potion had been intended for the apprentice mechanic at the village garage, which was a thriving little business. However, through a simple twist of fate, the doctored mug of coffee had been drunk, not by the young mechanic, but by the owner, a widower, repulsive to look at and so grossly overweight that he would have needed a heart the size of his backside to transport blood around his minuscule arteries with any chance of long-term survival. Naturally the bride-to-be was delighted at the mix-up, for in a few months' time she would be free again, mistress of the garage and able to afford any number of love potions. Messalina was very much the hen-night's guest of honour.

When Father Gutierrez arrived just before kick-off (his devotion to meticulous preparation of the Sunday sermon generally overriding his earthly desire to take in the full delicious anticipation created by the pre-match build-up) and headed towards his usual seat at the bar, he was spotted by Messalina. And not only spotted, but targeted. She stared at him across the room as if seeing him for the first time. Perhaps she was attracted by his clear blue eyes – unusual for the rich brown skin and Hispanic features of his face; eyes which suggested an ancestor of Northern European heritage, from the days when English buccaneers roamed the coast of the Spanish Main – and the firmness of will implied by their steady gaze. Perhaps she was attracted by his warm smile, which implied a generous spirit. Certainly she was attracted by how his cassock billowed below his waist, and implied he was hung like a donkey.

I remember seeing at that moment her eyes glinting with that look of mysterious devilment which I knew always heralded some memorable event, which, be it large or small, hilarious or horrifying, contained one constant – anecdotal potential. As he squeezed past her table, Messalina looked up through lowered eyebrows, and a smile sneaked across her beautiful face. The look of the wily cayman, lurking among the mangroves awaiting a careless wading bird or ingenuous monkey. She gently silenced the bride, who, for the hundredth time that evening was slurring out her gratitude and appreciation for the love potion, and proclaimed suddenly: 'That's nothing. Watch this.'

She rose and glid silently, like a bird of prey surfing the thermals, or a water-snake insinuating the reed beds, until she stood beside Father Ramón, who was now leaning at the bar between the Space Invaders machine and the shrine to the harvest God Tezcatlipoca. Messalina wiggled her chin in that disarming, coquettish way she has, reached out a dark bejewelled hand, and gently, but firmly, grabbed Father Gutierrez by . . . well, by the billow of his lower cassock, and squeezed. But not too hard. In fact, just hard enough, as the father later told me.

'Just hard enough for what?' I would reply. But he would never elaborate.

'Bless me father, for I have sinned,' said Melissa de las Manitas de Oro, calmly.

'So I see,' replied the priest, less calmly.

The whole bar was silent, watching.

'Would you mind letting go of my balls please, Messalina?'

Ramón perhaps had assumed Messalina would shrink away, humiliated by the public exposure of her boldness. He was wrong.

'I would mind very much so, father. I hate to see anything designed so well by Nature go to waste, its purpose unfulfilled.' Now she slowly did release her grip, but not her stare, while the whole bar stifled a collective guffaw, and the priest it was who blushed.

'Perhaps it is time for you to repent your sinful ways, my child,' he retorted, stiffly.

'Perhaps you are right, father. Well, see you at the wedding tomorrow.'

The priest cleared his throat, and turned away, attempting to catch my eye. This was not difficult, as my mission in life – to observe and interpret human nature – had compelled me to follow the whole incident from as close a vantage point as politeness would allow.

'Get me a whisky. A large one. And stop smirking.'

Messalina was still watching. As the priest knocked back the double shot, she grinned to herself and turned to bask in the cackling chuckles and mortified gasps of her half-cut companions.

The following day, after the wedding, Father Ramón Gutierrez took Messalina de las Manitas de Oro discreetly to one side and suggested that for the good of her mortal soul it was time she considered attending confession. She made a fair job of appearing surprised at the priest's suggestion, accepted immediately, and the priest was done for. Not usually a vain man, he made the mistake of assuming her ready compliance was a sign of contrition and a mark of the ultimate superiority of his creed over hers. Thus, he was off guard, and from the first moment she entered the confessional, his arse, as the Yankees put it, was hers.

Day upon day, hour upon hour, Messalina whispered salacious revelation upon salacious revelation into his ear, each one drifting through the grille wrapped in beguiling perfumes concocted from freshly-trapped civet cat, orchids and a hundred secret ingredients gathered from the plants of the ancient forest (although some maintain it was Allure, by Chanel). The lascivious odours permeated the hapless priest's raiment; he carried her scent home with him, and it worked its magic as he slept, his sacred garments drenched with olefactory stimulation just as his mind was overloaded with staggering visual images of her decidedly unchaste life. Messalina began to attend Mass once, twice or even three times a day, always sitting in the front pew, never releasing the priest from the predatory gaze of her knowing brown eyes. Still the priest did not guard against his vanity, for he prided himself in the knowledge it was virtually extinct, which of course made it all the more dangerous, and allowed him to believe Messalina's assiduous attendance indicated a genuine desire to repent. Perhaps he had not noticed the way he had taken to standing at least a pace back in the pulpit when delivering his sermon in order to accommodate the now virtually permanent billow in his lower cassock. Messalina had noticed, and bided her time.

Father Gutierrez was devastated when Messalina let slip in the confessional one day that she had never been baptised, let alone taken communion. This, of course, was calculated to make the priest take his next irreversible step; he offered to give her instruction prior to being received into the faith. She would arrive at his house every Wednesday promptly at six in the evening, and it became clear she was an avid pupil, for her sessions lasted longer and longer. A pupil eager to please her master, too, for each day she would flicker her eyelids demurely and present him with a basket of sumptuous apples. Who knows if Father Gutierrez felt the presence of the serpent stirring? If he did, he clearly didn't mind, or thought he could handle it.

Whatever the truth of the matter, Father Gutierrez was for his part, no less fervent, and began to miss even key Italian Serie A fixtures, so firm was his resolve to bring home this little lamb who had strayed so far and so wide – and so often; and indeed so athletically, and inventively – from the flock.

And of course, there was now no grille between them.

Marta, the father's housekeeper, saw where his relationship with Messalina was heading long before he did, and was not impressed. Although whether her objections were strictly on moral grounds, or whether she sensed with distaste the possibility of two people falling in love and finding some kind of happiness, is debatable. A portly woman of an uncertain age, she had two facial expressions. Disapproving and disgusted. However, the surface belied the reality, for underneath she had but one mood, and it was neither disgust nor disapproval. It was grudging malicious resentment for all creatures that walked the earth, swam in the waters or flew in the firmament. For instance, for most of us, the occasional backpackers who find their way to Mondongo are always welcome, because they see the wondrous bounties of Nature that surround us day in day out in a different light, making us look at what we consider commonplace and mundane with fresh eyes, and reminding us that although we may not be rich, we possess beauty in abundance, and this makes us very happy. (That, and knowing that judging by the ostentatious brand names plastered all over the backpackers' equipment, we can hike all prices astronomically without them batting an eye.)

Marta the housekeeper, should she overhear them gasp in astonishment at the polychrome magnificence of the Resplendent Quetzal, or of the Slaty Tailed Trogon, would merely mutter about the vanity implicit in such colourful birds, how once one crapped on her washing, and how she would be much happier without gawping groups of

Nature-loving gringo tourists getting in her way while she's shopping.

'Father, I cannot help noticing that Messalina has been spending a lot of time in your confessional recently.'

'She has a lot to confess, Marta.'

'I don't doubt it. She is a witch, father.'

'She is a sinner seeking redemption.'

'Yes, and in the old days she would have had a fast-track to redemption. Involving two dozen bundles of brushwood and a stake.'

'That was in the old days.'

Marta scowled, and turned on her heel.

Finally, at around nine o'clock one humid night on the brink of the rainy season, the whole town heard from behind the wooden shutters of the priest's study windows, his ecstatic declamation of triumph:

'Jesus Christ! Oh God! Oh Christ Almighty!!!' he howled at the top of his voice.

'Yes! Yes! Yes!!!' concurred the voodoo priestess in a shrill soprano; at that instant the long-awaited rains came with a crack of thunder and sheet of lightning that dispelled the overwhelming electricity in the air, and it became clear that, her conversion complete, Messalina had been received into the bosom of the Church. Or something.

The next morning, Marta packed her bags, left a stern note saying she could not carry out her duties for one who had strayed from righteousness, and departed for the city to work for the chaplain to the Internal Security Police. (Our country is blessed with a leader who is a noble and tireless defender of human rights and a relentless crusader against Communism. He has the official commendations of several United States Presidents on the matter, and even in these post-*Glasnost* days, he and his National Security Police can sniff out the seedlings of potential socialist tyranny in the most apparently innocuous places – workers striking ostensibly for a living wage, students demonstrating, journalists reporting, lawyers arguing – and, luckily for us, just as quickly snuff it out. We are not as well protected up here in the remote highlands; there is a Chinese saying: The Mountains Are High, and the Emperor Is Far Away. We are pretty much left to fend for ourselves. Surprisingly, we do quite well most of the time.)

From this point on, Messalina and Ramón were inseparable. Naturally, Father Gutierrez was somewhat disturbed by the moral implications of his eccentric behaviour, but Messalina took pity on him and tried to draw the pangs of his guilt. As he confided to me one afternoon, while the rest of the town enjoyed the siesta, every time she took him to bed, she made him forget he was a priest at all, and when the knowledge came flooding back over him afterwards, she would rationalise away his self-recrimination by pointing out that we all have our crosses to bear, and that as far as crosses go, passionate, unbridled unquenchable passion for another human being wasn't a bad one.

He would reply that he was a priest and had taken a vow of chastity.

'Don't split hairs,' she would counter.

· * * *

A week before their wedding, he decided he would have to leave the priesthood. Messalina was horrified.

'It would take all the fun out of it.'

'Are you marrying the man or the uniform?'

'A bit of both, I suppose.'

'You mean you don't love me for myself?'

'Of course I do. But the gear does add a bit of spice, be honest. I mean, you wouldn't get half the thrill either if I stopped being a pagan worshipper of false idols.'

'Aha! So you admit they're false idols!'

'Cheap shot, Ramón. I was simply trying to see things from your point of view.'

'Well, actually I was kind of wondering if you might think of at least toning down the Black Magic.'

'"Black Magic." Thanks for the reciprocated empathy. The phrase is Natural Magic: how many times do I have to tell you? Besides, don't forget we get a good discount on chickens, buying in bulk.'

'The other thing that's bothering me . . . what will the neighbours say?'

'At least if you stay in the church we've *got* neighbours. Where would we live if you had to give up the presbytery house?'

This silenced Gutierrez for a moment. Setting aside the sins of pride and covetousness, he contemplated the prospect of vacating the adobe presbytery with great trepidation. It was the oldest and finest building in town. The thick, breathing clay walls afforded highly agreeable temperature variation all year round. He decided however, to bluff it.

'That is not a consideration. True love conquers all.'

'What's that got to do with leaving a perfectly good house?'

'What I'm saying is, it doesn't matter where we live as long as we have each other.'

'Yeah right.'

'What's wrong with your place?'

'You've been to my place. It's a tin shack.'

'So?'

'"So."' She shook her head. 'Get real, will you?'

'We could go to the city and live with your mother.'

'I told you. She hates priests. Never forgiven them for burning my grandpapa.'

'I wouldn't be a priest, would I?'

'To her you still would. Anyway, the priesthood is a good living for someone who's taken a vow of poverty. What other job could you get?'

'Well, I'd find something.'

'What are your qualifications?'

'I can read and write. I'm good with people. I know the Bible, and quite a lot of Latin.'

'Oh excellent. Just the ticket for say, a career in merchant banking or selling rotten fruit at traffic lights.'

'It just doesn't seem right, marrying a witch and continuing to be a Roman Catholic priest. I don't know, I can't put it into words.'

'You're just worried about the archbishop finding out, aren't you?'

'Well, it's not going to do my promotion prospects much good, is it?'

'You're not interested in promotion.'

'No. But I might get fired.'

'Unfrocked.'

'Whatever. I'm serious, Messalina. It really doesn't look good. I'll lose respect amongst the people.'

'Excuse me? This is South America. The home of machismo. You're shacked up with the hottest babe for miles around, and you're worried about losing respect? Don't give me that forlorn helpless look. Trust me – it's not a problem. It's unconventional, that's all.'

'Unconventional. What kind of self-serving excuse is that?'

Messalina shrugged. 'That's the way you should look at it. You love the Church, you love me. I'm cool with that, I don't feel threatened. The least you can do is meet me halfway.'

'But—'

'Enough. Now come on, give me a hand. I need to pick some herbs for a potion.'

'What kind of potion?'

'That's not important. Ramón, I've told you before, never ask me about business. Come on. Fetch that basket will you.'

She was already through the door, and heading across the Plaza del Liberador in the direction of the forest. Two old men were sitting in the shade of the fountain, watching the turkey buzzards tearing apart the carcass of a dog. Messalina smiled at them as she passed.

'Just promise me one thing,' insisted the priest as he caught up with her. 'You don't still do human sacrifice do you?'

'That's not the kind of thing you hear a priest ask his fiancée every day,' remarked one of the old men as the happy couple passed out of earshot.

His companion nodded and threw a pebble at one of the vultures who had waddled a little too close.

'True. That's why I like it round here. Unconventional.'

'Mind you, not going to do much for his promotion prospects.'

'Promotion? What would you care for promotion if you were hitched to a hot babe like that?'

The most entertaining moment of Messalina and Ramón's wedding was, in my opinion, when the officiating priest asked if anyone knew of any just cause why the two of them might not be joined in holy matrimony. The deadpan look on Ramón's face was betrayed only for a moment as his eyes flickered in admission of the travesty of it all. We, the congregation, could all see his face of course, for he was the officiating priest as well as the groom. For a moment that seemed like an eternity he waited for someone to object, but no one did. We were happy for the happy couple, and wished them only well. Besides, had anyone piped up, who knows what awful payback Messalina would have devised?

The couple spent their honeymoon in Europe. The priest had always harboured a longing to visit the stadia of all the major European clubs, but had never envisaged having the money to do it. However the whole town dug deep in their pockets for a collective present, and the priest was overwhelmed when he realised he could make his dream come true. While he attributed this miracle, as he called it, to the power of prayer, it was a simpler reason that prompted our generosity. Namely, that were Messalina not to be satisfied with the final total, she might well have the resources at her disposal to make life difficult for any one of us, or indeed, short. There were numerous examples and precedents to make us think this way, such as the incident of the exploding iguana-trapper, the mysterious haemorrhoid epidemic that had afflicted the entire village soccer team a few days after they had mooned at Messalina while celebrating their first away win in six seasons, and of course, perhaps most forcibly of all, the way she had shown Ramón what retribution awaited him should he ever try and back out of their matrimonial union.

She had promised she would invoke the gods of the forest and render him incapable of administering the duties of his office unless naked and made up to look like Marlene Dietrich. To demonstrate this was no idle threat, she muttered a few words from some hermetic language, and challenged him to recite the Lord's Prayer. He would stand there and move his mouth, soundlessly and uselessly like a freshly hooked parrot fish. Only when she then forced upon him a blonde curly wig, long cigarette holder and top hat, applied copious amounts of lipstick and vamped the opening chords to 'Falling in Love Again' on his battered old upright could he stutter feebly, 'Don't tell me, don't tell me . . . it's something to do with the lad with the beard from that book with the really thin pages and the random italics? Oh I know, I know . . . "Our Father, which art in heaven . . ." Can I put my clothes back on now? Dahlink? Plees?' If the Holy Priest himself were not immune to her powers, what chance did anyone else have?

*　　*　　*

Life proceeded uneventfully in their absence; a Virtual Priest, provided by Microsoft's Vatican branch, was downloaded into the parish laptop and conducted the church services; the voodoo worshippers were happy enough honing their orgiastic skills in a Leaderless Workshop Situation for a few weeks, the sun rose and set, the villagers laboured by day, drank in my bar by night, and that was it. The predictable rhythms of rural Latin American life carried us all gently along towards the grave and nothing worth speaking of interrupted. Just a brief civil war, the landing of an alien spaceship, a couple of earthquakes, and a few dozen television crews trampling several species into extinction underfoot each day they spent there filming their documentaries about biodiversity and the rape of the rainforest.

Then one day the priest returned, and our lives would never be the same again.

Of course, to say 'our lives would never be the same again' is to disguise a truism in spuriously portentous language, for in my opinion, change is the only constant in the universe (despite how Tony's tale may argue to the contrary). However, the employment of such phrases does with luck induce a turn of the page.

Mandy moaned and quivered as she felt his hot tongue

is another variation on the same device.

CHAPTER TWO

The day the priest and his bride returned, I was in the bar, as usual, waiting to play backgammon with my regulars.

Yankee John, the disgraced Los Angeleno psychiatrist, is always first to arrive, generally wearing old khaki chinos and a black T-shirt with the words 'Respect my lack of dignity' printed across the front.

Each morning at around ten o'clock he will appear from the fringe of the forest, trotting nimbly down the stony trail that leads up the hillside to his spacious cabin by the waterfall, give his friendly wave, and, disdaining the little wooden bridge, cross the stream with a running jump and skip up the three little steps into the cantina. He is conscientious about his physical fitness, although not obsessive, unlike most Southern Californians, who appear to believe that immortality is attainable for those who work up a sweat while wearing lycra and then drink huge quantities of bottled water. Since he arrived here two or three years ago, he has taken up cigarettes again, fearing that breathing our clean unadulterated air would be too great a shock to his system after so many years of obtaining his oxygen from the toxic cloud which passes for air in Southern California.

Unfortunately, he does seem to believe his bowel movements are of great and general interest and a splendid opening conversational topic. But we all have our faults.

He reminds me of Rocky Marciano, although slighter, and indeed his speech, with its Brooklyn accent, somehow reflects that great champion's fighting style. He delights in verbal sparring, hectoring and confrontational, constantly trying to force his counterpart into a corner. Perhaps it is a compliment to the relaxed pace of life in our village that this characteristic has mellowed within him with time, and he has achieved a comparative calmness which all his years on the Coast had failed to instil. (Consult our Website for details on fantastic all-inclusive special off-season 'Chill-Out' deals.)

The turning point in his life came one fateful day when he was sitting in his Beverly Hills office listening to a young, beautiful and incomprehensibly rich take-away carton heiress who was demanding he write a deposition to the LA County Court on her behalf. She had recently been convicted of drunk driving, and wanted Yankee John to explain to the judge that her conviction should be quashed, owing to the intense mental cruelty her parents had subjected her to on her eighteenth birthday when the brand-new Porsche 911 they had bought her turned out to be the wrong shade of blue. He had stared out of the window for a while, taken a deep breath, then in a slow and deliberate voice told her to read the newspapers, think of all the starving people in the Third World, remove her head from her immaculately irrigated colon and count her blessings. Incredibly, this eccentric tactic had been utterly successful. The heiress was initially stunned into silence, but had gone home, taken his advice, shaped up, settled down to academic study, gone to medical school, trained as a surgeon, set up a worldwide network of leper colonies and been shortlisted for the Nobel Peace Prize. (Although rumours persist of the jury being treated to long and extravagant lunches at her uncle Vinnie's restaurant in Little Italy.)

Yankee John had spent the next two weeks giving similar treatment to most of his other clients. Ironically, his business did not suffer. The vast majority of his longstanding patients left, but only to recommend him to all their friends, who came flocking to his door in search of the same blunt cure. His professional colleagues were less impressed, however, and, sensing a severe threat to their livelihood, forced him to leave town.

Pepe the postman had finished his round and joined us at the bar, while Doctor Herradura had crossed the square and taken his seat at the furthermost table, where he always sat reading the newspaper until Yankee John had finished his second coffee and called for a glass of water, which indicated his account of that morning's bowel movements had finished.

'Good morning gentlemen,' said the doctor, placing his silver-headed cane on the bar and bowing formally to us all in turn. 'A game of backgammon perhaps?'

But although Yankee John had finished his second coffee and was on to water, he had not yet finished delighting us with his report on the effects of the new granola-mix he had been testing. The doctor was horrified. He is naturally squeamish, but doesn't like to let on in case it affects his professional reputation. Just as it seemed the doctor would not be spared a most unseemly conversation, he was rescued when the air suddenly filled with a gentle tinkling of random musical notes. I thought for a moment that we were suffering another infestation of the giant centipedes who periodically nest in the church organ and can disturb our sleep for weeks at a time. But looking up, I saw coming down the gentle slope on the other side of the stream, Father Gutierrez and Messalina, mounted on burros, and expertly driving a team of sturdy pack-nuns who were dragging behind them the grand piano Messalina had requested as a present to replace the battered old upright.

'Ten sisters from the convent of Our Lady of Shifting and Humping in Cartagena, judging by the tattoos,' opined Dr Herradura from behind his binoculars. 'Must have cost him a pretty penny to hire them.' (They are renowned as the finest and most careful furniture removers in the entire Catholic Church.) 'But who is that on the third burro?'

On the third burro sat a haggard young man, dark and brooding, swigging from a bottle of tequila. His deep-set eyes gave him a haunted look, and he drank from the bottle greedily, as if the cactus spirit would somehow ease his troubled mind. He looked like Franz Kafka after a heavy session. But the pure redness of his sunburnt face told us something else. He was English. Now, I take my profession very seriously, and pride myself on being able to discern what drink any customer will want from the moment I see him or her. It's a question of body language, and being able to read its most subtle and tiny signals. Considering the Gringo for an instant, I made my judgement, and went to the cellar to dig out the keg of Watney's Red Barrel I had won in a Reader's Digest Prize Draw in 1973. We may live in the middle of nowhere, but we have our finger on the pulse.

By the time I returned, the priest was seated at the bar, the Englishman beside him, the grand piano silent now as Conchita, my cook, fed and watered the nuns.

'Welcome home father! Welcome home Messalina!'

'It's good to be back, Señor García. Two beers please. And allow me to introduce to you Señor Tony Hardstaff.'

'A pleasure to meet you, Señor Hardstaff. A pint of Red Barrel perhaps?'

He looked at me, amazed.

'You have Watney's Red Barrel?'

'Why yes sir; it is the first duty of my humble calling to make all travellers feel at home.'

'Feel at home?'

'Why yes.'

The Gringo's face emptied of all expression. Then he smiled. I smiled back. He laughed – a wry chuckle. Wryly, I chuckled back. His laugh swelled into a full flood of deep and troubled grunting. At this point I dropped out of the duet, feeling disconcerted and inferior, like Jon Voigt trying to keep up with the inbred banjo player in the film *Deliverance*. Tony continued the tortured noise, and nine or ten female howler monkeys approached, swinging through the trees, returning the call exactly. They then lowered themselves to the ground with none of their usual timidity around humans, and fell face down before him, presenting their genitalia in attitudes of abject submission. We had to set the nuns on them to drive them away. But the stranger's laughter did not stop. He cackled and screamed, then burst into tears.

'Make me feel at home? Just great. Just what the doctor ordered. What a great start.'

It was my first introduction to the famed English 'ironic sense of humour'. For Tony's words seemed to say that he was indeed delighted with the prospect of Red Barrel, and feeling at home. And yet when I had finished clamping the tap and pipe into position on the bar, and proudly set the little red plastic display barrel in its place, his face told a different story. All blood and tension drained from his features. He became very calm, tranquil, almost vapid. Then suddenly, the eruption. A roaring of anger, a snarling face and an explosion of violence as he smashed the barrel into pieces, beating it against the bar rythmically, over and over again. We smiled politely, suspecting this to be some traditional custom of the English, combining as it did those key elements of English culture (as we perceive it from afar): alcohol, incoherent neanderthal screaming and systematic destruction of inanimate objects, all done to a rhythmical beat in four–four time (albeit with the accent, rather pedestrianly, on the on-beat). It was only when Tony's grunts of aggression melted into whimpers and he then slumped on to the floor in a foetal position that we suspected something might be wrong.

'Perhaps he doesn't like Watney's Red Barrel,' someone whispered, helpfully.

By now Tony's sobs were causing his whole body to shudder.

'He's even shuddering on the on-beat. Man, these English are so square.'

'Anyway,' said the priest, grinning sheepishly, 'I thought you might be able to give him a job.'

Everyone turned to the priest and stared. Then in unison turned and stared at the pathetic quivering blob of snot and sandals and white socks and shorts and sunburn which lay huddled at our feet. Again in unison we swung back to stare at the priest.

'Look, I know his present behaviour is a little odd. But he's been under a lot of pressure recently.'

'He's sucking his thumb.'

'OK, so he's not quite as macho as you guys,' said Messalina. 'That makes you feel uncomfortable. But believe me, it's very rare for an English guy to behave this way. When he wakes up he'll probably deny it ever happened and assault anyone who tries to say different.'

No one was convinced by this attempt to reassure us.

'Oh come on guys. You've got to help me here,' pleaded Ramón.

'Why?'

'Why? Why?' The father used these two 'whys' to great dramatic effect, pirouetting on each to make eye-contact with us all as he moved away from the bar and took the centre of the floor. 'I ask you, my friends' (clasping head in right hand, anguished) 'my . . . oldest . . . dearest . . .' (sweeping the group, making eye-contact once more to embarrass us) 'friends . . . for your help to help another human being' (gestures to the Gringo, who now in some kind of coma, gurgles and farts slyly) 'and you ask me why?' (Hangs head in despair at man's inhumanity to man.) 'You know brothers and sisters . . .' (Raises head, tears streaming from eyes, fumbling to replace slice of onion in pocket without us noticing) 'last night I had a dream . . .' (Audience sighs collectively, rolls eyes. We have heard all Ramón's improvisations on Dr King's great oration before. Many times.)

As Tony lay there unconscious, with a beatific expression of peace on his face, the mottled sunlight casting a soothing glow upon him, and as the little village children came running to rifle through his pockets for change, the priest explained how he had been seated next to Tony on the plane from Leeds to Caracas, and they had struck up a conversation.

'He wasn't exactly forthcoming or even coherent,' the priest explained, 'but he was talking about killing himself for he was worthless and evil and brought misfortune to all he came in contact with.'

'And so you brought him here?' I asked.

'Oh come on Señor García, no one carries bad luck around with them like that – it's all superstition, touch wood. The poor boy has simply been going through a bad patch and it's got to him, that's all. So I proposed a wager: I would show him he was not beyond redemption, that, for him, happiness need not be just an illusion, and he bet me he would convince me that life was pointless.'

'And I told him that the skull of a suicide would be of great potency in certain rituals,' said Messalina, brightly.

'So you're on a bet?' said Yankee John.

'We're engaged in a struggle for his mortal soul', said Messalina. 'We decided it would be a great thing if we had a common hobby. Isn't that right darling?'

Father Gutierrez concurred. He explained that neither of them would seek to influence the Gringo's behaviour in any way, beyond helping him to find a job and thus a reason to stay in town. After that they would both simply sit back and see which way the fates would lead him.

'We thought you might be able to give him a job behind the bar,' said the priest.

'Well I'm pretty hard up at the moment.'

'Hey come on, García. You gotta admit it would be pretty entertaining, watching two priests test their views of human nature on a willing guinea pig.'

'It certainly would add a certain zest to the mundane quotidian routine,' added the doctor.

'You want me to employ as a barman a mentally deranged Englishman who cries in public and makes howler monkeys wild with sexual desire?'

'If you can, Señor García, we would be eternally grateful,' said Ramón.

'And if you can't,' said Messalina, staring at me unblinking 'well, you can't. There's no pressure. By the way, that coral snake really doesn't go with your shirt.'

She reached towards me slowly and lifted from my shoulder a brightly-coloured four-foot-long serpent which I could have sworn was not there earlier. It remained motionless in her hands, slithering off into the undergrowth the moment she released it.

'I would be delighted to employ the Gringo. I am sure he will be a model employee,' I said automatically, looking down at his inert body. 'If he's still alive.'

'Excellent. You see, Messalina, I told you we could count on Señor García's goodwill.'

'You stupid bugger!' screeched Hamish, our parrot. Although his English is limited, and the phrases of course mean nothing to him, and he utters them at random, he has an unnerving habit of making them seem apposite.

'Thank you so much, Señor García,' said Messalina, pecking me on the cheek. 'Conchita, would you help me round up the nuns? I want to get the piano into the house before noon.'

Father Gutierrez joined us for a few games of back-gammon and to catch up on what had been happening while he was away, before leaving to join his wife for the siesta.

Immediately he was out of earshot, we began excitedly to discuss the main event.

'So, you have a new barman,' observed the doctor, inhaling flamboyantly on a fresh cigarillo.

'Will he be saved or damned?' asked Pepe in a hushed and awed whisper. 'What has brought him to his present state?'

'Let's wake the guy and ask him.' Yankee John was off his stool and about to lift the sleeping Englishman by the shoulders.

'No, best let him sleep it off. He'll tell us when he's ready.'

And the Gringo slept on at our feet into the evening.

When the last customers had left, I removed the remnants of the Watney's Red Barrel equipment from the bar as quietly as possible, for Conchita was in the back room watching a rerun of *ER* and could be very irritable if disturbed, then tried to wake the Gringo. I was concerned for his welfare: the bar has a roof, but the walls are only waist high; just wooden pillars support it, and if he slept on the floor, he would be surely eaten alive in the night by all manner of insects. But I could not lift him. There was nothing for it.

'Conchita.'

'What is it?'

'We have a poor suffering Christian soul collapsed in a heap in the bar who needs to sleep off his fever in a comfortable bed with the tender care of a kind woman skilled in the arts of medicine.'

'I'm watching *ER*. It's the one with Ewan MacGregor. Give me twenty minutes. And anyway, why don't you ask the doctor.'

What a depressing reaction. No one cares about their fellow man (or woman) any longer, unless they are young, sexually attractive and on television. 'Ask the doctor' indeed! At the rates he charges I could buy a new video.

'But he is unconscious.'

'So stop shouting. You will wake him.'

'Conchita, if he lies all night on the barroom floor, the cockroaches will nest in his ears.'

'Just pour a bucket of water over him.'

She said this in the clenched, portentous voice she kept for special occasions, like the time she bit off the nose of a dog that had been howling while Robbie Coltrane was on the *Tonight Show*, or the time she embedded a nail file in a travelling tortilla salesman who had interrupted her viewing of *The Full Monty*. 'Right where Robert Carlyle dances for the first time.'

I began to detect a pattern. But surely, she would not assault me, her employer and friend, when it was a matter of . . . well, perhaps of life and death . . . ?

'But Conchita . . .'

A pause. Then, very gently, very patiently: 'Ye-es?'

'Nothing.'

The Gringo was now snoring long and loud. Indeeed so rich and powerful was his snoring – like the lowing of a bull – that had I not witnessed his earlier display of public softness and effeminacy for myself I would have judged him to be of fine, noble and upstanding male character and not the Northern European nancy boy his tears had shown him to be. However, I needed to get him inside, for the sound of his snoring was beginning to excite the heifers in the paddock beyond the soccer pitch. I could hear them shuffling about near the fence, their moos clearly infused with the tell-tale tones of sexual desire. And the last thing I wanted was a bunch of horny young cows stampeding through my cantina. What if they woke the howler monkeys? All hell would be let loose. I tried again to wake the Gringo, slapping him harder, with the edge of my palm, then with a skillet, then with a large spoon. I administered Conchita's most fiery chilli paste to his nostrils with an icing syringe. All to no avail. Not only did I fail to wake him, but he continued to snore his spuriously macho snoring all the while, and louder. And all the while the heifers in the paddock were growing more excited ... it did cross my mind that were they to escape and find their way into the bar, the Gringo would at least have the opportunity to restore his reputation, should he manage to sate them all. Then I rebuked myself for thinking such a terrible perverted thought, and made a mental note to bring it up next time I went to confession. In fact, I would go to Cartagena to make that particular confession. All the way down the river, and through the foetid mangrove swamps, braving the savage swarms of mosquitoes and the terrible call of the American tourist, all the way to Cartagena to confess to the really stern archdeacon at the cathedral. The one who looks a bit like Vincent Price and wears the rubber catsuit underneath his robes ... but I am telling you more than you ever need to know.

The point was, I did not want my bar destroyed in a stampede. Desperately I tried to drag the Gringo into the storeroom, but it was no use. He must have weighed almost fifty kilos, or eight stone, and although I am a strong man, there are limits to what the human frame can achieve. Hearing the latch, I looked up, to see Conchita silhouetted in the doorway by the hurricane lamps within, a dead ringer for the silhouette of Emma Peel in the opening credits of *The Avengers*. Except for the fact that Conchita is somewhat wider and her curves are exclusively convex. In spite of myself, I felt an involuntary twitching in my groin. I yelped, realising a cockroach had crawled up my trouser leg.

'What is the matter, Señor García? And why do you dance the hornpipe with your hand inside your underpants?'

'Cockroach up my trousers.'

'Again?' Her tone was sceptical.

'What do you mean?'

'Fourth time I've caught you at it this month.'

'Pure coincidence.'

'Hmm.'

'Look Conchita, think what you like; we have more pressing matters. This Gringo is disturbing the cows with his snoring.'

'I am not surprised,' she purred. 'It is very attractive.' She spat a jet of tobacco at a cockroach and considered the Gringo stranger. 'Hm . . . reminds me a little of that Scottish actor . . .'

'Never mind that now Conchita. We need to get him into the house.'

'So you're going to hire him?'

'What choice do I have? Messalina has asked me to. So yes, I am going to hire a Gringo barman who has cried in public, despite what this could do for our reputation.'

'You know, Señor Márquez. You really ought to relax off all this macho bullshit. Women respect a man who is in touch with his feelings, who is not afraid to cry, to reveal his vulnerability . . . a man who can show his female side . . . look at him, like a little boy,' she cooed.

'He is certainly proving his attractiveness to the howler monkeys and the cattle.'

'Don't take that petulant tone with me. At least they are mammals. You are prepared to settle for a cockroach up your trouser leg.'

'Just save it, Conchita. "A man who can show his female side." This is South America, not . . .'

'Yes? Not where?'

'Not . . . I don't know! Not somewhere full of effete blokes who pretend to like boxing *and* baking quiche. Here, men are men. Hard, tough, and male and strong and could you give me a hand please, he's a bit heavy for me to lift.'

Without taking her eyes off me, without changing their expression, Conchita spat a huge moth out of the air with another squitch of tobacco, picked up Tony with one hand, slung him over her shoulder and marched inside, dropped him on the couch and continued upstairs without breaking step.

The cattle were quiet now. There was just the noise of the crickets and the whistling frogs, the distant wash of waves and the occasional hoot of an owl, followed by the high-pitched terrified death-scream of its prey.

CHAPTER THREE

The next morning as I took my shower, I was alerted that something strange was happening in the bar when I heard Hamish squawking and whistling in a most excited manner. Hamish had been brought up in the North of Scotland, and given to us some years ago by his master, a Scottish merchant seaman who had suddenly felt terribly bad after watching a David Attenborough documentary and decided that his dear Hamish should be returned to the wild. The seaman now worked as a minicab driver, and perhaps it was the geographical ineptitude congenital to that profession which caused him to return an African parrot to the wild in South America. Fortunately, however, Hamish possessed a strong survival instinct and immediately took up permanent residence in the bar, where he lives on a diet of leftovers and the occasional berry.

I came out to see Hamish striding upside-down along the beams of the roof, cocking his head and declaiming, in his broad Highland Scottish accent,

'By Christ, I never seen the like!'

And he was right.

The bar had never looked so spick and span. Tony looked

up from polishing the beer taps, smiled and extended his hand to me. It really was difficult to believe this was the same bar I had left the night before. The glasses had all been rendered sparkling clean and glinted on the shelves where they now sat in neat rows, arranged according to type. The labels of all the bottles faced outwards. The duckboards which lay atop the earthen floor had all been swept, the wooden tables all scrubbed down, and the little circular dance floor shone brilliantly with a new coating of wax. 'I felt this was the least I could do after disgracing myself last night, Señor . . . ?'

'García. And if you're going to shake hands, take those rubber gloves off. And the apron.'

'What's the matter?'

'What's the matter? You look like some refugee from the *Rocky Horror Picture Show*, that's what's the matter. It was bad enough last night with the crying and everything. Now you're dressed like a woman doing woman's work, and Father Ramón wants you to work behind the bar here? There'll be no one for you to serve.'

'You're really uptight about sexual orientation and gender role-boundaries round here aren't you?'

'No. This is Latin America, *amigo*. There is no uptightness. There are just definite rules. And you ain't playing by them, my friend. I don't know how long you plan to stay, but if you plan on staying a while, you'd better change your behaviour. It's not that I object personally you understand. I am a broad-minded, liberal man of the world. But, at the risk of sounding self-satisfied, vain, self-important, verbose, pompous, I am an exception. I have travelled, I have experience of other cultures, other customs. But round here, it's not enough to know you have balls, you have to act so everyone knows it.'

'I see.'

'I hope you do. By the way, if anyone threatens you who comes in here today, you'd better fight them. It will be safer. If you back off, they'll take it as a sign of weakness and stab you down some back alley. But they're a great bunch of people. Once they get to know you, you'll like it here. Just be on the look out in case anyone decides to kill you before they get to know you.'

'Thank you for the candid advice. But to tell you the truth, Señor García, I don't much care whether I live or die, so I'll just take everything as it comes.'

He took a deep breath, and for a moment seemed to be elsewhere, a long way away; perhaps thinking of a long-lost sweetheart. Then he put back carefully in his wallet the snapshot of a girl at which he had been gazing wistfully, and almost imperceptibly whispered her name.

'Emily . . . love of my life, have I really lost you for-ever?'

I like to pride myself on my intuition, and something told me this man was less than happy. Furthermore, I got the feeling that perhaps his unhappiness had something to do with a girl, called Emily, and moreover, a girl who was the love of his life, and whom he believed he had lost forever. It was more of a feeling and a sixth sense that enabled me to construct this haphazard picture – random clues and tiny signs which are there to be read for those who know the language, but invisible to those who do not take the time to pause and consider the world in which they live.

I must hasten to add that I do not consider that this ability to understand the world better than many makes me in any way superior to my fellows; it is simply a gift one either has, or does not, that is all.

'Good morning gentlemen, I trust you slept well,' said Conchita without the merest hint of sincerity as she came through from the back room and began warming oil in a frying pan. 'Would you like your eggs scrambled or fried?'

'Fried please.'

Conchita nodded and began scrambling eggs in the pan. Señor Hardstaff noticed this, and smiled wryly.

I was curious to know what chain of events had brought him here, but judging from his behaviour so far, and what the priest had told me, I did not want to broach the subject too directly. As if he could read my mind, he changed the subject.

'Those bees . . .' He pointed to the three nests in the rafters at the far end of the roof. 'They are very big. Are they dangerous?'

'Not at all Señor Hardstaff; they are utterly gentle under normal circumstances.'

'Under normal circumstances?'

'Yes. You will notice the juke-box is positioned directly beneath them, by the huge round table. They will turn ferocious if anyone selects 122 01 – "Hi Ho Silver Lining". It is a song none of us can abide.'

'Then, why not take it off?'

'Then we would have no means of speedily evicting large groups of tiresome customers, who invariably occupy that table as it is the biggest in the bar. Otherwise you need not fear them. Their honey is quite excellent incidentally.'

Conchita brought over to our table the plates of eggs, rice and beans and motioned for me to assist with the bread and coffee. I looked around to check no passer-by was around to notice my domestic complicity, then jumped to my task in case Conchita gave me one of her looks.

A voice boomed out from the other side of the track.

'Hey García, nice to see you helping out with the breakfast chores.'

It was Yankee John, striding down the bank.

'OK, OK, keep your voice down.'

'So pretty soon,' Yankee John was now telling Tony, as they sat at the table and waved me over periodically to freshen their glasses, 'I'm getting referrals all over town, people quitting their therapists and paying me big capital letters hyphenated bucks ditto underlined even just to hear me tell it to them straight. I dunno, maybe my accent was part of it. Sometimes people say I sound a little bit like Al.'

'What?'

'Al Pacino. That I sound like him. A little bit. People say. Sometimes.'

'Oh right. Yeah you do, yeah. So then what happened?'

'I'm putting all the shrinks in LA out of business. The only people going to shrinks are shrinks with business anxiety. To cut a long story short, they run me out of town. Turned up on my front lawn one day. A deputation. Four, maybe five busloads of angry therapists. Freudians, neo-Freudians, Jungians, Kleinians, Classical Primal Screamists, neo-Classical Gestaltians . . . people who would not be seen dead in the same restaurant were suddenly talking to each other, riding in the same vehicle. Not just talking to each other – forming car pools. I'd done what no one has been able to do since Freud split with Adler and Jung. United the entire profession. It was unprecedented. They'll write a book about me one day. I'd invented a Grand Unifying Theory of Psychotherapy. Which in a way is nice, except the Unifying Factor was – they all hated me. Angry therapists – let me tell you, that is a scary sight, know what I'm saying? Cos you know, they're good at dealing with anger, it's like, what they do. So when they lose it, woa, watch out.'

'Right.'

'They get out of the cars; they're armed; they're wearing sheets. I make a mistake. I say "Hey, let's sit down and talk about this." Like I'm reminding them how much they've lost control, you know? And they don't like that at all. They take a leather consulting couch off the roof rack and set fire to it, right on my front lawn. I'm thinking, I don't need this. So I tell them – "I don't need this! I can retire already. Screw you!" That really gets them, showing I'm not intimidated? They back off, hide in the bushes; they break up into self-help groups and I can hear them confessing and catharting and debating next-step assertiveness strategies all through the night. They're in chaos now – no one can hear anything over the Primal Screamists anyway, but I know they won't attack while it's dark – too many of them carry deep-seated infant traumas to risk it. So I packed up and left at dawn. Just drove South and kept on going. Here is where I ended up. In this one-horse town in the back of beyond. Never made a better decision in my life. I am not bitter at what I left behind, I want to make that very clear. The free tickets to the Lakers and the Dodgers, the premières, luxury automobiles, being able to get good tables at the hot restaurants any time any notice, the TV appearances, the celebrities coming over to *my* table, the connections . . . it was all meaningless. Meaningless, you understand? Here, the weather is great, the forest and the mountains and the ocean are all just beautiful, my bowel movements have never been better, *in my life* . . . I spend most every day here in the bar drinking and playing backgammon and poker. What more is there?'

'Being in a successful loving relationship?' Tony seemed imediately horrified that the thought had passed his lips.

Yankee John went quiet. 'So limey, you play poker?'

'Occasionally.'

'Excellent. We start after the siesta. Always the same school. There's Pepe, here, the postman.'

The mestizo raised his glass in a friendly gesture and smiled his wide and almost toothless smile.

'This guy has a great life. State salary, and around here illiteracy runs at 99 per cent so he has about one letter a month. Then there's Doctor Herradura. You met him last night but you probably don't remember. He's a big fan of Salvador Dali. Dresses like him. Big hats. Edwardian suits. Spats. Long curvy moustache. Got sued once for stitching an appendix scar in the shape of a melting watch. Nice guy, but watch out. His most common remedies and prescriptions usually contain coffee, tequila, tobacco and chocolate.'

'Forgive me, Yankee John, but you misrepresent Doctor

Herradura's integrity and ignore what a great patriot the doctor is,' said Pepe, politely. 'You have neglected to say he believes the commonly propounded harmful effects of alcohol, coffee, tobacco, and to a lesser degree, chocolate, are vicious rumours spread by the Yankee imperialists to keep Latin America economically weak. He does not prescribe them to his patients out of irresponsibility, but as a contribution to the struggle against the global hegemony of the Gringos. No offence.'

'Right Pepe, I apologise. And of course, there's Señor García. A great guy – but you probably figured that out already. Runs a great bar, very generous, very wise man – seems to know something about most everything, speaks several languages, mixes killer cocktails, seems to have a incredible insight into human nature. In short, a modern Renaissance Man.'

(From this glowing representation of myself, dear reader, you may be thinking that as your narrator I have reconstructed this conversation between Tony and John with a certain imaginative bias in my own direction. However, all I can say is that I am an expert lip-reader and that while it might appear vain to reproduce this paean to my character, I decided ultimately that my natural inclination to modesty must defer to my obligation to tell the truth. I must report what I see, no more, no less, and with no regard for the consequences. It is a burden, but one I have no right to shy away from. It was not an easy decision, and furthermore I have suppressed much of the description, where John went on to speak of my distinguished appearance – I have been told many times I resemble that great and noble thespian Fernando Rey – of my effortless ability to converse with anyone from the highest to the lowest, my legendary charm and attractiveness to the opposite sex, my expertise in lepidoptery, in the natural and political history of the area in general and my youthful achievements as an amateur boxer and 'cunning midfielder with a cultured left foot' (*El Diario de Herradura*, June 7. 1951. p. 32, col 4, par. 8. Third line). But I digress. This tale is not about me – however much more fascinating that might be – but about Tony Hardstaff.)

And so Tony took to his new situation quite happily at first. I was able to give him accommodation in a simple yet comfortable wooden hut which stood a little way up the hillside behind the bar. The hut stood in a clearing on the edge of the cloud forest proper, and had a fine view across the valley. I proudly told him that Che Guevara himself had stayed there for a few days in the early fifties, when he made his famous trip round South America on his Norton 500.

'Let's hope his luck doesn't rub off on me!' said Tony with a laugh. The sky went black and a massive clap of thunder shattered the sky. When we went outside, we discovered the lightning bolt had incinerated Tony's little suitcase. Curiously, neither of us thought anything of it at the time.

He was happy with the arrangement, working in the bar for board and lodging, and was a great help to both Conchita and myself, dividing his time between kitchen and bar duties as the situation required.

The priest's account of how he had met Tony, and the

little clues he let slip, such as his mournful contemplation of his sweetheart's photograph, had made us all curious to learn more about our new arrival, but over the first few weeks, all attempts to draw him out on the subject failed. He would drink no alcohol, and just did his job as bartender with a quiet and seemingly contented dedication. Everyone had their own ideas on how to discover his secrets. Yankee John tried asking outright, and when Tony replied simply that he didn't want to talk about it, he resorted to provocation, taunting Tony about his 'typical Limey emotional constipation.' With a smile Tony hit back with the observation that constipation was at least less messy than the emotional diarrhoea of the Californians.

'And anyway, I'm not constipated, I just don't shit in public.'

Everyone laughed. 'Fucking asshole,' muttered the Harvard graduate to himself.

Doctor Herradura said Tony would talk when he was good and ready. This annoyed Yankee John, as he knew the doctor was right.

Pepe offered to steam open Tony's letters, which everyone was very excited about until Conchita pointed out no one wrote to him.

Then, one day, we were all gathered round, sipping tequila on the occasion of the Festival of the Insistence that all the Nonogenarian Germanic Refugees in the Country are Swiss, OK, Because They Make Huge Contributions to Ruling Party Funds, Tony too accepted a glass of tequila.

We were all openly helping Conchita with the dishes (it being a Feast Day, all normal rules of decent behaviour are stood on their heads) when there was a scream from the direction of the church.

'Sounds like Father Gutierrez has been involved in another bizarre ecclesiastical accident,' someone said.

'What do you mean?' asked Tony.

'The priest is an unlucky man,' I explained. 'Ever since he married Messalina he is maimed at least once a month in another bizarre ecclesiastical accident: incense explodes in his face . . .'

'Many times I have treated him for food poisoning which he received from the Sacrament . . .'

'. . . though no one else ever has . . .'

'Remember when he was trampled underfoot by stampeding nuns rushing to visit the mobile Ann Summers shop?' reflected Pepe.

Yankee John chuckled. 'One time he was trying to remove a hornets' nest from the church bell—'

'It fell on him, trapping him for three days.'

'With the nest still inside.'

Their laughter I found rather distasteful.

'Gentlemen, surely we should not derive pleasure from another's misfortune.'

'Of course not. But it is funny, kind of.'

'He is my best customer,' said the doctor. 'I have devised a new system of bulk discount charges based entirely on his experiences. And I admire him. However bizarre and regular his accidents and injuries, never does he complain.'

At that moment, the priest appeared at the steps, clutching his face and led by a small child.

'Father, is everything all right?'

'Not exactly, doctor. Could you manage to remove this candle from my nostril? I tripped while genuflecting.'

'Gentlemen, said the doctor, rising from his seat, but first laying his cards face down on the table, and placing a stack of coins upon them, and then in turn his half-smoked cigar, with an inch of ash at the end, upon them.

'Not that I don't trust you of course,' he said to the group with a graceful smile. 'In fact, gentlemen, I will need your assistance.'

It took a little time, because everyone decided to protect their cards in the same fashion as the doctor. As he was the only one who smoked cigars, and I temporarily had none in stock, the child had to be dispatched to the grocer's to fetch another box, the cigars selected, cut, and then smoked for a while to produce sufficient ash. But after twenty minutes or so, we were almost ready.

'It does hurt quite a bit,' said the priest, with only the merest hint of impatience.

The doctor doffed his hat politely. 'We're coming, Father. Gentlemen, seize Father Ramón by the head please, and pull on my command.'

The doctor grasped the candle, gave the command, and the candle slid out of the nostril with a most satisfying 'POP'.

'Thank you,' said the priest.

I handed him a glass of rum. 'Drink this, Father. And tell me, do you never find that your faith is tested by this terrible run of misfortune?'

He laughed. 'Never, Señor García – I know that whatever travails I undergo in this life are nothing compared to the paradise that awaits me in the next. But enough of me; how are you settling in, Tony?'

'Fine.'

'Good, and is the grief of the life you left behind in England beginning to recede?'

Involuntarily we all swung an inquiring, expectant gaze upon Tony, who looked bashful. 'Well . . . you know . . .'

We waited, but he would say no more.

'Well,' said the priest. 'See you all tomorrow.'

We stared at him blankly.

'It's Sunday,' he explained, with a hint of disappointment.

'Oh yes, of course, see you in church,' came the customary hurried reply, in unison.

'Raise you a hundred,' said Yankee John. And the priest smiled his long-suffering smile and left.

'You know,' Yankee John continued, 'the way that guy deals with his life is incredible. All those accidents, the guilt he feels at being married to a voodoo princess . . . and yet he takes it all in his stride.'

'He is surely an idiot, or a saint,' Pepe opined.

'True, Pepe. But remember, to be a saint, you must perform a miracle,' said the doctor.

'Whatever, the guy has a terrible cross to bear.'

'Ha!' said Tony. 'You think he's got problems!'

And we turned and waited.

Tony looked away, angry that he had let his mask of equanimity slip for a moment.

'So tell us *amigo*,' said Conchita gently. 'It may ease the pain I see in your eyes.'

'Well . . . I don't know where to begin quite frankly. In St Petersburg, where I met Natasha? Or in Grimedale, where I found Emily again, and then lost her a second time – lost her for good . . .'

He stared into his glass and chucked the whole shot down in one. He winced. I winced. This tequila was no run of the mill stuff – it was top-class, one hundred per cent wild-grown blue agave cactus tequila, smooth and delicate, with the taste of the sweet earth it came from elevated into an essence – true spirit of its place, made for sipping, not slugging.

'. . . or perhaps before that, when I left home in the first place . . .'

'For Christ's sake start somewhere,' I said to myself.

'For Christ's sake start somewhere,' said Conchita, out loud.

'Come on you Limey putz. Scared of a little self-revelation?'

Tony stared at Yankee John. There was menace in his eyes. I went to the juke-box and selected 'Angel' by Massive Attack. The bass line reflects perfectly the mood in Tony's face. (And also illustrates how hip and up to date our juke-box is should you fancy a change from Newquay or Ibiza this year.)

'Well, we seem to have finished the tequila. Perhaps I should get on with some work . . .'

'Sit down, my friend', said the doctor. 'I am sure that Señor García has another bottle of this excellent vintage tequila.'

'I don't believe so.'

'Oh yes, here we are,' said Conchita emerging from the storeroom with my last three bottles of the good stuff and an innocent grin for me.

Tony fidgeted and looked into the middle distance, pretending to be fascinated by Gregory, the fighting cock, who was strutting through the long grass outside the bar with the confident poise of a creature who knows he is much bigger than the insects he is hunting, and who has no notion that within the year he will be pitted – literally – against another cockerel, and with spurs on his claws and our money riding on his back will be expected to fight to the death for the honour and entertainment of the village.

'Come on Tony, have another drink and tell us your tale.'

With this she plonked another bottle of the very fine gold tequila on the table and poured out glasses for us all, set out the salt, and a few limes plucked from the nearest branch, sat back, folded her arms, and stared at the Gringo stranger. And this is the story he told . . .

PART TWO

walking into Grimedale

CHAPTER FOUR

'Before St Petersburg, I was in the States,' said Tony, staring into his glass. 'Working as a freelance filmmaker.'

'Oh yeah?' said Yankee John. 'Which restaurant?'

Tony ignored him. 'I'd made some experimental guerrilla videos,' he said, running his fingers through his hair, 'you know, very cutting edge, very *avant*, and basically, when I decided to move back to London, my body of work was enough to get me a job in a leading underground multi-media production house.'

'Doing what?'

'Well, I was jack of all trades really – it was a very non-hierarchical company structure. A bit of everything: producer . . . director . . . you name it. Anyway, the details aren't important,' he said, looking at his nails. 'Basically, I'd come to realise that the ferment and anarchy of post-Soviet Russia was the perfect symbol *for* and very crucible *of* late-twentieth-century millennial angst and spiritual doubt, and therefore the perfect place to create the defining Great Work of Art of Our Times. My preliminary agenda methodology was this: . . .'

'I'm going to take a piss,' said Yankee John, whose bladder capacity was legendary throughout the region.

'I'll wait until you get back,' said Tony.

'Don't worry, I'll catch up.'

'Right. OK. Well . . . as I was saying, the peculiar ferment of post-Soviet Russian society seemed to me to present the perfect context for, if you will, an in-depth defining examination of all the fundamental intellectual, socio-economic and moral dilemmas facing mankind – forgive me, I should of course say humankind –' (he nods obsequiously to Conchita) 'as we approach the millennium.'

Conchita swatted another cockroach with her steak tenderiser.

'Good gracious! That's incredible,' she exclaimed.

Tony smiled modestly. 'Thank you. Well, it's not such an amazing idea really, I guess I just got there first. But thank you.'

Conchita wrinkled her brow as she digested this. 'Oh, no. I meant, *this* is incredible.' She held up her copy of *Hello!* magazine for us all to see. 'What I wouldn't give to own a magnificent four-wheel-drive lawn-mower like that. Say what you like about Julio Iglesias, he has an unerring eye for top-quality horticultural machinery.'

She was exasperated when she realised from our imploring looks that we needed further explanation. She shook her head, scowled, and went on.

'A lot of people in his position would simply buy the most expensive model available, but not Julio. He's clearly made a thorough examination of the technical specifications and plumped for the machine that does the job best, regardless of the snob appeal of the more expensive models. An international star with his feet still firmly on the ground.

What more could a girl wish for? . . . Sorry Tony, I *was* listening.' She cupped her chin in her hands and gazed at the Gringo adoringly.

'Right. Well, I was asking myself, what form would it take?'

'Would what take?' said Conchita, kindly.

'My . . . Work of Art,' muttered Tony, a little less confidently than before. 'Would it be the Great Late-Twentieth-Century Novel, or an essay on the semiology of style-change in post-Soviet football for *When Saturday Comes*? Or maybe a seminal cutting-edge pop-video? I couldn't decide which of these could best contain and articulate – if that's the right word – the essential pulse of the *Zeitgeist*. There was only one way to find out . . .' We all looked blank.

'Go there and start,' he explained. 'But I didn't know if I had the courage to do it. Then fate took a hand. On the same day I won ten thousand pounds on the lottery, and had artistic differences with my co-producer.'

'What happened?'

'Well, at that time we were brainstorming a . . . well, massive project – real cutting-edge corporate-avant-garde crossover-point stuff, working on a total re-imaging concept for a major financial institution . . . radical stuff – real state-of-the-art boundary-redefinition-time . . .'

Conchita looked bewildered. 'They were trying to think of a trendy advert for a bank,' I translated.

'Whatever. Anyway, like I say, me and my co-producer, we had major creative differences.'

'What exactly?'

'It had all been brewing for some time, and then one

morning, he goes, "Hey arsehole, there's no fucking sugar in this cappuccino you've taken twenty minutes to bring me."' Tony paused, and even in the pale light of the storm lanterns (the generator was once more on the blink) it was possible to discern his blush as he realised he had spoken out loud. 'This tequila's strong isn't it?' he added. 'Well, I thought, sod it. I got the next plane to Petersburg and found a small apartment on the left bank of the Neva. I played the casinos by night to supplement my savings, and worked all day on my . . . work. I was getting nowhere, but then suddenly, one day, bingo! The answer leapt into my mind. There was only one possible form the work *could* take.'

'And this was?'

He gave me a look of withering disbelief.

'Notes, of course.'

'Notes?'

'Notes. Work In Progress. Fragments.' He lit another cigarette and began running his fingers through his hair.

'I mean, how can you express the essential paradox of the chaos and interconnectedness of the modern, information technology age . . . and when I say modern I mean it of course in the sense of postmodern – or should I say even post-postmodern . . . pre-post-postmodern at any rate . . .'

Conchita poured water over his head, where the cigarette had set fire to his hair.

'. . . Thank you. But you know, you've got like a total-information-overload society now, yeah? TV, cable, satellite, internet . . . multi-media, it's like total – you know, like digital technology, it's a Tower of Babel Knowledge–Information Polarity Thing, yeah? You can't express the multilayered – it's a remote-control society you know, attention span is like a thing of the past . . . it's like, the present is obsolete by the time your brain interprets it you know . . . so you know, like irony is the only . . . let me start again . . . the point is, right . . . how can you express any of that within a conventional closed-structure art form? They're totally outmoded, I mean, you know . . . it's a dinosaur thing – the dinosaur situation, right, I mean if you like, the Net, the Internet is the asteroid that blotted out the . . . the digital equivalent I mean, of the you know, meteorite that blotted out the sun and killed the dinosaurs – that's what the Information Age has done for conventional forms right, you see what I'm saying . . . it's a dinosaur thing?'

'A bit like Jurassic Park?' said Pepe, trying to help.

The jungle was quiet now, bar the whistling of the frogs. Monkeys were snoring in the trees above.

Conchita stared at the charred strands of hair on Tony's crown as if suddenly regretting she had put out the fire. I was happy just to observe, as usual. There was a screech from Hamish; we had encouraged him with bananas to roost over the table so that listening to an Englishman might help him widen his vocabulary. 'Please can I change to metalwork?' said the parrot.

'Can I just make a polite suggestion here?' said Yankee John. 'Thank you,' he went on, without waiting for a reply. 'Cut to the fucking chase. What was the big event in Petersburg?'

Tony was silent and took a deep breath.

'Natasha.'

'OK. Thank you. So tell us about Natasha.'

'Right. My landlady was an old Russian woman . . .'

'Is her name Natasha?'

'No.'

'"No." So is she relevant?'

'Yes. How can I describe her? Ah! I probably have a description of her in my organiser!' He switched on the little machine and pressed a few buttons. 'Here we are! "St Petersburg Notes" . . . The secret of great writing you see, is meticulous research and attention to detail . . . just a second . . . yes! "Mrs Yepanchin . . . Russian-looking. Old. Shawl.'

'Meticulous attention to detail. Right.'

'Exactly. Anyway, she was a fortune-teller, would read the Tarot, the crystal ball, palms. She had quite a reputation in the neighbourhood, although I wasn't keen myself. I didn't believe in destiny . . . in those days . . .' His voice shrank away into the darkness. 'Well,' he continued cheerily, 'one evening she was sitting there in the tiny decrepit little kitchen – there's paint peeling off the walls, an ancient two-ring cooker, a rickety table with a piece of old velvet curtain on it to make the place look exotic and mysterious, and she insists on sitting me down to do a reading.'

'The cards read well for you tonight Tony, they speak of much good fortune.'

'Can you be more specific?'

'Cross my palm again and I will tell.'

I pulled a few coins from my pocket and placed them in her hand.

'Thank you. Cards say . . . don't be so trusting and gullible. Negotiate more with your fortune-teller for cheaper rate. Cards also say . . . yes . . . much money coming to you . . . maybe a good day to visit the casino. I also see a beautiful woman . . . I see love, jealousy, a sea of tempestuous emotions . . . a long journey . . . I see you going home, just in time to see your mother before she dies.'

'A long journey? That's not something you hear from a fortune-teller every day. And as for home, that's the last place I'll ever go.'

She returned my sarcasm with a faint but cruel grin. 'Cards also say you will not return to these lodgings tonight.'

'What?'

'Tony, you have always been good tenant, always pay rent on time, translate cable channels for me, I like you; but this morning someone come, offer me twice the going rate for your room. So no hard feelings, but *dosvedanya* baby.'

'But I have a lease . . .'

'I renegotiate lease, with help of my lawyer.'

'What lawyer?'

'This my lawyer . . .' and she produced an automatic pistol from beneath her Arnold Schwarzenegger tea-cosy.

'I hate to do this to you Tony; but business is business. Surely you understand – you lived in UK under Thatcher? But wait one second. Take this. If cards speak truth, then maybe you meet beautiful woman tonight, and maybe there come time when you need this. Open only then.'

She made me promise not to open it, telling me that I would know when the time was right.

'All I will tell you, it is made of rubber. Now go.'

'And she slings me out. Once more I'm alone. Walking down a foreign street at twilight, the keen wind rushing off the Baltic, whipping me with frozen filaments of salty wire, blasting me along the icy streets like a cork adrift on the ocean of fate, shredding my very resolve and self-respect with sharp and cruel fingers, blowing rubbish from the gutter around me as if in blatant and delighted mockery of my inner state.'

'What a remarkably clever and versatile wind,' said Conchita. 'All we ever get round here are warm winds. Warm and dry, or warm and wet. But always warm. Apart from the occasional hurricane of course, but even the hurricanes seem to lack the talent of the European ones of which you speak.'

Tony lit another cigarette, biting into the filter. 'Well, anyway, it was very cold. I just wanted to lie down and die. But one thing kept me going.'

'Yes! Even in the depths of your despair,' interjected the priest, 'you knew that God's love still kept you warm.'

'Well, sort of. In the sense that Mrs Yepanchin had told me the cards said I was going to get laid.'

The priest looked disappointed.

'That's the way it is, father; the *id* will always win out over any manifestation of the *superego* as a primary survival instinct,' said Yankee John, smugly.

'So I reach the cab rank on the corner and get a taxi to the casino.

'Gambling has always been an uncontrollable passion for me. I don't know why. Before I was in New York – which is where I made the shorts, I'd been in Las Vegas—'

'Forgive me, I am confused,' said Pepe, politely. 'You say the story starts in St Petersburg, then you take us to London, and now New York and Las Vegas . . .'

'Well, Vegas really.'

Tony had moved to Las Vegas with a plan. A plan both original and thoroughly realistic. Namely, he would win so much money gambling that he need never work again. Remarkably, he succeeded in this, not once, but three times, at poker, which he played with considerable skill. Unfortunately, he also adored roulette, which he played solely for the thrill, and lost all three fortunes within a matter of hours. His reasoning was that winning a few million dollars through the hard work of poker was not enough. One day he would multiply his huge winnings from the cards, which he owed to his steel nerves, his ability to suss out his opponents and incredible powers of mental arithmetic and sheer stamina, with a correct guess on the destination of a little metal ball. The more times he lost a fortune, and the more times he felt the utter despair of plummeting from millionaire to destitute in seconds, he argued, would only make the delight of the ultimate win an absolutely unbeatable sensation. All he had to do was keep faith. One night, after an eight-day stud game where he had won several million dollars and lost it all again (bar a few hundred) in a matter of minutes, his adrenalised buzz had led him to wander around town aimlessly, until he stepped into a small hotel on the outskirts of town, ordered a beer and met Sarah Mae. She was working in a lounge act called Snakes Alive!

This consisted of Sarah Mae and her two sisters, dressed in costumes of Ancient Egypt, enacting the tragedy of Cleopatra as a tableau-ballet set to seventies disco classics with several increasingly spectacular demonstrations of snake-juggling, with live rattlesnakes. The roles of Antony, the Caesars and their armies were played by a trio of gay midgets called Pink Small But Hot!

Tony was captivated, and applauded loudly throughout the show. This was noticed by the performers, not unsurprisingly, since the only other customers were a group of Iceland's top carpet salesmen on a company junket who were asleep in the corner, and the stand-up comedian who would be topping the bill. He sat at the bar chainsmoking in disbelief, muttering to himself, 'How the hell am I going to follow that?' or casting a grim look round the room, trying to adapt his act for one strung-out Englishman and a group of tall blond people, who when they were awake sounded for all the world like the chef on the Muppets. He surmised that most of his references to the differences between New York and LA would go largely unpicked.

During the finale, enacted to the sound of 'Stayin' Alive', where Antony and Cleopatra rise from the dead (to provide the happy ending the management had insisted on), the stand-up raised his eyes to heaven and consoled himself by deciding it would all make a great anecdote when he finally made the *Tonight Show*. He then beckoned over the cocktail waitress and, in a tone of sombre resignation, ordered a large Jack Daniels on the rocks.

During the interval, Sarah Mae, nervously clutching a canvas tote bag, scoped the bar from the backstage door and came over to Tony to thank him for enjoying the show so much. When he asked her to join him for a drink and she realised he was English, she accepted, more readily than usual because the night before she had had a dream about Winston Churchill offering her a cigar. Details were vague after this, but she woke up feeling it had been a pleasurable dream, and meeting an Englishman the next day convinced her it was in some way pre-cognitive. She said she loved the way he talked. He was taken by her bright-eyed enthusiasm and in turn her accent, which reminded him of Daisy in the Dukes of Hazzard, with all the adolescent thrills this brought back. They strolled down the block to a Vietnamese pizza parlour, and talked. She was captivated by him because he was foreign (and Conchita, who is reading over my shoulder, wishes to add that he was also attractive in a little-boy-lost kind of a way – whatever that means); he was captivated by her because she was tall, young, innocent and pretty. In such situations, people can be enthralled by each other's conversation without even listening to it. At the end of the night he saw her politely into a cab, and promised to see her again the next evening. The next night he went to see the show again, and the night after that.

Within a few days the inevitable happened, and they shared a cab back to the mobile home she shared with her two sisters in one of the most fashionable trailer parks in town. Her two sisters, Lisa Marie and Priscilla (they had changed their names by deed-poll) were huge Elvis fans. The trailer was a shrine to the King, with every conceivable form of Graceland memorabilia and trinket on display, and a selection of vegetables in a glass case which the sisters claimed all bore the face of Elvis if you looked at them from the right angle.

Tony felt uncomfortable in the trailer, and suggested to Sarah Mae that they find a place together. Sarah Mae squealed with delight and declaimed to her sisters that she and Tony were to be married. It wasn't quite what Tony meant, but she was so excited that he didn't have the heart to set her right. Besides, in Vegas it seemed appropriate to get married spontaneously without quite knowing what you were doing and gamble on everything coming up trumps.

The wedding service was conducted that afternoon by a priest of the Church of Elvis Lookalikes whom Sarah Mae's sisters both recommended as the most spiritual man outside of Santa Fe. Whatever that meant.

Sarah Mae had explained on the night they met that she was raised in a Southern Baptist sect, who handled snakes as part of the regular Sunday service. The basic philosophy of these rattlesnake handlers, derived from a literal interpretation of a line in the Gospels, is that if the snake bites you, it's God's will. If it doesn't you're righteous. If it bites you and you're righteous, you will survive. But it was only now, as they sat together on their honeymoon (an evening in a booth at the Sands Hotel drinking margaritas), that a chance remark revealed what Sarah Mae assumed he already knew, that the rattlesnakes' venom glands were still in full working order.

Suddenly Sarah Mae's act, where the snakes writhed and coiled around her semi-naked body, or were hurled high into the air with a noise like angry rain sticks, seemed far more impressive than before. Tony felt his own compulsion to gamble against the odds was not much more adventurous than the little old ladies from the Midwest who stood at the one-armed bandits all day with their styrofoam cups full of quarters.

He was horrified as well, and found it harder to watch the show now he knew what constant danger Sarah Mae was in, and decided it was time to get her away from it. He started playing poker again, for modest stakes, just enough to buy groceries and contribute to the rent. He also took a regular job, in a gas station. One night a group of college students from UCLA film school with no money for gas bartered him a super 16 film camera in exchange for a full tank, which he then paid for out of his wages. He had no idea why he had accepted the deal. Perhaps he felt a desire to be charitable to struggling artists. Anyway, he began experimenting with the machine, and taking footage of Sarah Mae and their life together, first as simple home movies but then, having talked to a couple of backstage people who had some editing experience, he began to make weird little surreal montages and peculiar silent narratives.

'I guess I just liked filming my life and then cutting it about so it looked more interesting. Anyway, we used to show them once in a while, and I decided to go to film school.'

The next evening Tony took Sarah Mae to the Vietnamese pizza parlour where they had first dined together. He laid down his ultimatum – he was going to give up gambling; Sarah Mae must stop working in the act, because he loved her, and they would move to New York and make *avant-garde* films. Sarah Mae was staggered. She said it was her living and she couldn't give it up, and that she would never be bitten if she walked in the paths of righteousness. 'Besides, I can't walk out on my sisters. And if you give up gambling and I give up snake-juggling, how we gonna make a living?'

'Where there's a will there's a way.'

'Sure. But I ain't willin'.'

They finished their meal in silence.

About a week later, the three sisters were out after the show celebrating the birthday of a friend who worked as a croupier in one of the big hotels. It was a strictly all-female affair. Tony had bought a pair of long leather gauntlets from one of the fetish shops in town, sneaked into the dressing room, and then, trembling, put the eight rattlesnakes into their canvas travelling bag, and dumped it, open, in the desert. He stuck out his thumb and hitched all the way to New York in two days.

'You mean you left your wife and her two sisters, without a word of warning or explanation, and not only that, but deprived them of their livelihood also?' Pepe was clearly saddened that one of his drinking companions could be so utterly callous.

'Yes. In retrospect it wasn't the most intelligent or considerate plan. I suppose I knew the whole thing had been a mistake and, rather than admit it, I thought it was best to just, you know, run away and show what an arsehole

I was. That way I figured Sarah Mae wouldn't be upset at losing me.'

Yankee John shook his head and swigged another beer. 'Man if I was still in practice could I make a shitload of money out of you. So, anyway, you're in St Petersburg, on the way to the casino . . .'

'Yes. I hail a cab, haggle with the taxi driver, get a good price – he's an English guy who's been in Russia since he defected in 1961. Had some government job until 1990; then he had a nervous breakdown and was arrested for shoving his Order of Lenin up the arse of the manager of the McDonalds in Red Square.

'He drops me at the casino and . . . I walk in through the door, and . . .'

Whenever Tony reached this part of the story he would become hyperanimated. How can I put it? A bit like one of those nodding dogs on the back shelf of a car when you brake hard.

'There was this beautiful woman sitting at the bar, on her own, sipping a Martini and moulding condemned lard into babushka dolls.

'I remembered what Mrs Yepanchin had read in the cards, and thought, what is there to lose?'

'Excuse me, miss. Your lard moulding is first-rate.' She didn't even look up. 'Excuse me, I couldn't help admiring your babushkas. They are truly magnificent . . .'

'I heard you the first time,' she said in a tone which implied I was something she had stepped in.

'I was wondering . . .'

'Do you seriously believe that I, Nastassia Fillipovna Karamazov, so smoulderingly gorgeous that, with one look from my coal-black gypsy eyes, bromide addicts hyperventilate and break into chemical plants for fresh supplies; that I, Nastassia Fillipovna Karamazov, whose meta-natural curves are so amazing that they make professors of geometry burst into flames then smoulder and melt into tallow joyously, knowing they have seen such a collection of sines and cosines as Euclid could never have predicted nor Pygmalion expressed; do you believe that I, Nastassia Fillipovna Karamazov, with hair so rich and lustrous that men have seen their very souls reflected in it and spiralled into madness in the face of such beauty that even Pushkin could not have described; I, whose magnificent breasts have . . .'

'Yes all right, I get your drift. I was just wondering . . .'

'Yes?'

'. . . what a nice girl like you is doing in a place like this.'

'You think that I, Nastassia Fillipovna Karamazov, a force of Nature beyond Good and Evil, who can make adolescent boys explode with a single pout from my impossibly sensuous lips, need to explain myself to a gangly, English, art-student type in a tatty leather jacket and jeans? Beat it. I have lard to mould and you're cramping my style.'

She produced a solid silver nail file with a mother-of-pearl handle from her tiny Bulgari clutch bag, gouged a dollop of lard from beneath her exquisitely manicured nails, and flicked it into my face.

I sat down on the barstool next to her, and ordered a beer.

'Not very busy tonight, is it?'

She ignored me again.

'Can I get you another Martini?'

'Piss off,' she replied.

'Do you come here often?'

She rolled her eyes to heaven, her . . . wait a minute I have the exact description in my notes . . . her . . . 'gorgeous smouldering deep almost coal-black gypsy eyes' – and motioned to one of the two enormous Chechen doormen, who came over and pointed his .44 Magnum at me.

'Piss off, Englishman,' Natasha said once more, and the doorman cocked his piece. I could take a hint, and walked away.

The club was not busy, but there was enough money passing over the tables to make it worth a shout. I changed two hundred dollars into chips and headed for my lucky table. Within two or three rounds I was a thousand dollars up and no one in the room was talking any more – they were all looking at the action, and the action was me and the croupier. The croupier was nervous, and I was on a roll.

'Snap,' I said again, and yet another pile of chips was pushed across the table towards me. There was a film of perspiration on the croupier's upper lip. Or there would have been but for the moustache. She broke open another deck. I was unstoppable. When I'd won a million dollars, I pulled out, sat at a little table in the shadows and ordered vodka and caviar.

Vladimir, the cashier, came over to congratulate me. I

invited him to join me for a drink. He'd been a good friend to me over the past few months . . . slipping me free drinks and food when I was broke . . . pulling me in off the street that time I could have frozen to death when I passed out drunk in the snow . . . I proposed a toast – to friendship, and loyalty. Almost immediately Natasha was standing there, all silk and perfume and curves and pout and asked if she could sit down. The transparently mercenary change in her attitude towards me was nauseating.

'Vladimir,' I said, 'go away.'

'So, what does a girl have to do round here to get a guy to buy her a drink?'

'I wouldn't want to tear you away from your lard moulding.'

She laughed, and stroked my cheek.

'Funny English guy.'

I ordered champagne.

She raised her glass.

'Congratulations on your good fortune.'

'Yes, thank you. It was quite a big win'.

'I was thinking of the fact you are sitting with me. But yes . . . that too. Quite a chunky wad.'

'That's nothing. You should see my money belt.'

'What a sad comment on humanity,' said the priest (he had wandered over for a nightcap when he noticed our lanterns still burning at around three in the morning). 'That money can change a person's attitude to another so quickly. One moment she treats you like dirt, the next – as soon as you are rich – she is virtually throwing herself at you.'

'You're quite right, Father Ramón. It is a terrible indictment of the worst of human nature. And looking at her sitting there, smiling at me, brazenly flirting without the slightest embarrassment at her flagrant change of attitude, I thought, "how can someone so beautiful be so scheming and mercenary – you disgust me." I was about to tell her so. But then I looked at her again, long-legged, pneumatic and smouldering, and I thought, well, you could learn to live with it. I mean, every relationship requires compromise, doesn't it? So, I thought, maybe I'll give her a chance . . . maybe at the bar, when she'd ignored me, insulted me and threatened to have me killed, maybe I'd just caught her at a bad moment. Maybe this was the real Natasha; the one that was hanging on my every word, giggling at my jokes and stroking my hand gently as I lit her cigarettes. Maybe that was the real her. It was worth a guess. I could do no wrong, Señor García. Everything I said was funny. Just one of those times where everything works.

'We're talking for a while – I forget exactly what . . .'

'Thank Christ for that,' said Yankee John. 'We just want to know if you got laid or not.'

Tony gave one of his cheap hang-dog expressions which somehow always gained him female sympathy. I don't know how – Conchita attributes it to his 'little-boy-lost look, his slight build, which with his sad eyes, gives him an air of vulnerability.'

'It always all comes down to sex with you, doesn't it Yankee John,' said Conchita.

'Sure. I trained as a Freudian.'

*   *   *

Natasha put her arms around my neck and suggested we went somewhere else. I'm thinking:

'Yes! My luck is changing.' Then I'm thinking, 'Get real – we get outside and someone knocks me on the head . . .'

I said no, I wanted to get to know her better first. She looked at me like I had two heads and sat back down again.

'You are interested? In me? As . . . a person?'

'Of course.'

'You were bullshitting, right?' said Yankee John.

'No. And I told her "I must know who you are, not what you are."'

'He's definitely bullshitting,' Conchita whispered to Yankee John. But Tony did not hear them, and continued, attempting to portray the character of the impossibly beautiful and probably entirely fictional Russian girl.

Natasha shrugged diffidently. 'OK, Englishman, ask me what you want.'

'Have you always lived in St Petersburg?'

'No,' she said. 'I come from far away. To the East.'

'And what brought you here to St Petersburg?'

'Why do you ask me this? You are police?'

'No, I'm not police. I'm just interested.'

'Always since I was little girl I wanted to dance, to be ballerina; my parents say no, I should get proper trade. They make me stay in school, they want me go to college. But still, I want to dance. So, when I was fourteen I run away to St Petersburg, audition for Kirov Ballet.'

She stopped, and looked at me.

'Tony,' she said. 'I don't know what it is – maybe that little-boy-lost look, perhaps it is something to do with your slight build, which with your sad eyes, gives you an air of vulnerability . . . but . . . I want you . . . now.'

Conchita swatted another cockroach with the meat tenderiser.

'Yeah right,' we chorused, inadvertently.

'It's true.'

'So you're asking us to be believe that not only does she start coming on to you because you have a wad load of money, but she's also genuinely hot for you? This incredible broad, this gangster's moll, is suddenly looking to make out with a skinny Limey punk just like that?'

'Yes.'

Pepe, as usual, felt constrained to ease the tension. 'I must say, Tony, it does sound somewhat unlikely – although more of a comment on her nature than your own.'

'Well, there was one other small thing,' said Tony, sheepishly. 'I'd put on Mrs Yepanchin's rubber present.'

'Already?'

'I sit down in the corner, after I've won, and I see Natasha looking over; I figure she might be interested now I'm flush, I take out the package to make sure it's there. Anyway, it wasn't what I expected it to be. It was a latex, professional model, one-size-fits-all Daniel Day-Lewis mask. Natasha had hardly even looked at me when she gave me the brush off . . . I slip it on, and . . . well, as you've heard from Natasha's reaction, it seemed to work.'

'So now she's drooling for you, because you've made a fortune playing snap and you're wearing a rubber mask.'

'Yes.'

'I'm outta here. It's almost dawn.'

'Might as well finish this bottle before you go, Yankee John.' Conchita can always find an extra twist of the knife. The last bottle of my finest tequila was barely touched.

'One last glass. OK, so finish the story Tony. You got this much tequila before we go to bed. Salud.'

'OK. She's telling me her story, how she fails the audition for the Kirov, gets a job in a nightclub.'

'It is tough life Tony – long hours, little money. But then I meet Peter. He is a businessman, from Odessa. Import–export, you know.'

'You mean, Peter . . . Kropotkin?' I said in a strangled voice.

'You have heard of him?!'

'He does crop up in the papers now and then. When he was fourteen, didn't he strangle a bishop with his own intestines?'

'That's right! I mean, officially no. But yes. He was a very mixed-up teenager. But he is great guy! So kind to me – and generous . . . buys me an apartment. Cars to take me everywhere, restaurants, health spas, monthly allowance, trips to all the fashion shows of Europe. A little dog . . .' The pain showed on her face for an instant. 'I know I am fallen woman, but it was not just me who needed the money: there was my family – my father, my mother, my little brothers. Living in terrible conditions in Siberia: they can't stop shagging, you know – it is only way to keep warm. Always my mother is pregnant . . . the babies nearly all dies – the funeral bills and midwives' fees alone nearly took all their savings. And the ones that survive are even more of a burden. So I send them money when I can. For I love my parents, even though they never supported my dreams, denied me love, affection: I don't know why, I'm a crazy mixed-up kid I guess. You see, my father's income as a psychiatric electrotherapist had really gone downhill – the political prisoner business has really dried up in the last few years. So being a gangster's moll was all that I could aspire to, the limits of my horizons . . . until you came along.'

'Actually, perhaps I should be going.'

'It's OK! He's out of town, and this is safest place to be: no one would seriously believe you would dare to hit on the girlfriend of Peter Kropotkin in his own casino.'

'No. No, I don't expect they would. Well, nice to meet you. I really must go.'

I leave, I hail a taxi, she gets in beside me and tells it to go to the Grand Hotel. The foyer echoes to the sound of men's necks incurring whiplash as we walk up to the desk.

Natasha insisted on the largest suite in the hotel, and when told it was unavailable, demanded to see the manager.

'Sir, madam; allow me to present myself: I am Vladimir Ilyich Harpo Ossipon, the hotel manager, and I would be honoured to show you personally to your room.'

'Thank you,' said Tony, anxious to proceed.

'You're sure it's your largest suite?'

'Actually second largest, *madame*. But the difference is minimal – merely a matter of millimetres, *madame*.'

'Your alliteration does not impress me. We asked for the largest.'

'I deeply regret, *madame*, that our largest suite is currently occupied.'

'By?'

The manager was powerless to observe the usual rules of discretion and privacy under Natasha's gaze.

'Signor Stromboli, eminent Professor of Geometry at the University of Padua.'

'Geometry? I wish to speak to him.'

'I will attempt to arrange it *madame*, but I assure you our second largest suite is . . . oh, there he is now, stepping from the lift.'

Natasha turned, shifted all her weight on to one leg to accentuate the curve of her hip and purred out the professor's name.

'Signor Stromboli?'

'*Si*? *Mama mia*! Such curves! Such perfect geometry! Such . . .' Natasha pouted and there was a fizzing sound, and where the professor had stood, a cloud of sputtering smoke that smelled of old chip fat. When it cleared, there was nothing but a pair of expensive Italian shoes slopped over with a sludgy grey ash.

'What a shame. A tragedy for the world of geometry. However, I take it he will not now be needing his rooms.'

'No, I suppose not.'

'Good. I expect them ready for us immediately.'

And we stepped into the lift, delicately stepping round the professor, who was being swept up with a dustpan and brush.

* * *

The manager himself delivered our room service. I think he was disappointed that Natasha was in the shower.

'Champagne, caviar, and I'm afraid the steak tartare is off, sir, but as a substitute, I did manage to get you a fresh beetroot.'

Not that I was hungry, but I decided to play it starry. 'Hardly the same as steak tartare, is it?'

'But much better for the teeth, I can assure you. And very high quality – the rats put up a hell of a fight when I pulled it off them.'

I tipped him and he turned to go, when I noticed he had forgotten the vodka.

'I'm sorry sir. We only have six cases left in stock, and Mr Yeltsin is in town tomorrow for the finals of the All-Russia Ted Heath Lookalike Championships. It would be more than my life is worth if we ran out before breakfast.'

I couldn't argue with that.

'Oh, your companion also ordered this.'

He opened the door wide and led in a blindfolded gypsy string quartet, who began setting up somewhat clumsily in the corner.

(Incidentally, none of us in the bar was believing any of this any more, but we felt we might as well let him continue with his story. It was a way of passing the time.)

Natasha comes out of the bathroom.

'Tony, you must tell me the truth. Have you ever been in love?'

I thought of my dear teenage sweeheart, Emily. I thought of Sarah Mae. But there was only one answer I could give.

'No.'

'Only one answer you could give if you wanted to get laid,' said Yankee John.

'I prefer to say, only one answer I could give that would have been appropriate to the moment.'

'That's lovely,' said Conchita, beaming.

I asked Natasha the same question.

'Oh,' she sighed, 'I suppose I thought I was in love with Kropotkin. He attends to my material needs, he looks after me, but I don't know, there's something about his business methods that makes me uneasy.'

'In what way?'

'Well, for example, when he wanted to buy a bank that time, and the board wouldn't sell to him, so he arranged a special helicopter trip for them.'

'Like corporate entertainment; that's perfectly accept-able business practice.'

'I don't think they wanted to go. Anyway, he forced them to vote in his favour by dropping a board member out of helicopter each time they say no. They turn around opinion pretty quick.'

'Oh my God.'

'And then you know, there was time he pistol-whipped this guy in a restaurant, then poured a bottle of hot chilli sauce into the guy's face. It's all pulp you know, like stewed tomatoes. The guy is screaming, never have I heard such screams of pain. Well, in a restaurant. Quite often from Peter's office.'

'What had the guy done?'

'He looked at me.'

'Looked at you?'

'Yes, you know, looked at me – like he find me attractive.'

'So Kropotkin beat him to a pulp, just for looking at you?'

'Yes. But never mind that now. Kiss me.'

'I don't know if I'm in the mood any more.'

'What do you mean? Open your eyes. Am I not worth the risk? Besides, I have never been rejected by a man I wanted. If you reject me, maybe Peter find out you come on to me. He will track you down. He has long tentacles. Now relax, and make love with me.'

We make love. Passionate, tender, violent, thesaurus-challenging love. In the course of it, my Daniel Day-Lewis mask splits; but she doesn't mind! It's like she really does like me for myself now. Ten minutes later . . . three hours later I mean – several hours later, we're fast asleep when there's a hammering on the door, completely shattering the soothing effects of the string quartet playing Brahms' lullaby.

'Natasha! Open the door!'

'It's Peter! With one of his trained gorillas no doubt. Quick, get dressed!'

The gypsies quickly hit an appropriate dramatic chord and waited silently for further instruction.

'Natasha! I know that you're in there.' Kropotkin's voice was calm. He knew we had no way out.

The bass player improvised a low, menacing two-note measure.

'Natasha, I know you are in there. It was on the news that a professor of geometry has exploded in the lobby of this hotel. Things like that don't just *happen*. Now open the door.'

I was dressed. Natasha told me to shin down the drainpipe.

'We're eight floors up.'

'Better chancing the drainpipe than staying here and being thrown out. I'll bluff it out, and then you can come back in the front and gun them down and we can leave the country on the next flight and be together for ever.'

'Gun them down? What with?'

'A machine gun of course. You can get one in the newsagent's. Or borrow one from hotel security. They'd swap you for that watch. But hurry!'

I walked to the window with my legs jerking around like a stoat on heat.

The gypsy musicians slid into scene one to the *Magic Flute*, where the hero is being pursued by a serpent.

'Quickly Tony, quickly!' cried Natasha.

The hammering continued, and the violinist asked politely:

'Can you ask the gentleman beating down the door to swing his axe in time please? It's very hard to keep the rhythm against such random thumps.'

And I climbed down the drainpipe . . .

'And did you immediately rush back into the hotel, gun

down the gangsters and rescue Natasha?' asked Conchita. But the look on his face told the whole story. Who do you think I am? the look on his face seemed to say – James Bond? Looking more closely, his expression continued to unfold the narrative. The faint lines around his mouth, implying he was only a couple of steps away from bursting into tears, said that once he reached the pavement, his only thought was for self-preservation. From the way he sucked his lips into his mouth, I knew that his logic was that, while he regretted his fear, Natasha might have a chance of bluffing it out on her own, and even convincing Kropotkin that she had hired the blindfold musicians as the perfect accompaniment to a quiet night on her own, whereas if he did make any attempt to get into a gunfight, he would stand little chance of success (the imploring bend in his eyebrows reminding us he was almost completely unfamiliar with all types of Russian military hardware). The slight flush in his cheeks reemphasised that of course he was terrified as well, but that running away was, as far as he could see, the best chance that either of them had. As his lips slid back out into view, and the corners of his mouth sank down, it was obvious that he knew it wasn't entirely foolproof, that maybe one of the musicians would crack under heavy interrogation. As he wrinkled his brow, I realised that he was sure there was a good chance that even a jealous psychopath would forgive someone of Natasha's beauty anyway. And on top of that, the slight duck of his head added, he'd only known her a few hours.

'What about "commitment" and "undying love"?' asked Conchita with a contemptuous sneer.

'That was before he'd had her,' said Yankee John with a world-weary shrug.

The priest was looking confused. 'Did I miss something?' he said out loud, breaking the silence for the first time in many minutes.

'I ran away,' said Tony.

'And left her to her fate?'

'I reckoned she could talk him round.'

I smiled smugly at this confirmation of my face-reading.

'But . . . you abandoned her, my son?! Surely with a little more resolve you could have risen above your fear and operated according to a higher nobler moral code, and tried to save her. I mean, yes perhaps you would have ended up dead, but even as the bullets ripped into your flesh, you would have known that your death was contributing to the sum of human goodness, of noble self-sacrifice – for do not the scriptures tell us "No greater love hath a man than that he lay down his life for his friends"?'

Opinion was divided. 'There was nothing he could have done.'

'I'd only just met her! OK we'd had sex, but I wouldn't automatically call her a *friend*. Maybe it wouldn't have worked out after all. Besides, she did evidently get round Kropotkin, and got her revenge.'

'Well my son, I am not impressed. We should always take full responsibility for our actions according to the highest moral principles.'

Tony hung his head. 'On reflection, perhaps you are right.'

'Come come, we all make mistakes, father,' I said.

The priest knew where this was heading, made his excuses and left.

'Give my regards to your wife,' Conchita said, driving the point home. 'Now,' she said, turning to Tony, 'Father Gutierrez tells me you mentioned on the plane that you are the eldest son of a very rich family.'

'Yes, very rich.'

'With a big English country house?'

'Pretty big.'

'With huge grounds?'

'I suppose they're pretty big, yes.'

'So tell me, do your parents have a four-wheel lawn-mower?'

Tony was momentarily nonplussed, but then continued.

'When I reached the street, I looked up and saw Natasha leaning out of the window.'

'Be quick to come back and overpower them, my love,' she cried. 'The door is nearly broken through. Wait! Do that speech from Last of The Mohicans – you know, when Daniel Day-Lewis has to leave Madeleine Stowe at the waterfall.'

'Yeah yeah,' said Tony, rolling his eyes at a passer-by in an attempt to dissolve his embarrassment. 'OK. I'm on the ground.'

'Ready to rush back in and take them unawares?' shouted Natasha.

'Yeah yeah. Throw me the money belt.'

'But you can collect it when you come back up.'

'Er . . . I may need cash. For taxis. To buy a machine gun I mean.'

'How do I know you won't desert me?'

'If we can't trust each other Natasha, what hope is there?' he pleaded, pulling the tattered Daniel Day-Lewis mask back on to preserve some disguise. 'Taxi!'

'What did you say?'

'Nothing.'

'Here.' She threw the belt. And he hailed a taxi. This whole incident filled him with great regret and pain. He hated seeing her there, so beautiful and perfect, and so vulnerable and afraid. He felt a warm rush flood his body with an almost unbearable delight – like a large shot of vodka on a cold winter's night or a small line of pharmaceutical-grade heroin – when he saw how genuine the feeling between himself and Natasha had become in such a short time and despite all the odds. He was brought back to the present by the cab driver.

'Do you want me to wait for your friend, Mr Day-Lewis?'

'What?'

'That gorilla that's just jumped out of the window with a machine gun seems to want us to wait for him.'

Tony was stunned to see a large male silverback picking himself up from the pavement and brushing shards of glass from his pelt.

'No, just drive.'

'OK. Don't see that very much these days in Petersburg, gorillas with machine guns. Hardly any armed primates of any description in fact.

'Loved *My Beautiful Laundrette* by the way. I must ask though – what's it like snogging a bloke?'

'Well . . .'

'Don't think I could do that myself even if you paid me – course they did pay you didn't they least I hope they did not much call for that kind of thing in this line of work although don't get me wrong live and let live that's what I say.'

'Please, just be quiet and take me to the airport.'

He could still see Natasha, leaning out of the window, furious and betrayed, her hair so bouncy, shiny and full of life he was reminded for a moment of a Pedigree Chum advert. He then found himself wondering if she used Pantene New Formula Conditioner (for all hair types), whether the flick-curls at the end of Natasha's raven tresses were natural, or the perfect example of what Redken Smart Hairspray, with its revolutionary genetically engineered organic microchip shaping enzyme, could do for the busy woman about town of today.

Then, before he could speculate further, she was calling down imprecations on his head.

'I curse you Tony Hardstaff! I curse you for abandoning me. I will track you to the ends of the earth for vengeance!'

For a flashing moment they had stood together miraculously on the threshold of another kind of life, and just as suddenly he had dashed it from both their lips. Not that you can dash a threshold from anyone's lips, of course.

At the airport he asked to get on the very next plane to England and, after passing a few bribes here and there, found himself sitting aboard a flight bound for Yeadon airport near Leeds, amidst the members of the Purston-St Petersburg Friendship Society. This had been founded in the days of Peter the Great, as the members of the local proto-Rugby League team (in those days the ball used was a live British bulldog) had developed a great admiration for the Russian Czar when they learnt of his curious combination of progressive genius in socio-economic policy and propensity for random acts of terrifying violence. Indeed, to this day, there is not a member of a West Yorkshire Town Council's controlling group who is not fully appraised of all biographies of Czar Peter.

Tony took another huge slug of my prize tequila.

'It seemed as if fate was taking me home. I had nowhere else to run. Maybe the fortune-teller was right. At any rate, I had no other options. It was the only place on earth no one would consider looking for me.'

'Nobody should have to apologise for wanting to visit their parents,' said Conchita kindly.

'Huh,' said Tony, and slowly ground a cigarette out on his forearm.

CHAPTER FIVE

S o it was that a few hours later Tony found himself at
Leeds railway station investigating the cheapest ticket
deal he could get to travel the twenty miles to Grimedale,
the town he had left behind so many years before. After
the six-hour wait in the queue, Tony finally understood
how it had been moving so slowly, as the booking clerk
needed two hours and a variety of highly sophisticated
visual display technology to explain to Tony the various
ticket options available to him. He then shoved a pile of
handbooks through the grille so that Tony could reflect at
his leisure. Tony chose the cheapest, travelling via Torquay
with a compulsory stopover at a Noel Edmonds Theme Park,
for £8 inclusive. He arrived in Grimedale four days later.

It was a Saturday morning when he stepped down from
the train. The ticket collector – a small, wizened man –
had been working at the station since Tony was born. He
was like some menacing lizard from a detoxing alcoholic's
hallucinations. It always seemed he was poised to spring
forward and bite you in the throat, and infant nightmares
on this theme were swirling out of Tony's dormant memory
like the flying monkeys in the *Wizard of Oz*. He skulked

through the gate at the furthermost possible point from the rattlesnake man, whose fierce eyes, like two tiny lead split-shots, followed him contemptuously the whole way.

'See lad, I told thee to gerra return ticket all them years since,' he sneered. 'I knew tha'd be back even if thy dint. Tha can tek t'lad out o' Grimedale but tha waint tek Grimedale out o'lad,' he added, almost logically.

Tony stood in the station car-park and looked around him. The canal still led out eastwards across the lower, flatter terrain towards Wakefield and far beyond where it met the River Calder and ultimately the Ouse and Humber. The high moorland still surrounded the town on its other three sides. He was disappointed to find himself scanning the northern slopes until he spotted the line of black trees which concealed the house he had been born in from the road. Only then did he turn and look for Emily's house, which stood in a similar position to the south.

Dominating the whole town, casting a long shadow down its main street, was the huge black monolith which was the headquarters of the Hardstaff Corporation. A thousand different enterprises in a hundred different countries. The building – black marble, reflective windows, a waterfall cascading down one terraced side of the structure, nourishing a variety of exotic plants, a huge bronze statue of Obadiah Hardstaff bestriding the entrance-way, uniformed security guards with Dobermans patrolling day and night. Seventy-two floors. Office space for four thousand. A gym and a swimming pool in the basement. A helipad on the roof. And it was all for show. Empty. Nowadays, the Hardstaff

Corporation, thanks to computer technology, consisted of billions and billions of little chunks of electronic information, and two people – Obadiah, and his daughter Jane, who analysed and redeployed this electronic information with the tapping of a few keys. The building stood simply as a monument to Obadiah Hardstaff's megalomania.

Tony stood and stared at the statue of his father, and was disturbed, when he caught his own reflection in the black marble plinth, to see how similar in frame and build they were. The same sharp features, the same cocky stance, the firm look of determination in the set of the jaw and the jutting upward tilt of the head. He suspected the sculptor had been under orders to flatter Obadiah's girth, but knowing his father was somewhat fatter was scant consolation. Essentially all that differed between them in appearance was age.

Pepe was fascinated, and confused. 'Señor Tony, could you explain in more detail about the operation of the family business?'

'Hey – this story is about me, OK, not them. All you need to know is that they're very very rich, OK?'

'OK. I only asked.'

Tony needed a drink. It started to rain as he walked on towards the centre, and soon the hills were hidden by low cloud slouching in from Lancashire, sucking all colour from the dirty sandstone terraces.

The main road at the other end of the station access-road was now one-way. Not one of the line of cars halted by the pelican crossing was less than eight years old. The nightclub on the other side, a brick shoebox, had changed its name. It was no longer 'Coco's, Grimedale's Polynesian Nite Klub Scene', but proudly announced itself in green and pink neon letters as 'Phuk-Et! Thai One On ToNite!' There was a tiny neon palm tree at each end of the name.

Leading up to the town hall was a grey concrete pedestrianised zone half full of half-empty market stalls which Tony, straining to remember, had last known as a busy little street full of old independent shops and a coffee bar called the Alhambra where he and Dave had enjoyed putting a Fleetwood Mac song called 'Someone's Gonna Get Their Head Kicked in Tonite' on the juke-box and staring at youths they didn't know. It was now a Dunkin' Donuts. A pale-faced teenager perched on a high plastic stool glared at him aggressively through the window. The fish and chip shop on the corner had been extended next door, where formerly had stood an ancient foul-smelling red-brick public convenience. The new development was no longer a fish shop, but a burger bar called the Mechanically Recovered Meat Emporium. It was not clear which building had colonised the other.

Shoppers walked around like prisoners in a Gulag. It was *Blade Runner* painted by L.S. Lowry.

The main street was now another pedestrianised zone. Most of the buildings Tony remembered had disappeared. The neo-Gothic town hall at one end was still there, and the eighteenth-century church, with its domed bell-tower that always reminded Tony of a plastic pepper pot, the kind you got at school. The fine Georgian front of the Black Lion, plastered with adverts for happy hours, strippers, disco nights and Thai (spelt Thie) food. That was about it.

Half the shop units were boarded up, the rest occupied exclusively by high-street chains. They all had bright lettering and posters in the windows screaming out incredible and fantastic and unbeatable special deals and offers with dozens of exclamation marks and aberrant apostrophes. The intention behind all this, as with the various pastel shades of brickwork in the disturbingly vulgar neo-Classical Prince Charles-style architecture, must have been to appear cheerful and irresistibly attractive, but in their dismal surroundings it just seemed like they were taking the piss. Or maybe a drowning woman trying to keep her lipstick and smile just before she went under for the third time.

Overweight extended families all dressed in the latest prestige sportswear waddled around eating takeaways. He flicked his cigarette end into the burnt-out remains of a litter bin and sat down on a bench at the foot of the Billy Bremner Memorial Clocktower and breathed deeply. He felt suddenly very anxious, a growing panic he had experienced before only once, when he had visited an Ikea store and felt very uneasy, alienated in a new and incomprehensible environment composed of recognisable objects in unreal settings, and surrounded by swarms of families who, unlike him, all seemed to know how the system worked. His meditations were broken by a sharp pain in his leg, and he turned to see a small boy with a diamond earring with the word 'Leet' shaved into his crew cut stabbing him with a plastic chip-fork.

The boy's father, an exact copy of the son, except bigger and with no discernible neck, slapped the child round the head without apparently looking up from his own takeaway.

As the slap landed, the boy automatically sank his head into his shoulders and took the full force of the blow without spilling a chip. Evolution demonstrated. Tony realised he might have been seeing the past through a tinted wash. One thing was certain though. He needed a drink.

Most of the pubs where he had done his teenage drinking had new names, but at least the street was pretty much the same. Eighteen pubs side by side, all presumably profitable enough to resist the developer's bullozer. His father's bulldozer.

What once was the Blue Bell was now called 'The Glue Boilers' Arms'. But he realised that he was going to have to accept that just about everything had changed in some way. He walked in and every drinker turned to look at him as he approached the bar. No doubt they would have all stopped talking too, but for the fact no one was. Constant conversation had always been looked on suspiciously in West Yorkshire. It might lead to intimacy. Before you knew it someone would have found something out about you, and then where would you be? The juke-box was playing Thin Lizzy's version of 'Whiskey in the Jar'. A girl in a black mini-dress and permed hair tottered past him on white sling-backs and vomited outside the door. It all gave him a feeling of reassurance. In here at least, in fifteen years, nothing had changed in the slightest.

Certainly not the barman. The same man, the two patches of hair on either side of his bald head greyer, but otherwise not much different at all.

'Hello Derek,' said Tony, recalling the name automatically.

'Now then Tony.' The tone was on the undemonstrative side of phlegmatic. 'You haven't been in for a while.'

'No. Must be fifteen years.'

'T'usual?'

'Aye.'

Tony sat at a corner table where he could see the poster of Marianne Faithful in *Girl on a Motor Cycle* and still overhear conversation at the bar. There was none, for about two pints. Then, from outside, something was blocking what meagre light was managing to squeeze through the bull's-eyed window panes. A moment later a huge man filled the doorway and in three massive steps reached the bar. He wore old combat trousers, boots, a worn NCB donkey jacket with an old Fred Perry and a Pringle sweater underneath. Tony caught his eye.

'Now then Tony, you've not been in for a while.'

'Aye, must be fifteen years, Dave.'

'T'usual?'

'Aye.'

Dave handed Tony a pint of bitter without looking at him, and then went and sat at the very far end of the bench which Tony occupied.

Dave and Tony had been mates forever, since their first day at primary school, when they were five. No one had spoken to Tony for four days, because they all knew what family he was from. Even the teachers ignored him. The only person who had not sent him to Coventry was Dave, who would come up to him at playtime and say:

'I'm gonna bray thee tha posh bastard.'

This went on until the Thursday, each boy eyeballing the other, until Dave snapped Tony's pencil at morning playtime and Tony smashed his milk bottle over Dave's head and a furious fight ensued. Both boys had been cut by the flying glass, but if they noticed it at all it only served to fire their rage and aggression. They thrashed away at each other for a good ten minutes, surrounded by a thick ring of screaming, chanting schoolmates until finally a teacher stepped in and pulled them apart, though only because Tony – the rich kid – appeared to be winning. They were taken to the casualty ward, in separate cars, for the moment they were both put in the back seat of the headmistress's Toyota (the first Japanese car in Grimedale, and a topic of considerable discussion and less than approving comment in 1966) they had started fighting again. Dave needed four stitches in his head, Tony six in his hand, all of which had been reopened the next day, even before the nine o'clock bell, as the two boys piled in on each other once more in the playground. After a week of this, they had somehow gained a respect for each other's ability to throw and take a punch, and were also beginning to consider themselves separate from the baying crowds who simply stood around them and watched the action. They both now had their gangs of acolytes who flattered them and wanted to be their best friends, but somehow they knew that being prepared to slug it out set them apart, and sensed that the only admiration worth anything was the other's.

Of course, it took a while to express this, although the frequency of their fights came down to one or two a year, with results pretty much even. By the time they were eleven or twelve, both were going to watch Leeds United on a regular basis, or rather to hang around on the fringes of the hooligan element. Here they still kept their distance from each other as best they could, but were looked on as two peas from the same pod as far as the older hardcore lunatics were concerned. They would travel on the same buses and trains, and ignore each other, but then, in the action, often stand side by side as they taunted rival fans with the ritual chanted insults, kicking at the same isolated fan who lay in the street, like a couple of hyenas lurking behind a lion-pride. Then they would travel home again, barely acknowledging each other. Until one day, both were trapped in a compartment with a dozen Sheffield Wednesday fans. When both refused to stuff their Leeds scarves down the toilet, they were subjected to a beating, but stood shoulder to shoulder fighting for what they would have claimed was the honour of their team until someone pulled the communication cord and they were carried in the same ambulance to Wakefield Infirmary. This time they did not fight but shook hands, and then embraced, finally able to admit what they had felt for each other since that first Thursday seven years before.

They stopped going to football after that; they fished, chased girls round Woolworth's on a Saturday afternoon, bought bottles of cider and drank them in pub car-parks or wherever they could find a low wall to sit on, compared penis sizes (erect and flaccid), passed on garbled gobbets of the 'facts of life', learnt how to spit long distances, invited girls to parties, played strip poker and spin the bottle and postman's knock, shot rats, went to rock concerts, swapped

LPs, learnt how to vomit and carry on drinking, chased girls round town on Saturday nights, took girls on double dates, learnt how to repair old bangers, told each other 'how much they'd got' off their girlfriends, learnt what a hangover was, how to put on a condom, how to talk to policemen who had pulled you over when you'd had three pints. How to roll a joint, to call it 'rocky' or 'red leb'. Where to buy it. They were mates. Then Tony had left home.

And they now sat a few feet apart after an absence of fifteen years. Neither of them spoke for another ten minutes or so. Tony had an indelible sense-memory of ten to twelve minutes being the optimum time to spend on a pint at this stage of the session. Anything longer would have been considered strong evidence that the drinker had 'gone soft' as a result of being away from Grimedale, with all the moral deficiencies that implied. He whacked down the three-quarter pint that remained in his glass and walked to the bar.

'T'usual Dave?'

'Yes please Tony.'

After another round each, bought this time without any words being exchanged, nor indeed looks, the preliminaries had been observed, and some kind of conversation was considered permissible.

'So, Dave . . . you're still weight-training then I see.'

'Aye. Got some great new tattoos and all.' He removed his jacket and rolled up the sleeve of his huge left arm. If they ever had a fight now, there would only be one winner.

'Milton's *Paradise Lost* tattooed round this bicep. And *Paradise Regained* round the other.'

'Great, Dave.'

'Aye. Bit more sophisticated than *Love* and *Hate* on your knuckles.'

'Aye.'

'Students did it at rag week. I'm in t'*Guinness Book of Records* for that.'

'Fantastic.'

'Means you've always summat to read on't bog.'

'How long has this been a theme pub then?'

'Theme pub? No, it really is a glue boilers'. You can fetch your dead pets in and that and boil their bones up for glue. They've vats at the back. Bit of pin money, you know. There's not much going round here in the way of work you see. Whereas, it's very popular in Harrogate, is glue. They collect stamps and have scrapbooks and all sorts so I hear, in Harrogate. So what you been doing?'

Tony wanted to be forthcoming enough to imply an invitation to friendship, and yet knew he should keep the story brief. He thought he'd got the balance about right, although still attracted several disapproving looks from the silent drinkers at the bar.

Dave murmured occasionally as Tony spoke, though whether it was interest or contempt was not always easy to tell.

'. . . and so here I am back again.'

Dave nodded and remained silent for a full quarter of an hour.

'I got your postcards,' said Dave.

'Good. How about you?'

'Not a lot.' He paused again, then turned to half-face Tony.

'It's very much more Ken Loach than Busby Berkeley round here you know, since the pits went and that. Ducking, diving, scrimping and saving, devoting myself to the wife and kids, getting pissed through despair, committing acts of terrible violence that nonetheless have their causes in social conditions . . . I tell you, if I could've afforded Mike Mansfield QC as my barrister, I wouldn't have done a day's time in me life . . . Morris dancing to preserve some vestige of the internal spirit within me which the system attempts to crush and snuff out – and the system round here incidentally is symbolised by your family; no offence – That's about it really. Bit of gardening. Come on, sup up, you've still four pints left.'

'I'm not used to drinking at this pace.'

'Get 'em down thee or landlord'll set dogs on thee for being Southern.'

They left the Glue Boilers' and headed to the Greyhound. It was now dark outside.

'We'll have one in there, then we'll do the Crown and Artichoke,' said Dave. 'Then we'll have two in the Trout and Slide Rule then the Rottweiler and Child. All right?'

As they approached the market place, they could hear the noise of a crowd shouting. There was a serious fist-fight going on. One group of about fifty young men were driving another group of about the same size towards a coach. Some were dressed in ordinary street clothes: shell suits, jeans, bomber jackets. Some had donkey jackets and miners' helmets. Others appeared to be a brass band, in uniform. Another group were dressed as redcoats, and fighting side by side with a group of eighteenth-century peasants. Women in crinoline dresses ran screaming away from the seat of the action, while a mixed group in skiing anoraks and designer hiking boots cowered behind a minibus . . .

'Scabs!' said Dave, and piled into the fight. Tony hesitated. 'What's up with you?' screamed Dave over his shoulder. 'You yitten or what?' It was true, partly, Tony was afraid. 'I don't know who I'm supposed to be hitting,' he said. And might have added 'Or why,' but didn't. 'Scabs' was good enough reason to hit first and get details later. Besides, he needed a bed for the night and he wasn't going to get one from Big Dave if he didn't show willing.

'Just stick next to me then.'

Dave picked someone up, butted him in the face and threw him to one side. Tony kicked him in the chest and ran into the main group. Dave was in the process of throttling a stocky ginger-haired man with one hand. As Dave dropped his victim on to the pavement, Tony was struck by how pale and sickly his complexion was and found himself thinking it must have been months since he'd eaten any fresh fruit or vegetables. He whacked the ginger boy in the ear. Dave was now holding a Roundhead high in the air, and hurled him at an oncoming crowd of brass bandsmen. Tony had no idea what was happening, assumed he was having an acid flashback, took a deep breath and tried to make the best of it.

Suddenly there were sirens and blue lights all around

them and two dozen riot police were piling out of Black Marias and baton-charging them in a flying wedge. Everyone scattered to the far end of the square. Then, without a word or a look, both the scabs and their former assailants turned and charged the police together. Tony was confused, for he now noticed that at the head of their charge were a dozen or so riot police. The police at the other side of the market place, who were now advancing slowly, as if giving the rioters time to disperse, faltered in their step, obviously thrown by being confronted by their colleagues. Dave pulled Tony by the shoulder.

'Come on, that's enough. We've buggered their filming for the night, that's main thing.' They slipped down an alleyway and into the Woodbine and Whippet.

'What was all that about?'

'Bloody film crews, wasn't it? Since the pits shut down, all these film crews have started turning up from down South, making feature films about life in the post-industrial north, and the miners' strike, and the Brontës and whatever the fuck else has happened in Yorkshire in the last five hundred years. Remember Wardy? He had a job at Pontefract castle reenacting th'death of Richard the Second. Had to sit in a dungeon for eight hours a day pretending he was starving to death.'

'He always was thin.'

'Thin? I've seen more fat on a chip. That's how he got t'job in the first place. Any road, you get seventy-five quid a day for being an extra. It was great for a while, you'd get one or two days a month. But then this agency sets up in Wakefield getting people to do it for fifty. Well we're not having that. I mean, scabs playing miners fighting scabs? Bloody ridiculous, in't it? By the way, it's your round.'

They stayed in the Whippet until closing time, as there was a lot of activity outside. A couple of Dave's friends had joined them about nine thirty, and said there was a rumour that the whole riot may have been incited by a documentary crew making a film about warring feature-film crews in West Yorkshire. 'It's postmodernism gone mad if you ask me,' said one of them, putting his pint pot down on the bar with a conviction that forbade any further debate.

'Mind you,' said Dave, 'good preparation for the inevitable conflict to come.'

'Aye.'

Tony had missed something. 'Sorry?'

'You know – the Big One. Or, as it is more correctly known, Ragnarok.'

'Ragnarok?'

'Ragnarok, Tony – it is written. In the mythology of our Aryan forebears. Ragnarok – Twilight of the Gods, when They try and take over, and t'world will be consumed by fire and only the righteous shall survive.'

'When "they" try and take over?'

'"They." You know – federal government, international financiers, transnational-Zionist conspiracy, Arabs . . . I've got a list somewhere – anyway they're going to weaken us with localised nuclear attacks first to paralyse communications right. I can't remember exactly but it's all in *Guns and Ammo*, you know. Not sure if t'Vatican's in on it or not . . . I'll lend it you. So, any road up point is, we'll have to live rough for a while, on us wits and that, you know, and then come back out fighting like, when they move in to try and steal us womenfolk off us. Want a bag of pork scratchings?'

'What are you talking about?'

'We're in constant training to preserve the ancient traditions of our Aryan blood, and survive the Big One. Me and the rest of the lads in the Morris Dancers.'

'Survivalist Morris Dancers?'

'That's it. We go training up on t'moors at weekends. Take twelve bore, shoot a few rabbits, sleep in tent, get in't sweat-lodge, bond, beat up anyone who betrays physical excitement at the homoerotic undertones of it all, back Sunday night in time for a curry. You'd love it.'

'Sounds great. Perhaps I should be going.'

Suddenly Tony realised that they were on their eighth round. He knew this because Dave had lurched across the distance between them and put Tony in a painful headlock.

'Tha's going nowhere Tony lad,' said Dave with genuine passion, 'it's good to see thee again,' and ground Tony's forehead into the dark wooden table. (Eight pints was generally the point where inhibitions were relaxed to the point where affection could be expressed through physical contact.)

'So Tony lad, where are you stopping tonight?' Dave was slapping his throat to bring him round.

'Hadn't really thought about it.'

'You can't go round to your mum and dad's in this state. You'd best stop wi' me.'

'Great. So is there no regular work around here at all now?' said Tony, dazed, and for no clear reason.

Everyone turned and looked at him as if he had just arrived from a different planet.

'Bloody hell! Now I know who you are. It's Tony Hardstaff! What brings you back?'

Tony kind of recognised everyone. The only problem was they all seemed to look the same. Thick necks, inscrutable faces, short-cropped hair, polo shirts.

'I dunno really.'

'He's trying to get a share of Jacob Earnshaw's will.'

'I didn't even know he'd died.'

'Aye, yesterday afternoon. Our Terry was there – you know he does the garden . . . anyhow from what I heard, yon batty lass of his threw a party for him . . .'

'Emily?' Tony noticed, along with everyone else, the excitement in his voice.

'Aye, Emily. Well she read out this poem she'd writ and said she loved him.'

'What, in front of company?'

'Aye.'

'What, and he killed himself out of embarrassment did he?'

'No. He started . . . crying.'

There was a pause of utter amazement.

'Crying?'

'In front of guests?'

'Aye, couldn't stop. Weeping and weeping he was, collapsed, went into a coma, that was it.'

'Just goes to show.'

'Aye.'

'There was this . . . psychiatrist on Radio Cutsyke, she

said it was because for the first time in all his life he'd let out an ... emotion ...' Everyone fidgeted uncomfortably at the word '... and there were so much pain and anger and fear and I don't know what bottled up inside him, letting it out were just too much for his system.'

'Like a volcanic eruption.'

'There you are then.'

'Aye. But then she went on to say that it was a lesson for us all to ... get in touch with us feelings.'

'Bollocks. Just shows what happens when you do.'

'Southerner was she?'

'Course she was.'

'If you ask me it all started going wrong when they started having in substitutes in Rugby League,' said an ancient man in a cloth cap at the end of the bar, who looked like he'd spent several centuries asleep in a peat bog. 'Made people give in to pain.'

Everyone stared into their pints to consider the possible truth of this.

'Look at the Brisbane Test of 1914,' the old man went on.

(He referred, of course, to the famous 'Rorke's Drift' Test Match.)

'Nine men against thirteen and we still held out and beat the Aussies. Nowadays we've got subs and physios and God knows fucking what and they piss on us even with half their best players missing. *And* that were in Australia.'

Everyone looked back into their pints again. He might have a point. Nobody spoke for a while. The danger of talking about showing emotions was that you might show them by talking about them.

'So have you come back for a share of the will then?' There was a sense of relief that the conversation had got back to material things.

'Like I say,' said Tony. 'I didn't know he was dead; I thought he must have died years ago.'

'Had a good innings. How old was he?'

'A hundred and eighty-three,' said Dave. 'It was the bet with your dad kept 'em both alive, Tony. They might have been a pair of ruthless capitalist bastards, but they were hard. Well, your dad still is. Hundred eighty-three and still going strong. Pretty good is that.'

'I assumed he must be dead by now, actually.'

'Oh. Well, best get some more ale in.'

The whistling of the frogs in the dusk around us swelled and sustained momentarily in reaction to this incredible piece of information, as if they could understand the Gringo's narrative; but I suspect it was no more than a convenient pathetic fallacy. Pepe raised his hand politely.

'Excuse me Señor Tony, I have a question. Have I understood correctly that you just said your father was one hundred and eighty-three years old?'

'Yes,' said Tony.

Although it may sound bizarre, this is the explanation that Tony gave us, and it was one part of his unlikely narrative which never differed in the slightest detail. He explained that his father and Jacob Earnshaw were exact contemporaries, to within a couple of months, and had always been fierce business rivals. At the age of twenty, with the Industrial Revolution in full spate, they were both very wealthy and powerful men. Their business interests spread over many areas – mining, steel, shipping, weaving, woollen mills – but neither could quite get the better of the other commercially, and so they began inventing other ways of locking antlers, and fell into a pattern of cunning and relentless oneupmanship. One began setting up sickness benefits for his workforce, the other would tolerate trade unions; the first embarked on a programme of building model dwellings; the other would institute holiday pay. For each knew the other could not bear to part with money, and yet had to compete with the other for the public popularity their apparent altruism engendered. Philanthropic contributions to churches, hospitals, schools, sports clubs followed. Then the field of conflict widened. They began to challenge each other with a series of outrageous bets. Who could be first to seduce a Brontë sister (all three died before either succeeded – and indeed some say the constant attentions of these two boorish men hastened the decline of the frail but passionate geniuses) . . . both ran for Parliament. Both were elected. The bet then became who could make the most apparently sincere but actually insulting speech about Florence Nightingale. Obadiah Hardstaff gracefully conceded that Jacob Earnshaw's speech was the winner, in which he argued that by improving conditions in the Crimean hospitals, Miss Nightingale was encouraging the British troops to be careless on the battlefield. But this defeat rankled deeply, and Obadiah Hardstaff was determined to have the last laugh. One evening, when they were riding home together from heckling William Wilberforce at a Friends' Meeting House, Hardstaff hit upon the ultimate challenge. He was in a furious mood, as Earnshaw had once more won the evening's bet, that he could provoke a Quaker into physical violence, and was exultantly nursing a broken nose to prove it. Hardstaff was beside himself. Suddenly he had the next challenge. The ultimate wager. He would bet Jacob Earnshaw that he would outlive him. Furthermore, the first to die would surrender all his possessions and assets to the other. 'Imagine the pain of defeat on your deathbed, Earnshaw! Imagine the despair with which you will slip out of this world, knowing that at the last, your bitterest rival takes all that you have striven to outdo him with. The knowledge that, effectively, you have failed in everything!'

And of course, Earnshaw could do nothing but accept, for a refusal would in itself be an immediate admission of defeat – even to imply in the faintest terms that his rival had a scintilla of possibility of winning the bet was to lose it, psychologically, on the spot. The terror of the final defeat was impossible to concede. No fear or showing of pain or the anticipation of it could be brooked. They shook hands, making a precautionary pact that assassination would make the bet null and void, and dined that night famously, celebrating the way they could both – unspoken acknowledgement though it was – look utter desolation in the face and risk all upon it.

So it was that willpower, greed and naked hatred kept them living through the years. They both threw themselves into the administration of their empires, each thinking the other's health would perhaps be adversely affected by missing a trick, the other making a shrewd new investment, exploiting a new territory or making some startling technical innovation. Of these, the most famous was the spirit level. Obadiah cornered the market in manufacturing these essential building tools, even though he had to visit Birmingham to do it. It was the furthest south he ever travelled, apart from the minimal and perfunctory visits he made to the House of Commons when he was a member. For decades neither thought of marriage, or families, until, in 1936, he encountered Quintillia.

A shameless libertine, Obadiah would use women but never wanted to marry one until he met Quintillia. His desire was clear and simple: he had slept with women whose names began with every letter of the alphabet but Q, and was determined not to be denied. She was the fifth daughter of the Earl of Tanshelf, an impoverished nobleman. A voluptuous Bright Young Thing, she was an extraordinary example of her aristocratic class, combining a low native cunning and self-serving ruthlessness on an instinctive level with the intellect of a greyhound. She was twenty-one when Obadiah met her at a fundraising ball for Sir Oswald Mosley's Blackshirts. Her family had been landowners in West Yorkshire for hundreds of years, possessing huge tracts of the most beautiful countryside in the county. When Obadiah surveyed the rolling pastures on his first visit, he was captivated by their ancient timeless beauty and the potential he saw in them for overspill development for the several overcrowded mill-towns he owned, and decided on the spot that Quintillia was the only one for him. On her part Quintillia saw her chance to refresh her ancient and noble bloodline with some unfamiliar genes for the first time since the Crusades, and with the one practical thing the family lacked: money. Quintillia's family seat was situated high on the hill above Grimedale, on the north side of the valley. Its original structure had been built during the reigns of Stephen and Matilda, when vicious civil war savaged England for twenty years. The first Earl Tanshelf was descended from the Digger of the Royal Latrines, and generations had loyally served each monarch from William the Conqueror onwards in their campaigns. Personal hygiene was nobody's strong point in those days, but the Tanshelfs were exceptionally odoriferous, even by contemporary standards. Thus, when the Fourth Earl embarked on an ambitious strategy to win the ear of the King, and advancement perhaps to some junior post in the Keeper of the Royal Bedchamber's employ, the court was always aware when he was in the room, but less than gleeful about it. At first, a simple execution was considered: some trumped-up offence could easily be invented, and indeed, in 1147, an act was passed in Parliament – the Offensive Odours Act – which forbade anyone who stank, in the Lord Chamberlain's opinion, from standing within ten yards of the Royal Presence, and twenty yards if upwind. The Earl of Tanshelf was undeterred, however, and merely took to shouting his compliments from without the stipulated distance. Moreover, he did his job very well, with no complaints, even after the famous skirmish at Whitstable, where, fighting a remnant band of Hereward the Wake's guerrillas, the army had lived for three weeks on dodgy oysters and stale Kentish beer. So while the King had no qualms about charging anyone with treason, there was a sense of indebtedness which kept the Earl alive, together with two further reasons: firstly, a humble petition on behalf of the Guild of Master Torturers and Executioners begged him not to make any of them spend more than five minutes in the same cell as the Earl were he ever arrested, and secondly, despite widespread tendering, no one else in the kingdom of sufficient rank was prepared to take over responsibility for the latrines. So a compromise was reached. The Earl was allotted a small estate in Yorkshire, and in return would send his eldest son to court to carry out the time-honoured service, with the stipulation that he must not talk to or approach any member of the court unless spoken to, and that he wore a shirt of lavender flowers and violets at all times. The Earl repaired to the North, convinced it was reward for his loyal service and shrewd flattery, when in fact it was simply because he was a victim of that all too common human failing, thinking his shit didn't stink. Even when his feudal tenants presented him constantly with posies of sweet-smelling moorland flowers, he was none the wiser. Since that time, the Tanshelfs had cunningly and industriously built on their good fortune. They trained the sons of local peasantry in the tricks of the family business, and hired them out to surrounding landowners for handsome profits. The Earl wrote treatises on latrines – or rather, about them – conducting scholarly experiments as to the best type of woods for both seat and handrail, the best method of cleaning oneself afterwards (after much trial and error, the Earl pronounced the finest, most efficient and pleasurable means was the neck of a live yearling goose. This last is thought to have given rise to the local expression, 'as angry as a goose on its first birthday'). He also developed the best method of breaking down the waste material into quality compost, which he then sold at great profit to various estates across the Pennines in Lancashire, to the huge and constant delight of all the great houses of Yorkshire, and the less great ones as well. Various legends have been handed down as to why the Lancastrians did not use their own waste for this purpose – that they were too stupid; that their own waste, on account of the wetter climate, was too soft to mature into decent compost, and that they bought out of snobbery, in that the Tanshelfs were Latrine Keepers by Appointment to the King, with their famous Coat of Arms, Two Shovels Crossed on a Bed of Jaune, with Geese Sheepish and the motto beneath, *'Felicitas Foramen in Recto Est'*.

The Tanshelf family had shrewdly exploited the strategic situation of their property, offering protection to the sur-rounding populace behind high limestone walls in return for money, goods, ownership of farms and whatever else they could think of. Gradually the estates and the house grew, and by the mid-nineteenth century it had reached its present state, an imposing building, an eclectic mixture of various architectural styles.

Obadiah's wooing was perfunctory, but it seems both sides knew what was on the table. Obadiah's age was no obstacle in Quintillia's eyes, when matched against the size of his assets and within six months they were mar-ried. Shortly after the wedding, Quintillia's four sisters, her parents and her elder brother all perished in a freak accident, falling down a mineshaft which collapsed beneath their weight when they were out for their customary constitutional stroll on the moor.

Thus Obadiah became master of the estate, and the ancestral home, in recognition of one of the best-known goods in his industrial empire, became known round about as The House of the Spirit Levels.

Obadiah was too busy during the War to think of children; he was too busy working for the nation, as he put it. And certainly he worked very hard. Although for which nation was a subject of some debate. Certainly he supplied the Allies with substantial amounts of hardware, but his enterprising spirit, as he himself described it, led him into other areas. It was not easy to travel between Britain, Switzerland and South America in the War years, but he managed it.

It was only in the late fifties that Obadiah allowed the possibility of his death to cross his mind even for a brief moment, but when he did, it stirred him to procreate as soon as possible. If he won the bet, having heirs to take possession of Jacob Earnshaw's wealth was, he suddenly realised, essential, to provide the salt to rub in the wounds. Furthermore, if he lost the bet – a prospect he refused to give much headroom, but it lurked – then he would gain satisfaction from knowing how his devastation would be borne also by his offspring, and he gained solace from the fact that materially they would find the sudden change in their social situation even harder to deal with than he would. They had a daughter, Jane, and one son, Tony.

Doctors were baffled by Obadiah's longevity. He had a very strong constitution, certainly, but this was something else. There were rumours of satanic rites, of vampirism, even of vegetarian diets, but the truth was simple: 'Greed, willpower and hatred'.

All that was known of Obadiah Hardstaff's past was that he had been a foundling, brought up by a childless local farmer as his own. There was nothing to suggest in his early days that he would turn out to be such a monster. He had been baptised like any other child, and the ceremony had passed like any other. Superstitious minds point out that the day he had been christened there was a total eclipse of the sun, a terrible storm had raged for twenty-four hours during which it rained frogs, rain and fish, and a bolt of lightning severed the church spire, bringing down a hail of masonry just as the congregation moved outside. A number of small stones hit the baby, marking him on the forehead with three small scars which resembled the figures 666. But there's no stopping idle chit-chat.

Jacob Earnshaw was similarly hale and hearty. Tall and fair, he was walking evidence of how far the Vikings penetrated into West Yorkshire. His father had been a local lawyer and landowner. He had married a woman he actually loved, and perhaps in this lay his eventual downfall. The daughter of schoolteachers, Methodists from Baildon way, Elizabeth Sykes was a bright and self-confident girl. She was a respectable pianist and was also encouraged wholeheartedly in her academic activities, eventually winning a scholarship at Christ Church, Oxford, where she studied Natural Sciences. Oxford in those days admitted few women, and Christ Church none. She had been rejected from Lady Margaret Hall for being too Northern, and applied to Christ Church under a false male name. At the interview she had been considered somewhat effeminate despite her disguise, but the dons decided that when all was said and done she was no more so than the bulk of their usual intake.

After graduating she worked in one of Earnshaw's chemical factories. Earnshaw at that time had pondered on the strategies behind Hardstaff's marriage, and concluded it was a challenge which he had to meet in kind. He therefore held a series of Grand Balls for his various companies. This was partly to see if any of his employees were eligible prospective partners, in a way that saved time spent being introduced to people who didn't know who he was and who would perhaps need convincing that he was an impressive and important and desirable bachelor. A secondary motive was to taunt Hardstaff, who disliked socialising not only as a waste of time and money, but also because he was not very good at it. He knew, as well as Earnshaw did, that his awkwardness in social situations was a sign of his fundamental lack of self-esteem.

Earnshaw met Miss Sykes, was taken by her beauty and her intellect. She was not the kind to be impressed or swayed merely by Earnshaw's status. However, she saw in him the potential to be a warmer human being than he generally appeared, and decided to marry him. They were a happy couple, and although Earnshaw remained a cunning businessman, under the influence of his wife, his ruthlessness abated and he began to develop interests in other areas, arts and culture, and appeared to enjoy them for their own sake rather than simply for appearances. This did not worry Hardstaff at first: in fact he was quite pleased as he was certain that these signs of softness guaranteed Earnshaw would be the first to fade away. He became more anxious when it appeared that Earnshaw's outside interests in fact seemed to make him stronger. The Earnshaws had one daughter, Emily, who was beautiful and who carried the artistic sensitivity of her mother, and seemed to bring out even more of the hidden warmth in her father, especially after Elizabeth's tragic death in the foot and mouth epidemic of 1966. Wearing a sheepskin coat she was shot by a drunken gamekeeper who mistook her for a wolverine after he had hallucinated while fasting over Lent.

Emily was an exact contemporary of Tony's.

Finally Earnshaw had given in to death with his outpouring of more than a century's stifled emotion, and the bet was won by Obadiah Hardstaff. This seemed to vindicate Obadiah's tougher, more single-minded attitude to the world. Earnshaw left a deathbed message, assuring his rival that he died happy, which Obadiah naturally took as complete bluff.

Returning from the bar with the next round, Tony tried to sound casual and disinterested.

'How is Emily?' he said. Inside, he was wondering if this was why fate had led him back home: to make it up with Emily, his childhood sweetheart, to atone for his cruel abandonment of her and find happiness in her arms.

Perhaps Emily was the beautiful woman that Mrs Yepanchin had seen in the cards.

Suddenly, Dave had Tony in another asphyxiating head-lock, and was rubbing his ears with his free hand. Tony was bent over with his face very close to the floor.

'Hey!' yelled the landlord from the other end of the bar. 'Mind that spittoon!'

Tony, opening his eyes, closed them again immediately, having seen enough to know he was within a cigarette paper of having his face shoved in the Woodbine and Whippet's internationally famous spittoon, which had not been emptied since 1660, when the Restoration of the Monarchy had caused such resentment amongst the staunch Levellers who drank in the Woodbine that they vowed to fill the spittoon on the day the monarch came back, and to empty it over the head of the departing one. It must be said that they had expected this to happen almost immediately, but the spittoon stood there as a reminder to all who cared to pay it any mind never to speak too soon.

'I said, careful with that spittoon.'

Tony was a little disappointed that the landlord seemd more concerned about the spittoon than he was about Tony's head ending up in it, but this was understandable in a way. The spittoon's fame and symbolism had spread far and wide, and was a big enough attraction for Japanese tourists to help the landlord shift a fair few more barrels of bitter through the year than otherwise. If it were spilt prematurely, he'd be out of pocket.

'I love this lad like a brother,' said Dave, slackening

the lock slightly so that he could assault the other side of Tony's head.

The next moment Tony realised he was upright again, and able to breathe. This gave him considerable pleasure, and he made a mental note never again to overlook the simple things in life, like oxygen, and being able to get it regularly. He collapsed on to one of the red velvet banquettes. A group of ladies came in and sat on him, apologising but claiming they hadn't noticed him. It was true – his red face blended in with the red velvet almost exactly. After ten minutes or so he had got his breath back.

'Bloody hell Dave . . .'

Everyone looked at him appalled, and he remembered how it was. It was common unspoken knowledge in Grimedale that if you liked someone you couldn't possibly hurt them however hard you hit them, because they were your friend, and so the violence was inflicted with an entirely different mental attitude. You were paying your friend the compliment of assuming he was hard enough to take his pain, and the least you could do, as a mate, was pay your assailant the compliment of confirming his trust in you, by not registering the pain. The rest of the bar was staring at Tony, waiting to see how he would finish his sentence.

'Bloody hell Dave, I thought for a moment you'd nearly hurt me there,' said Tony nonchalantly, and straightened his nose in the mirror. Everyone laughed and slapped him on the back. Someone got the pints in. He had come home. All he had to do now was go back to his parents, apologise for his past behaviour, the acrimonious nature of his parting and his fifteen years' absence, reconcile with them, become their son once more instead of the rebel outcast, gain their trust, and then repay their faith in him by getting hold of a big enough chunk of the family fortune to be able to disappear again, this time forever. And, if possible, make it up with Emily and take her with him. He ordered large whiskies all round.

CHAPTER SIX

W hen Tony awoke next morning a horde of Valkyrie were swooping down at him out of an immense bank of storm clouds. It was Dave's living-room ceiling.

He sat up carefully and was surprised to feel no pain or dizziness in his head, only a dull ache in his shoulder. He tried to recall how this had come about, couldn't, shrugged his shoulders and then cursed himself as the ache sharpened, mockingly pointed out his crapulous short-term memory-loss. Next to the empty Chinese takeaway containers on the coffee table there was a pint glass with a little water still in it, which he drank, and congratulated himself for having downed so much last night before crashing out on the couch. He was staring blankly at his socks, trying to decide which one to put on first, when Dave came in and set a mug of tea and a bacon sandwich on the table in front of him.

'Fantastic. Thanks Dave.'

'Just like the old days, eh?'

'You can't beat a bacon sandwich after a night on the ale.'

'You can't. There's plenty more in the kitchen if you

want one yourself. Just kidding!' He slapped Tony playfully round the head and Tony realised he wasn't completely unhungover after all.

'Here's a question though,' continued Dave, shouting as he disappeared back into the kitchen to fetch his own sandwich and tea, 'You know how they reckon pigs are really intelligent . . .'

'Yeah?'

Tony had followed Dave into the kitchen. He was not keen on walking around, but he needed to stop Dave shouting.

'Well, what if they proved that pigs knew what was going to happen to them in the abattoir . . . would you still be able to eat bacon with a clear conscience?'

'I've no idea. What's the answer?'

'I've no idea. It just occurred to me, that's all, while I was making the sandwiches.'

'Hey, you've got all my postcards on the wall.' Tony was touched, but didn't say so, obviously.

'Aye. You've done some travelling, eh?'

'Yeah. And now I'm back where I started. Well, anyway, pigs. I think they probably do know, don't they? I mean, seeing the pig in front of them get strung upside down and then getting his throat cut must be a bit of a clue.'

The challenge of thinking while vertical was proving too much for Tony. He took a deep breath, returned to the sofa and slumped into it.

'Aye, but I'm not talking about just before they get their throats cut, I'm talking about when they're on the farm, hanging out with their mates, having a stroll round the field – hopefully: I'm not a big fan of factory farming – getting fed, and all that . . . are they so intelligent that they know what's going to happen to them? And if they do, why don't they try and escape?'

'Well they do, some of them, don't they?'

'Not that many. Which leads me to ask – do you want some mustard? No? – do the bulk of pigs not try and escape because they're not as intelligent as we think they are, or because they meekly accept their fate?'

'I don't bloody know, Dave; it's eight o'clock in the morning. Can I have a bath here before I go . . . ?'

'Not if you don't venture an opinion on the pig question.'

'Bloody hell. What's the point of this?'

'I dunno, I just found it intellectually stimulating when it popped into me head.'

'OK. So you're asking is it wrong to eat pigs if they're intelligent enough to know what's going to happen to them?'

'Yeah.'

'Well you can't say, can you? Maybe they accept it. Maybe they decide to settle for a couple of years living . . .'

'. . . like a pig in shit—'

'Yeah, exactly, in exchange for you know, being, killed and eaten.'

'So you're saying they accept their destiny.'

'Am I? S'pose so.'

'OK, that's an opinion. Do you like me mural then?'

'Twilight of the Gods is it?'

'Got it in one. Beryl wanted me to paper over it. The kids kept having nightmares over the battle scenes.'

'You're really into this stuff, aren't you?'

Dave stared at him through the mist of his steaming 'I love the Teletubbies' jumbo mug. 'It's not a hobby Tony. That's *my* destiny. I'd have liked a better shade of pink on that sunset though eh? It's a bit kitschy in my opinion.'

'Yeah; but it has a certain . . . other-worldly quality to it . . . which is appropriate, given that the heroes are being transported beyond the evening sun to Valhalla. I take it that is Valhalla above the fish tank?'

'Yeah. It's doubly relaxing, having the fish swimming gently about at one level, and a representation of one's final resting place directly above. Puts things in perspective. More tea?'

'Please. You . . . you're headed for Valhalla then?'

'Aye, to be hoped, provided I perform well enough on the field of battle come the final conflict, you know. Would you like a creme egg with that?'

'No thanks, tea's fine. Yeah . . . I've been meaning to ask – how come all you lot are Odin worshippers anyway?'

'Very tough on crime was Odin. Basically you had no recidivists in them days. It was transgression equals blood debt equals local law enforcement gives thee a clip round the lughole with a two-bladed axe. It's very appealing, in today's complex global village, to have a few simple certainties. And you don't get much simpler than a two-bladed axe round the lughole.'

'Right, and how did you get into all this stuff in the first place?'

'Well, when the pits went, there was nothing left here in the way of jobs. Your dad had shifted all his capital into Third World sweatshops years since. All that's left is the chemical works, which is fine if you don't mind shrinking. Not blaming you for any of this by the way. So, anyway, JobCentre set up all these activity workshops. I chose shamanic drumming.'

'Shamanic drumming?'

'It was either that or they stopped your dole. Bird who taught it were gorgeous. Bit of a hippy, you know, with them blonde dreadlocks but you should have seen tits on her. So anyway, I'm a fully qualified shamanic drum instructor now you know.'

'Great.'

'Me and four hundred other blokes between here and Doncaster. Anyhow, one summer we all went out to this village pub up in Wharfedale and all these Morris Dancers turned up. They start giving it the prancing bells and hankies and smacking each other with sticks and that, so we started taking the piss, obviously, and they all totally ignored us. Then it occurred to us; you go round pubs dressed as a Morris Dancer, you're bound to have the piss taken out of you, right? So, therefore, you can always get into a fight. It's a great way of getting rid of pent-up aggression, Tony. Beats Anger Management Workshops any day. And it all snowballed from there.'

'But what about all this survivalist militia stuff? And the Odin worshipping? How does that fit in?'

'Well, just started getting into all sorts off the back of the drumming really, you know – rituals, ceremonies, all that stuff. She were right into it, Ayesha – hippy with the tits who were teachin' us. Very knowledgeable. Then some of the lads started fishing around on the Internet, checking out these militiamen in America, talking to them, and one thing led to another. Before we knew it, we were worshipping Odin and preparing for the Final Conflict. But short answer is, it were destiny, that's all. Makes you listen to Led Zeppelin in a totally new way and all.'

'Are you sure it all makes sense?'

'Of course it does! You know where you are and what you should be doing.'

'But . . . I thought Morris Dancing was Celtic, whereas Odin is a Norse God and . . .'

'And any nit-picking and clever arguing that it's not so is the tricks of the enemy.' Dave was looking at Tony, who noticed Dave hadn't blinked for some considerable time.

'Right. Who is it exactly, the enemy you'll be fighting come this final conflict then, Dave?'

'I've told you – international Zionist United Nations Bolshevik Conspiracy.'

'OK. Just trying to, you know, get it straight in my own mind.' He was relieved to see Dave blink.

'And we've to be ready at all times for when it happens. Nearer that time, there shall be signs, and portents. It's all made very clear in the Book of Revelations.'

'Of course.' Tony pulled on his socks, suddenly not worrying which should go on first, and shook out his shirt.

In Tony's experience, when someone used the phrase 'it's all very clear in the Book of Revelations', it was always time to leave.

'You'll have to come up on the moor with us some time, if you're going to be stopping here for a while.'

'I will, yeah, that'd be very interesting. What does Beryl think of it all?'

Dave's huge and fierce and impassive face, that looked like it had been carved and fitted to his shoulders on Easter Island, suddenly crumpled and a ripple of sadness ran down it for an instant. Then it was solid again.

'She left me six months back, Tony. Took the kids, she's staying at her mother's. She said I was barmy. She said I looked stupid in a Morris Man's costume. Everyone does for heaven's sake. She's missing the point: it's a sign of your hardness just being able to go out wearing one looking that stupid. But she didn't understand. She just said I wasn't the man she married. That a teacher couldn't be seen raising her kids with a right-wing extremist lunatic who believes in the literal existence of the Norse Pantheon. She told me to seek psychiatric help, Tony. What does that tell you?'

'Well . . . it tells me . . .'

'It tells you they'd got to her, turned her against me.'

'"They"?'

'Aye. You know, agents of the global military-industrial conspiracy . . . My own wife and kids . . . it hurts, Tony. It hurts me. But what can I do?'

'You could . . . you have changed, Dave. You're less happy-go-lucky.'

'You'd be less happy-go-lucky if your wife had walked out on you and taken the kids.'

'Yes, but . . .'

Tony decided he owed it to Dave to be a compassionate ear. 'Why don't you tell me all about it. Beryl leaving I mean.'

'I just have told you all about it. She left me.'

Dave's eyes were as dense as a black hole. There was no point pursuing it.

'And anyway, we all change, Tony. Your hair's completely different from last time I saw you.'

'Yeah. It has been fifteen years, Dave.'

'Still, you see my point.'

'But Dave, what you're doing, it does all sound a bit . . . unusual.'

'Thing is, how can you resist your destiny?'

'Well, perhaps we've all got free will.'

'That's rich coming from you on top of your pig theory.'

'It was only a theory, Dave. Look Dave, I'd better get going.'

'And what you were saying about Emily on the way back from the Chinky.'

'What was I saying about Emily?'

'How you should never have left her. How fate had brought you back to claim her. It was so moving I had to dislocate your shoulder twice. It's OK, I put it back in.'

'I see. Well, I'd best be off.'

'I thought you wanted a bath.'

'It's OK, if I look a bit dishevelled they might take pity on me.'

'Your family? Take pity?'

CHAPTER SEVEN

Meanwhile, across the valley, in her brand new mock Queen Anne ranch-style mansion, Tony's sister Jane was preparing for the day in a rare good mood.

'Eeh, isn't it a lovely day, Jeff, love. Lovely blue skies, autumn sunshine and that beautiful brown strip of smog hanging over the chemical works . . . *our* chemical works. It might say pollution to some folk, but to me it says burgeoning profit margins and a winter break in Barbados.'

Jeff shuffled across the carpet and timidly pecked his wife on the cheek.

'Aye Jane love, you're quite right.'

'You know, there's nothing quite like standing here on an enclosed all-weather patio and gazing through high-quality armour-plated smoked-glass down on to the valley below.'

'Nothing like it; specially when you own everything in the valley.'

'Yes. Do you know Jeff, it makes me feel a little bit like Jesus.'

'How do you work that out?'

'You know, that bit in the Bible where Jesus looks down from a high place and is Lord of all he surveys – well we're the same: we own that whole town, everything you can see.'

'Yes, from the market place and the shopping centre and the squash club and the abattoir . . .'

'To the JobCentre and the hospital and the off-licences and the rehabilitation clinic . . . and just think, from today, even the moors belong to us!'

'Yes, well your dad.'

'Same difference, he can't last much longer can he? Poor soul, I mean. Pour me some more champagne will you love?'

'Surely love.'

As Jeff went to fetch the champagne, Jane was assailed by the terrible prospect of a moment alone in silence and repose, and a dreaded moment of self-contemplation. She shivered and, as usual, looked around for a diversion, something to nag at or attack. Her head twitched this way and that like a blackbird listening for worms. Then she had it, and yelled up the open-plan staircase:

'Joanna! Will you get out of that bathroom! We're going to grandma and grandad's.'

'That's why I'm in the bathroom, Mum. I'm getting ready.'

'We'll be late. Get a move on.'

'How can I when you're talking to me?'

There was no need to pursue the argument – the main purpose of the attack had been served, for now Jeff had returned with the champagne.

'Are you sure that was Jesus?' he said, handing her a glass.

'Eh?'

'Are you sure it was Jesus, who was Lord of all he surveyed . . . I thought that was the Devil, tempting Jesus . . .'

'Oh don't split hairs – the point is, it's got a religious air about it, don't you think? And anyway, who are you to come over all bloody Sunday school teacher correcting me and picking me up on biblical minutiae? If it wasn't for me you wouldn't be living here at all.'

'Now now love, I didn't mean any harm.'

'I should hope not too. Just remember who's boss around here. Without me would you be living in a house with shag-pile carpets and underfloor heating?'

'No love, I wouldn't. You're the boss, love.'

'Yes. And you're just—'

'"A jumped-up PE teacher."'

'Exactly.'

'With a finely toned body.'

'Very finely toned.' There was a quiver in her voice now.

'And amazing stamina . . .'

'Jeff . . .'

'Yes love?' As if he didn't know what was coming next.

'Take me. Now.'

'You've a full glass of champagne.'

She hurled the glass into the fireplace, and herself round his neck.

'Take me.' She growled, and bit his neck. Aroused

137

they both might be, but Jeff's sense of domestic protocol was severely infringed. 'Oh Jane! You broke that glass on purpose.'

'Of course I did.'

'Well that's very irresponsible.'

'Scold me then. It's because I'm mad with passion for you. Slake it Jeffrey. Slake my passion. Slake it now.'

'Slaking will have to get in the queue and wait its turn,' he said, prising her arms from his neck and holding her still. 'There's broken glass and Moët all over the fireplace. I'll fetch a dustpan and brush.'

'But . . . oh . . . forget it.'

'I'm sorry love, but I just wouldn't be able to concentrate with all this mess all over . . .'

'Never mind. Get me another glass will you.'

'I thought you were going to drive.'

'I am.'

'But . . .'

'We'll take the jeep, OK? That way anything we hit will come off second best. Good God! What on earth are you wearing?'

Jeff was a little confused. He'd been wearing his grey tweed trousers and multi-coloured diamond-pattern golf sweater for several hours. If Jane was going to give him a row about it, surely she'd have done it by now. Moreover, he was especially proud of the trousers. They were very similar to a pair worn by someone at the golf club who'd been to Cambridge University.

'Is it the shoes, love? I know you don't like pale blue, but they're very in just now you know.'

'Not you! Her!'

Jeff looked up to see his seventeen-year-old daughter Joanna fold languidly into a black leather armchair and cross her legs, which Jeff was surprised to notice were suddenly very long. She scowled up at her parents, flicking her hair away from her face. Since when had Joanna's hair been blue? he wondered.

'What?' said Joanna, and began filing an electric green nail.

'What on earth are you wearing?'

'You are not going to your grandad's dressed like that?'

'What do you mean?'

'You're half-naked.'

Joanna rolled her eyes and took a long patient breath before explaining carefully to a point on the ceiling:

'I am not half-naked. I am wearing a fashionably short dress with a plunging neckline designed to give the odd tantalising glimpse of my nipple rings.'

'Love, it'll upset your grandma,' suggested Jeff. He knew that force would only create a blazing row, and they couldn't afford to be late today.

'Only until she sees the label. Then she'll be really impressed.'

Jane was shaking slightly, like the valve on a pressure cooker, and hanging on to the marble mantelpiece for support – and, by the look of it, as a surrogate throat to strangle.

'And what will your grandad say?' What Jeff meant was, 'What would your grandad say if he was an ordinary decent grandad like children have in books and cosy television shows at Christmas?' Joanna stared at him with a sardonic contempt.

'He'll say "I suppose you're too old to sit on my knee any more young lady." Then he'll ask me to sit on his knee and he'll give me a tenner.'

Jeff was beaten. Jane sort of clucked in despair, but could not speak. There was nothing she could say. But Joanna decided to sprinkle salt on the wounds.

'I don't see why we have to go to Grandma and Grandad's every Sunday anyway. It's not as if there's anyone else they'd leave all their money to.'

'What are you implying?' said Jeff, feebly acting a man indignant.

Jane was more assertive.

'Rubbish is what she's implying! They're my parents. And I love them.'

'Right. And I love you too, Mum.'

'Listen young lady – you don't know those malicious bastards like I do. And I tell you, they could well leave it to a Cats' Home or Arthur Scargill just out of spite. So knuckle down to the job in question and learn some proper "Life Skills" – like Ingratiation and Dissembling for Personal Gain. Mark my words young lady – you'll thank me one day.'

'Well it just so happens I don't want to live my life by your decadent values. I want to live by honest principles and refined social accomplishments.'

'Oh my! . . . "honest principles and refined social accomplishments"! Like what?'

'Like socialism, the arts, and mind-altering drugs.'

'Really? Well learn the bloody piano then – see how far that gets you up the social ladder these days. "Refined social accomplishments!" Who do you think you are anyway? Jane bloody Austen?'

'Yes, lighten up, Joanna,' Jeff chipped in. 'You sound just like your uncle.'

The glass fell from Jane's hand and smashed in the fireplace.

'Don't you ever mention that name in this house!'

'I didn't mention his name,' said Jeff, fussing.

'You know it gives me a nosebleed.'

'I know it gives you a nosebleed love, that's why I purposely didn't say his name.'

'You didn't say his name but it's obvious you meant Uncle Tony,' said Joanna, and managed to look shocked as her mother slumped on to the couch with blood pulsing from each nostril. 'Ooops. I'll go and get some ice.'

The older Joanna got, the more mystified and distressed she became at her parents being a couple. As far as she could see they had nothing whatever in common except she hated both of them.

She liked to think that perhaps somewhere in their early courtship there had been something real, some spark, and that they had stayed together in the hope of some day finding a way to rekindle it. But she would have been disappointed. Not that she would have permitted herself to admit it.

Jeff and Jane's relationship began when they were

teenagers, at a Young Conservatives disco. (Joanna felt physically ill whenever she thought of this. The idea of her parents disco dancing was bad enough on its own. The possibility that her own existence owed anything to a Young Conservatives' social event made her feel unclean and burn for vengeance. She could not bear mention of the way her parents met, and if anyone spoke of it in her hearing she would often be physically sick.)

In the late sixties, Jeff's parents had turned a quiet little village inn into the most successful gentrified country pub in the area. Mixing every day with a more refined clientèle had been a revelation for Billy and Doreen, a window on a wider world. It was such a joy in itself to serve bar meals to sophisticated customers who commonly wore blazers and a nattier standard of casual clothing, but there was more than this. Some of them had experience of dauphinoise potatoes and even spaghetti bolognese in the native country. It was positively cosmopolitan. (There was even one chap – an architect – who'd worked in Hong Kong!)

They were astounded by the wisdom and sagacity of their new customers. Whatever crisis or problem, national or international, which haunted the front pages and the television news, they had a definite and practical solution for it. (Generally involving corporal punishment, national service, armoured cars, capital punishment, martial law, strict immigration controls, and legal restrictions on male hair-length.) It was a constant mystery to Billy and Doreen that these worldly-wise sagacious men (their wives didn't talk much in male company) were generally speaking middle-management, or provincial professionals, with the odd smattering of small-businessmen with their own companies, when it was clear they had more common sense than all the politicians put together. There was obviously a conspiracy to keep them back. There was no other explanation. To see all this talent denied its rightful place at the helm of the nation was nothing short of criminal. As their little boy Jeff approached secondary-school age, Billy and Doreen began to make inquiries about the right place to send him. A major public school was out of the question of course; that was out of their league, beyond them in money and connections. But there was a principle at stake too: they didn't want to buy his way into the Establishment and lose touch with his roots. As was clear from how many politicians came from the major public schools, they received an inferior education even if the old-school tie was a passport to success.

Billy and Doreen wanted Jeff to receive the same excellent academic instruction their hallowed customers had clearly had. It was possible to get to the very top without being an insider, if you were good enough, and they had a prime example just up the road, and his name was Obadiah Hardstaff. A multi-millionaire, many times over, and he'd pulled himself up by nothing but his bootstraps.

All they wanted for Jeff was a level playing field. So in the end, after a quiet word in an ear here and a reliable opinion garnered over a brandy on the house there, the decision was made, and Jeff had been sent to a private school near Wakefield with high fees and low entrance requirements, which together guaranteed the pupils were all the right sort of person. Determined to repay his parents' solicitous investment, Jeff applied himself at school, and two years later qualified without much difficulty as a PE teacher.

Jane had been educated at a private school on the North Yorkshire coast and then, her sights always set on joining the family firm, taken a business degree in Leeds. Each knew who the other was. During school holidays they had both been active Young Conservatives, attended dances held by the local hunt, the Pony Club and the Young Farmers, but never been friends. Jeff admired Jane from afar, as did most of the young men of the same set. They all took care not to be caught looking, for her fierce little eyes could burn a hole through you, and her narrow, thin-lipped mouth seemed naturally to carry the hint of a frown, pursed to restrain the imminent caustic remark always set ready behind it on a hair-trigger. She was capable of a smile, although it was always quickly replaced by an unsettled reflective look, as if she was concerned that betraying warmth might put her at some disadvantage. She had an attractive build (though privately wished she was either slightly taller or not quite as broad), and light brown hair which in those days was generally tied up in a tight bun. She rarely let it down.

Jeff was fairly tall, dark and handsome. An unimagi-native description, but accurate and entirely appropriate, as he was also virtually dead from the neck up. Conse-quently, although he was pretty successful with women, his relationships never lasted very long. He was too stu-pid and dull to realise that this was because he was stupid and dull, and too stupid and young to worry about it.

Jane didn't need an intellectual companion. She had her father and the firm to exercise that part of her. What she needed was a devoted subordinate who would do as he was told and give her physical release from her devotion to business and empire building when they were between the sheets. One summer, at the social event that could not be spoken of in Joanna's presence, towards the end of Jeff's time at PE college, Jane noticed how impressively muscular the course had made him, and smiled at him when they were introduced. Even Jeff, stupid as he was, knew that Jane Hardstaff smiling was a big sign, and he asked her to dance.

When the courtship became public, Billy and Doreen were overwhelmed with delight. There was no bigger catch than Jane Hardstaff. Yes, she was fearsomely volatile, sharp-tongued and unfriendly; yes she expected immediate unquestioning deference and returned it with contempt; no, she did not have a sense of humour, as far as anyone knew, but, as Doreen put it, everyone has their faults. On the other hand, she was very, very rich, and her father was over one hundred and sixty years old.

Jane's parents were less delighted at the prospect. Obadiah had always assumed Jane had sufficient sense of duty to choose a husband with a shrewd business brain, as insurance in case anything happened to Tony, who at the age of fourteen was already showing disturbing signs of permanent delinquency. Jeff was clearly not that man. Obadiah made the mistake of telling Jane this straight out. Jane was furious. In her opinion, she was the only business brain the next generation of the company would ever need, and Obadiah's continued hope that Tony would turn out all right, despite all the evidence, just because he was male, was both insulting and impossibly optimistic. She was hurt on a personal level as well as offended on the more pragmatic one, although she would never admit to the former.

Obadiah retreated, and tried a more wheedling and possibly more convincing tack – namely that Jeff wasn't good enough for her.

But Jane was stubborn enough when holding out for something that she knew would upset other people. When she also actually wanted it herself, she was immovable.

Everyone enjoyed the wedding ceremony, except Obadiah and Quintillia, but they made up for it at the reception, where the groom's family were catered for in a separate room, and Jane cried for the first and only time in her life at the humiliation. Even Tony felt sorry for her. (Jeff didn't quite understand what the problem was: there was loads of booze and a disco.)

What was really disturbing, Tony noticed, was that once she got over the actual moment, Obadiah's cruelty seemed to make Jane respect him even more.

From the moment they returned from their three-week honeymoon in the Caribbean, Jane and Jeff knuckled down to the routine they would follow to the grave. Jane ran the company with Obadiah; Jeff was given a nominal position, and did what Jane told him.

After long discussions, where all views were taken into

consideration, they both decided that children would just get in the way of everything, and Jeff agreed with her. Of course, there would come a time when producing an heir was necessary, but not right away. Jane could not dare to take time away from work until she had made her position in the company unassailable.

It should have been enough that she was an excellent businesswoman, but she knew that her father still believed absurdly in male primogeniture, so it was clear she had to do something about Tony.

Tony was already doing his best to outrage his parents, but Jane was not confident it was enough. However, she had a plan, which suddenly had to be accelerated in its execution when Jane, to her fury, discovered she was pregnant: however ambitious she was, she just couldn't keep her hands off Jeff. This, of course, enraged her more: she hated not being in control. The fact that she had such uncontrollable passion for such a dolt made her even more angry and tense – an anger and tension that could only be quenched by vigorous and frequent sexual congress with the dolt. As she became increasingly aware of being caught in this terrible vicious circle, Jane, of course, became more and more angry, and needed Jeff's body even more . . . which in turn, made her more and more angry . . .

She took it out on the world.

'She always had a plan,' said Tony. There was a bitterness in his voice. The bitterness that masks powerless rage.

Suddenly, Jane became Tony's friend. She would slip him fivers here and there with a sly wink, financing his drinking, his rock music habit, his occasional joint smoking. Of course, she pretended not to know where the money went, not to worry: it wasn't her business to know as long as she could help her little brother; presented the image of a kind and generous elder sibling, gained Tony's trust. It was a brilliant performance. She would defend him when their parents raged at his school reports, at his occasional weekend-long disappearances, the company he kept.

'It's just a phase he's going through, Dad.' 'He's bound to come round in time.' 'You're too hard on him.'

She would manufacture private moments together, when she would sit him down and try to be solicitous, pleading with him to think of his future, of how he was in danger of throwing away the chance to one day head a huge profitable company. Tony insisted he didn't want it.

'You say that now Tony, but one day you might change your mind. I'd hate it to be too late.'

'It's not for me. You're welcome to it. All I want is to play my music, see the world, make it big, then disappear – go East, to Tibet, to Katmandu, gain enlightenment.'

'Please bear in mind, Señor García, I was only fifteen at the time.'

Jane slid the milk jug across the kitchen table. 'Well Tony, it's your life, you should do whatever you want with it. I applaud you for it.'

'What about you? Don't you want to travel, go places, experience things, find out who you are?'

'I know who I am Tony, I'm happy with what I've

got. Part of me wishes I had your courage, I suppose, but I don't.'

'You might think different, if—'

'What?'

'Nothing.'

'No, come on. You can trust me . . .'

'You might think different . . . if you had the odd smoke now and then.'

Jane's pulse was racing. The trap was about to be set.

'How do you mean, smoke?'

'You know, hash.'

'You mean . . . pot?'

'Yes. It's great. Relaxes you, you know, gives you a sort of buzz. You get all these . . . thoughts . . . sometimes it's like tentacles, coming out of your brain . . .'

'What would I want tentacles coming out of my brain for?'

'What I'm trying to say is, it makes you look at everything differently.'

She didn't want to seem too eager. 'I'll think about it.'

'Well, any time. Just let me know.'

She thought about it all right. About a week later, when Tony was round one evening to play his new Led Zeppelin LP on her vastly superior stereo system (Jeff was at the golf club), she casually asked him if the offer was still on, and he smiled and promised he would sort it out.

In the mid-Seventies, scoring a little lump of hashish in a small English town was a considerable operation for teenage schoolboys. It involved a long chain of contacts and middlemen. In every small town in the country, this chain always included certain invariable links: the school's major Pink Fairies fan (typical obligatory polite conversation: 'Did you go to't Reading Festival?' 'Did I go?' 'Were t'Fairies good?' 'Were they *good*? They were that loud I couldn't hear 'em.'), someone who worked in a record shop, and someone who owned an Afghan coat and always – even during a drought – looked like they'd just been caught out in a rainstorm. Eventually, Tony succeeded in acquiring a quarter-ounce. He rang Jane from a callbox in town and cryptically indicated that the Eagle had landed. She suggested Friday night.

Friday night came and as Dave and Tony walked along the misty road, huddled into their duffle-coats, each with a selection of appropriate LPs under their arms (*Sticky Fingers*, *Every Picture Tells a Story*, *Weasels Ripped My Flesh*, something by Neil Young, The Doors, *Led Zeppelin IV*) a panda car drew up beside them, and ten minutes later they were busted.

It was obvious immediately that Jane had grassed them up. There was no other explanation. Tony was speechless with rage. He couldn't bear to think how patiently and coolly she had strung him along, gained his confidence. He was chilled to realise how much antipathy she bore him. He hadn't realised you could understand another person so well and hate them. Until that point he had thought understanding went with affection. It really really hurt. But he would get his own back, and when he did, it would hurt her more. Worst of all, Dave was actually carrying the lump. Although Tony tried to insist on equal responsibility, he got off with a fine while Dave was sent to an approved school.

There was a bit of a fuss in the local paper about 'one law for the rich' and so on, generated by a corruscating article entitled '*J'accuse*' which angered Obadiah greatly, especially because Tony wrote the article.

Tony thought of all the obvious measures for getting his own back directly on Jane, like burning down her house, killing her, pouring clutch fluid all over her new Mercedes. The problem was that she would be expecting something crude and brutal, and so would everyone else. It wasn't really the fear of prison that stopped him in the end though (or so he claimed), it was the need to make the retribution something equally subtle and psychologically damaging.

His parents reacted just as Jane had presumed they would, with outrage and extreme measures. Tony was exposed as a black sheep through and through, written out of the will, disowned. Jane's position was safe. But she should have realised Tony was planning something when he and Dave both refused to implicate her in any way at the trial. Convincing the magistrates she was even peripherally involved would have been difficult of course, but desperate, frightened schoolboys might have tried, to dilute the blame.

She had failed to consider the innate talent of the family for mental sadism.

Tony first promised Dave he would make it up to him, but that it might take a while. Next, he went round to visit Jane and Jeff. They wouldn't let him in to the house, for fear of him damaging either them or their possessions, but Tony was calm and conciliatory. He simply told Jane he was glad she had got what she wanted, and only sorry she had to stoop so low to get it. He wished her well, and walked back down the drive.

Next Sunday, with Jane and Jeff over for lunch as usual, Tony calmly announced that he would be leaving home on his seventeenth birthday, which was two weeks away. He apologised to his parents for bringing shame on the family, and said he now understood how stupid he had been, what opportunities he had thrown away. He realised that Obadiah would much rather hand the fortune down the male line, even if this was unfair to Jane considering her complete devotion. (Noticed in the corner of his eye, with concealed pleasure, Jane's cheek twitching.) He said that after the way he had been the last few years, he understood that his words would probably count for nothing, but that some day he hoped to prove through his actions that he was a changed person, and that some day he would come home, prove Obadiah's preference for male succession to be ultimately justified despite all the current evidence to the contrary, and become in the end a worthy successor as head of the family business. (His parents laughed, but Jane's whole face went into spasm.) He had anticipated the derision, but he had deduced two things.

Firstly, however much Jane dismissed his promises, she would not be able to rid her mind of the nagging fear that any day he could return. Secondly, even if he had burnt his bridges irredeemably with his father, he was pretty sure his father would never confirm this to Jane; he knew enough about how his father's mind worked to be reasonably sure he would exploit the possibility of a reformed Tony's return as a stick to beat Jane with, and so she would never be quite as secure as she thought.

Furthermore, he remembered the way Jane had encouraged him to live a life, go his own way, take a risk, find himself. He could not be sure, but he had an instinct that although she had clearly used this as a tactic to gain his confidence, her envious undertones could not be entirely artificial. He resolved to send her postcards sporadically, the odd letter even, creating a picture of him having a wonderful time on his travels, finding excitement, fulfilling experiences, seeing the world, being happy, implying she was missing out, whatever the reality.

It was a hunch, but a pretty good one he figured, especially when Jane's nose started bleeding.

It never occurred to him that the family might take measures to make him stay. Neither did it occur to the family.

After lunch he went out. Bought a bottle of cider, and headed up to the moor. He had a favourite spot, a place where the shoulders of four summits created a deep hollow with a spinny of ash trees at its bottom. Ten feet down the bank and you felt invisible, sheltered from the wind, from the outside world, even as if you'd stepped out of time. There were the remains of an old shepherd's cottage halfway down, just the shape of the walls marked out by a few remaining blocks of moss-covered limestone.

Whenever I think of Tony telling this part of his story, I see him smiling, leaning against the whitewashed wall at the far end of the bar, the dappled sunlight filtering through the banana thatch and infusing him with a vibrant glow. 'There was a girl standing on one of the blocks of limestone.' He looked distantly, longingly, into the past. 'She had her back to me. She was slim and blonde and . . . she went up on tip-toe, and all the muscles of her legs tensed . . . the curve of her hips was the most wonderful thing I'd ever seen . . . and then she turned towards me; like—'

'—Meryl Streep in *The French Lieutenant's Woman* . . . ?' said Conchita.

'—like a meerkat on the African veldt?' asked Pepe.

'—like a sunflower seeking the refulgent solar orb?' (this last was mine.)

'—like a virgin? Rolling Stone? Bird on the wire?'

'—Like as not surprised as me to discover another person in this secluded place,' concluded Tony, flatly.

'I didn't expect to meet anyone else up here at this time of day.' She languidly swept a strand of wayward hair from her face.

'So I see. Is that why you've got no clothes on?'

'Peripherally. I'm communing with nature. Becoming one with the earth and the sky.' Her eyes were pale blue and cold. (Tony refused to go into further detail about the exquisite proportions of her naked body because he declared that it was his business and nobody else's.)

'Oh. Right.'

'Care to join me?'

'Don't you know who I am?'

'You're Tony Hardstaff, aren't you?'

'Yes. And you're Emily Earnshaw.'

'Yes.' She had closed her eyes and turned away from him once more. She turned back again and her mouth spread into the warmest, widest smile Tony had ever seen before or since. Her eyes seemed to have a light behind them now. Somehow they were deeper blue and no longer so forbidding. 'Don't you think it would be appropriate if, as a result of this chance meeting, we fell madly and inseparably in love?'

'How do you mean appropriate?'

'After all the pains our fathers have taken over the years to keep us apart? Do you realise my father sent me to the convent school in Switzerland simply on your account? It would have a marvellous ironic justice to it, don't you think, if today marked the first day of our lives in togetherness until the grave? Nature triumphing over the mean and pointless conflicts of old and megalomaniacal men; pure and noble desire and uncontrived affinity finding a way to break whatever shackles and chains the worldly vanities of self-serving power-mad capitalist bastards sought to bind them with?'

''Appen.'

'Haven't you ever thought the same?'

'I don't know. Not in those words, anyway. How come you know I'm Tony Hardstaff? You've never set eyes on me before in your life to my knowledge.'

'Neither *have* I. But you have to be. It would ruin the romantic and possibly life-changing nature of this chance encounter otherwise. Consider it. A perfect summer's evening, the cloudless blue sky being tinged red by the slowly setting sun, a gentle breeze whispering through the ash grove, bees buzzing among the heather, undisturbed by our presence as if we both belong here with them, the heather a gorgeous warm purple, synchromatic with – if I may neologise, or if I may not, the same shade of purple as – the head of a tumescent virile member, not that I've ever seen one. I'm only sixteen and I go to school in a convent, remember.'

'Would you like a drink of cider, Emily Earnshaw?'

'Is it sweet or dry, Tony Hardstaff?'

'Dry.'

'Smashin'.'

She got down off the stones and sat down beside him. 'It'd be a bit like that painting, *Le déjeuner sur l'herbe*, if we had a couple more blokes here.'

'I'm glad we don't.'

'There you are, you see, you can be romantic.'

She was home for the school holidays, and had sneaked out of the house to come to this spot on the moor which she loved so dearly and could visit so rarely. Tony told her excitedly it was his favourite spot too.

'Forces of fate, drawing us together.' Tony blushed after this slipped out.

'You're blushing! I find that very sweet. It shows a sensitivity that most boys of our age have learnt to mask completely. Who's your favourite existentialist?'

'Franz Kafka.'

'You consider Kafka an existentialist?'

'Er, yeah, in a sense.'

'What sense?'

'In that he . . . expressed the absurdity of existence.'

There is no need to reproduce any more of this conversation between two sixteen-year-old would-be intellectual lovers. Indeed, there is a need not to, even though it is documented meticulously in Tony's diary, and despite the fact it was one of the few episodes of the story that he could and did recite verbatim and exactly each time he told it. Perhaps the summarising first line of his diary entry will suffice:

Met Emily Earnshaw on the moor. We talked about everything and she is dead intellectual. Want to shag her more than anything else in the world.

They talked as the darkness closed around them. It got chillier, and Emily put her clothes back on.

They agreed to meet again next day. Tony said he would be there at dawn and wait for her to get away however long it took.

They met every day. They talked, drank, explored the moor, fell in love, declared love, made love, swore undying love. Tony felt sick as his birthday approached, for he was determined still to leave, but did not know how to break it to Emily. He wanted her to ditch school and come with him. When, on their last evening together, he told her, she was silent. He felt obliged to fill the gap with words hoping they would reach across the distance between them.

'I have to go. I want to fuck them all up. I can't go back on what I've said. I need to avenge myself, and Dave, by screwing my sister up. I promised I would, and if I stay they'll think it's because I lost my nerve. Don't cry Emily, please don't cry. If you want, you can come with me.'

'I'm not crying. I think it's a great idea, you going away to spite your family.'

'Come with me.'

'Why?'

'Because I love you.'

'If you love me, you'll always love me, and one day you'll come back, and we'll be together. But spiting your family's much more important. And I have my life to lead thank you very much. I'm not just your puppy, Tony Hardstaff. I've my sacred gifts of poetic vision to hone and develop.'

'You never told me you wanted to be a poet.'

'You never bloody asked did you? It's been you you you all week just about.'

'That's not true. I've asked you loads of questions.'

'Well anyway. I've many years of study and meditation before me just now to prepare myself for my sacred calling. I can't possibly just shoot off to London to go on the piss with a would-be rock star. And besides, the wait will only make your return all the sweeter.'

That final night they spent upon the moor, making love, getting bitten by creepy-crawlies, scratched by the bracken, stiff limbs from the damp ground. Next morning they limped and scratched their way to the station. Tony bought his single ticket from the lizard man. They kissed passionately until the train came in; he begged her again to come with him, and again she refused and promised she would wait for him until he was ready to return.

'That way Tony my love, when next we meet, we shall both be older, wiser, and gagging for each other like a couple of horny ferrets. Now get on the train and seek your fortune.'

The family had a leaving party for Tony, after he had left. They were certain it was for the best, although Obadiah still felt betrayed and angry that Tony had not turned out to be just a younger version of himself. Apart from the problems of inheritance this threw up, Obadiah was disturbed because it demonstrated there were things he could not control. He also played with the idea of suing Tony for all the free food and accommodation he had received so ungratefully for over a decade and a half. In the end his pragmatism gained the upper hand and he resolved simply to bind and mould Jane even more rigorously than hitherto.

When Jane and Jeff's first issue turned out to be female, they were both disappointed. Jane blamed Jeff, on the grounds that all his years as a househusband had altered the balance of his chromosomes.

Joanna grew up sensing she was an outsider, unwelcome, that somehow she had displeased her parents. It wasn't her fault of course that they hardly communicated, except physically, but it felt that way.

'Here we are,' said Joanna returning from the kitchen, and applied the ice pack to her mother's nose. 'Is that better?'

'Yes love, thank you.'

'You're welcome. And I'm sorry I mentioned Uncle Tony.' She tried not to giggle as Jane's nose once more cascaded dark red blood.

'Joanna! We'll be late now!'

'Oh damn, what was I thinking? I'll go and get some more ice.'

Up on the moor, two figures battling against the wind towards the summit. Ahead, behind and around them, a darting golden ball of energy, yapping and snapping, wheeling away in larger and larger orbits, scuttling back to attack them playfully then bouncing away again through the gorse, its pink tongue lolling like a stunned, freshly-caught spam. Partridge and grouse leapt flustered into the air as the spaniel pounced and snuffled in the scrub, while flocks of highly-strung-looking sheep sifted this way and that across the pale hillside like a monochrome kalei-doscope before plummeting, a bleating, trundling skein, into a sudden scar that lay concealed in a fold of the tawny moor.

Obadiah Hardstaff, gaunt and stern, was not impressed. 'That was an act of pointless cruelty on behalf of the dog. I trust he wasn't doing it to try and impress me.'

'Of course he wasn't, Mr Hardstaff,' said Quintillia. 'He was just fulfilling his nature. Weren't you boy?' The canine mass murderer had come gasping back for affection and reward.

'It may be my moor but there'll still be compensation to be paid on account of those sheep.'

'Well, let's not think about that now. Let's just enjoy.'

'Yes, you're right. I've won the bet. Finally this whole moor is mine.'

'Yes, Mr Hardstaff. Congratulations.'

'Who'd have thought when I made that bet with Jacob Earnshaw all those years ago it would have taken me a hundred and sixty years to collect?'

'It is a great compliment to your determination, Mr Hardstaff, surviving to the age of 183 simply in order to win a wager.'

'And my greed, Mrs Hardstaff, don't forget that. In the end I was the greedier. That's what swung it. Superior greed. Earnshaw lost interest in material things toward the end; that's what finished him off, if you ask me.'

'Mrs Womersley tells me he's very happy.'

'You and your seances and talking to spirits. I suppose they just happened to meet up on the other side the moment he popped his clogs then did they?'

'Actually yes. She describes Mr Earnshaw as being in a state of enhanced spiritual bliss.'

'Pah! That's as maybe, but I own his moor now, and that's what counts.'

'Yes . . . I suppose so.'

'You don't sound overjoyed.'

'Well, no, not really. I don't really like moorlands. I've never seen the point of them, aside from walking the dog on. I know some people find them beautiful but I can't see the point of that either. They're just huge lumps of earth that smell of sheep and get in the way. You can't wear stilettos on them; they blow your hair out of place; the driving rain wreaks havoc with one's make-up and complexion; if there's ever anyone to notice your jewellery it's a bunch of ridiculous-looking hikers in hideous anoraks who smirk at one for being what they consider overdressed . . . you can't build on them; you can't put motorways through them; so you can't make money out of them.'

'Well that's where you're wrong, woman. We're going to turn this desolate – what did the council call it? Area of Outstanding Natural Beauty – into a goldmine.'

'But you've already got one in South Africa.'

'Not literally, woman—'

'What then?'

'I'll explain at dinner. Come on. We'll be late.'

'All right. I'm coming. Hold on, where's the dog got to?'

'Got sucked into a bog if there's any justice.'

'That's no way to talk about Elvis. Here he is. Come on boy.'

The dog leapt obediently into the back of the Range Rover, disdaining the old rug laid out for it in order to scramble all over the upholstery, rubbing its wet and filthy body against as many soft surfaces as possible, obeying an ancient primal instinct which has operated within dogs since ever their owners first had cars.

'Oh! Look what it's done now! Mud all over the place! Bloody drain on our assets, that's what that dog is. Does it do anything to earn his dog food? No. Who'd have ever thought I'd be running a Welfare State in my own house.'

'Well, I'm very fond of him.'

'Fond. What kind of talk is that? Socialist talk, that's what.'

'Don't be ridiculous. And anyway, he *is* useful.'

'Oh aye. Useful. If you call being a spirit medium useful. It's plain daft. Whoever heard of a spaniel being a spirit guide? Preposterous! You want something smaller, like a pekinese that you could fit up your sleeve.'

'Well if he didn't have psychic powers I shouldn't be able to communicate with Mrs Womersley.'

'That's another good reason for getting rid of him. Since that woman died you spend more time talking to her than you do at the hairdresser's. Besides, if you ask me, it's all in your mind. You're just trying to justify the exorbitant amount of money you spent on the damn dog by attributing magical powers to it. Hell's teeth! It's got its nose in my ear now!'

'*His*! *He* has *his* nose in your ear.'

'He or it, it's still not too big to be drowned in a bucket. My point is, what do you want to communicate with Mrs Womersley all the time for anyway?'

'I'm very fond of Mrs Womersley.'

'She was only the housekeeper for heaven's sake.'

'She was my friend.'

'There you go again with your socialist nonsense.'

They drove in silence for a few minutes.

'Talking of Mrs Womersley, will Joanna be coming to lunch?'

'Of course she will.'

'Oh well, that's something to look forward to.'

'Yes. And we all know why.'

'She's my grandchild. The heir of my line.'

'She practises witchcraft you know.'

'That's just a vicious rumour. Anyway, you're biased because of what happened to Mrs Womersley.'

'Perhaps I am.'

'Well the jury found her not guilty.'

'The jury were all flown to Barbados within three days of delivering their verdict.'

'That was just my way of expressing relief and gratitude.'

'Sometimes I think you actually believe that. Look at the facts: the Monday, Joanna declares she's a vegetarian. Tuesday, comes round here for her tea. Asks Mrs Womersley if the soup has been made from a vegetable stock. Mrs Womersley assures her it has been.'

'And she was lying, don't forget.'

'She was not lying. She's just a simple country woman. She genuinely thought rabbits were a vegetable. Joanna finds out. Gives Mrs Womersley an odd look, borrows your pocket watch. Goes to help Mrs Womersley wash up. Next morning, Mrs Womersley, a simple countrywoman of eighty-eight years of age, gets up at the crack of dawn, yells to a passing paperboy she's got a "mighty yen to go in for a bit of skateboarding" and is last seen alive plummeting over the balustrade of the Rigg Valley Viaduct.'

'And what, pray, has that got to do with Joanna? Nothing.'

'She hypnotised her. Eighty-eight-year-old women don't just get out of bed at the crack of dawn to go skateboarding.'

'That's a bit stereotyping isn't it?'

'Mrs Womersley was wearing a ra-ra skirt.'

'She'd probably been overdoing the Sanatogen. Just

because Joanna learnt how to say the Lord's Prayer back-wards when she was six, people have been leaping to conclusions ever since.'

'Mrs Womersley told me that's what happened.'

'Mrs Womersley always was a stirrer.'

'I'm not saying I don't like Joanna – she's cunning, ruthless, devious, vicious; in many ways she's a credit to the family – but I just wish you'd see her for what she is.'

'I know what she is. A shameless hussy who exploits her sexuality for material gain. Remind you of anyone else we know? Or did you marry me for my personal charm and warm human qualities?'

'Of course I did,' said Quintillia, sheepishly.

Obadiah chuckled sarcastically, and accelerated to try and squash a baby rabbit that had strayed on to the road.

Dave had insisted on giving Tony a lift up to his parents', which had made Tony feel a little guilty. He knew he was scared of Dave now, and he knew he was entitled to be; on the other hand, was he really entitled to run away? OK, Dave was probably clinically insane and prone to violence; OK, he was a member of a right-wing Morris-dancing militia who worshipped Norse Gods and generally had a worldview that was clearly derived obscurely and incompletely from some deranged and twisted neo-Nazi inadequate with the IQ of a mini-cab controller, but he was still Tony's mate. Tony knew he should really have postponed the visit to his parents to embark on the long and heavy session which would have been necessary to break down Dave's defences and enable him to open up about his divorce; it would have involved several bottles of whisky, incoherent phone calls to Beryl and long sleepless hours listening to the same stuff over and over again. Not to mention sudden painful bouts of headlocks and joints dislocated in playful physical expression of affection and eternal loyalty. But was this not part of being a friend? Just as Dave was now speeding him across town, having hot-wired an appropriate vehicle in the town centre? But instead of wanting to listen to Dave, or instead of making himself listen to Dave, Tony was making himself scarce. He had been away for fifteen years, he told himself. There was no reason to get involved, it wasn't his business. But on the other hand Dave had greeted him as if the interval had been a couple of days . . . It would all work itself out in its own time, Tony told himself.

They were outside the town now. On either side of the road were semi-moorland sheep pastures divided by quite grand drystone walls.

'Do you want me to take you up to the door?' said Dave. They were stopped at the gateposts.

'No,' said Tony, 'I think I'll walk up – get me head together. Thanks Dave. I'll see you soon.'

'What if they're not in? Want me to wait?'

'They'll be in. It's Sunday lunchtime.'

Sunday lunch had always been a rigid part of life at the House of the Spirit Levels. Always at twelve thirty; always roast meat, rarely any guests outside the family. Having procreated and provided a next generation through whom the family fortune could be kept alive, Obadiah was horrified and not a little annoyed that hard work would be involved in ensuring his children behaved according to his will. It should just happen. Life was so unfair. But Obadiah was nothing if not resilient, and made the best of the situation. Thus Sunday lunch became a period where he could place Tony and Jane under observation for two hours or so, inculcated with the codes of behaviour that Obadiah wished to see observed, play mind games with them. Where, for many a family, the meal table might have been a place over which to exchange ideas, to ask questions, give answers, and to see how its younger members were developing, what interests they were pursuing, and to delight in the process of seeing a child slowly unfolding and discovering its personality and character, with a gentle encouragement here or word of concerned admonishment or warning here, with the Hardstaffs it was different. At the Hardstaff table, the children were not asked in a spirit of warm nurturing and curiosity, they were interrogated. Trick questions were asked, traps set, to see how well they were turning into Obadiah's preconceived notions of what he wanted them to be. There was no choice involved. You either did it Obadiah's way, saw it Obadiah's way, were interested in what Obadiah wanted you to be interested in, or you were in the wrong. And if you were in the wrong, you were in trouble. This was his house, and the idea of giving material support and a roof to subversives who saw things differently, and said so, had different points of view and disagreed with his opinion, this simply wasn't on. It was treachery. They had no right to.

So every Sunday from the moment Tony was able to

handle a knife and fork with some degree of competence and decorum, and saw how his first moves towards self-expression were treated with disapproval and suspicion, he learnt how to be more sullen, more secretive, more dissembling, how to convincingly mouth platitudes that his father would accept. Of course, Obadiah was too shrewd never to notice that Tony was putting up a front, but Tony became better and better at hiding himself behind some version of what his father wanted. And possibly Obadiah gained as much satisfaction from knowing he was driving Tony's real nature far far underground as he would from assuming he was seeing the real boy. Sunday lunches became for Tony ascetic meditation sessions where he learnt how to dissociate himself from his feelings, so they would not betray him with an unacceptable reaction when provoked. He came to view everything from a distance through a long dark tunnel of contemplation, turned everything inwards, so that anger at something preposterous his father had said, if so great that it could not be suppressed and hidden completely, would be shown in subtle sarcasm or self-denial, apart from when it occasionally all erupted uncontrollably and he did something spectacular like burn down his school. But most of the time he managed to keep the violence for football matches, and on the home front acted much more subtly.

Eventually he became a vegetarian – a calculated act of utter revolt. He claimed nutritional and moral grounds, and could express the arguments cogently and in considerable depth. But the real motive was always to say Fuck Off in a way that was not utterly dangerous to him.

His sister, on the other hand, bought the whole Hardstaff ethos unquestioningly. By the age of ten she was studying stock markets, closely following the treatment and handling of trade unions by the heads of government in various South American countries, subtly betraying her brother or members of the housekeeping staff over minor misdemeanours, courting her father's favour and learning from her mother's cunning without trying to appear too much of a long-term threat.

When Tony began to show signs of having a conscience – collecting for Blue Peter appeals, doing favours for his friends with no thought of reward – Obadiah was appalled: he had created a monster who had natural inclinations to behave decently towards other human beings even when there was no prospect of personal gain. Obadiah decided he needed toughening up – or breaking.

One Christmas when Tony was about eight or nine years old, Obadiah wrapped up a packing case in Christmas paper and Tony naturally was thrilled at the anticipation of such a huge present. In the years that followed Obadiah would still reflect warmly on the look on Tony's face when he unwrapped all the layers and finally found there was nothing inside but a plastic submarine from a cornflakes packet. Tony was caught by this one. He couldn't believe his own father could be so mean, and went round pretending that a plastic submarine was the best present a boy could have. Never showed a trace of bitterness. But Obadiah knew he was upset inside, having noticed the hint of a hidden tear in the corner of Tony's eye when he watched his sister unwrap her huge pile of varied and expensive gifts. This momentary betrayal of emotion was some consolation to Obadiah, but it was disturbing that the boy did not buckle completely under the calculated cruelty and disappointment.

At twelve Tony was briefly sent away to school. Up until this point he had attended a primary school in the town, as politically it suited the Hardstaffs to appear democratic and approachable at that time. But Tony was clearly enjoying it too much, and this was something his father could not abide. Tony had cried when he realised he was to be separated from his friends, and again Obadiah gained some pleasure from knowing he had inflicted pain; and yet this was mixed at seeing how much work there was still to be done to knock all the useless sentimentality out of the boy and make him an acceptable heir to the family millions.

The school he was sent to was run by a group of renegade Irish schoolteacher monks who had been drummed out of the Christian Brothers – and indeed the Catholic Church – for being too strict with their charges. (Although Obadiah was Church of England, his high regard for sadistic and terrifying teaching methods was ecumenical.) The school was in the Scottish Highlands, eight miles from the nearest road and in the middle of an army night-firing rifle-range, which was a very effective, if severe, way of enforcing the curfew.

Food portions were gradually reduced as the term went on as part of a deliberate policy to set pupil against pupil by encouraging stealing, duplicity, in-fighting and all the other essential components of building and running an Empire.

Shorts were compulsory until the age of seventeen. But somehow, Tony survived the experience intact, until after six months he was expelled under suspicion of having burnt the school down. It was clear that Tony had done the deed, it was just that no witness would testify against him. (This was partly because he was popular amongst his schoolmates, and partly because they knew that terrible reprisal would follow the breaking of the silence.)

Again, Obadiah's reaction was mixed. On the one hand, here was a ruthlessness that any Hardstaff would be proud of, but on the other hand it was being employed for questionable ends. Once back at school in Grimedale, Tony became a typical teenage delinquent radical. After his period as a football hooligan, he became more and more interested in intellectual and cultural pursuits and particularly music, learning guitar, piano and percussion, practising assiduously. This was not so much to feed any develop any great obvious and natural talent, more because he knew his father disapproved. In everything he showed his contempt for authority with every breath and gesture, and even suggested to his father that he should get medical treatment for his sadistic megalomania. Obadiah was outraged, and once again the causes seemed mixed: it was an outright flouting of Obadiah's absolute authority; it was also possibly done out of genuine concern for Obadiah's well-being. This implied an affection that utterly revolted Obadiah. And given all the blatant attempts Obadiah had made to cauterise such feelings, and replace them with fear and respect and nothing else, it was very very annoying. For two years they barely spoke, and on the rare occasions they were in the same room together, one could sense the electricity building up and almost visible black clouds gathering around the cornicing.

He had no terribly clear memories of his mother. She seemed to smell of nail polish and spend all her time under a hairdrier, or bustling round the house trying to scare people and make you feel as if whatever you were doing was something you shouldn't.

His sister Jane continued to be more of a successful breeding exercise in his parents' eyes. Somehow she became very quickly, or perhaps always was, an extension of their will within another body. She would boss and intimidate the servants, haggle in shops, torture her dolls, accumulate money at her friends' expense, disapprove of Tony's attempts and instincts to play and explore rather than appropriate and exploit . . .

This was the place he had left on his seventeenth birthday.

And now he was about to walk back up the drive, not understanding why. Had he given up? Was he ready to become like them? Did he finally have to admit that he had no one else who could help him, that he needed them? How come he had nowhere else on Earth to hide from the Russian gangsters? He was convinced on one level that it was purely shrewd tactics, that were Kropotkin to make extensive enquiries, he would find out about Tony's relationship with his family and conclude that the last place Tony would ever run to was home. But beyond that, he feared there were maybe other motives. Was there some hope in his heart that they might have changed, that they might be pleased to see him, beg forgiveness for their cruelty and be ready to slay the fatted calf? Fat chance, he retorted, and he took a deep breath and walked across the cattle grid. Why was he doing this? He still hated them. The gravel scrunched under his feet and the house came into view through the trees. A murder of crows scattered across the beech trees to his left. He had no idea what he was doing. Maybe he did want Emily back. Or maybe he just felt it was time to make something happen. For from the moment he pulled on the ancient bell-pull at the House of the Spirit Levels that Sunday lunchtime, things certainly started happening.

CHAPTER EIGHT

Obadiah was outlining his new business plan to the family, except for Joanna, who had slunk off and locked herself in the bathroom to listen to her walkman.

Quintillia was loyally attentive as usual; Jeff was doing his customary impression of a man pretending to understand a drunken lunatic speaking an unknown language; and Jane was wondering if her father had finally gone completely mad. The modern folly which was the Hardstaff Tower was disturbing enough proof in itself of Obadiah's megalomania, but what he was telling them now trumped even it as a way of wasting money.

They had observed perfunctory formalities to celebrate Obadiah's victory over Earnshaw with a token glass of champagne, but now Obadiah was doing what he did best – getting down to brass tacks.

'Right. Ludolf Moor. A site of Outstanding Natural Beauty. And no profits. Until now.

'British costume drama movies. Incredibly successful worldwide. Why? Information overload. Global village. Cultural homogenisation. The whole world is getting cut off from its cultural roots. People feel they need a connection with the past, but they're in such a hurry running to keep still, hold down a job, maintain the payments on the house, the car, the school fees and the insurance and pension . . . they're too busy doing, to keep track of who they are. Costume dramas connect them with a time when culture and society were simpler, values clearer. All bollocks of course, but people believe it and that's what counts. Doesn't even matter if it's their culture or not: it's the spiritual equivalent of international fast-food. They wonder where these movies were filmed, as if the location has some kind of spiritual significance. They maybe even try to read the book. But that takes effort. Here's where we come in. We offer them the Yorkshire Moors Experience. The Yorkshire Moors – Home of the Brontës, Robin Hood, Jane Austen, Winnie the Pooh, Hugh Grant and Liz Hurley, *The Full Monty*, Princess Diana, Long John Silver . . . whoever you want, we can airbrush them into the picture – think Trotsky in reverse. Think Irish bitter ales – all of them less than ten years old, but you make an advert with some waif-like freckly colleen swanning about in a misty peat bog to a fiddle track and everyone thinks they've been brewed since the Middle Ages.

'The only thing against us is the weather. So, here's my grand solution. Are you ready?' His eyes darted excitedly around his audience. He smiled his vulpine smile and rubbed his hands together portentously. 'We encase the whole of Ludolf Moor in a plastic dome and whack in some air-conditioning: problem solved. Think of it: state of the art monorails ferrying nostalgia-hungry tourists from America and Japan through beautiful unspoilt countryside from hotel to point of historical significance and back again. Unemployed people wandering around dressed up as the Brontës and Robin Hood and his Merrie Men, and whatever else we can think of for a minimum wage ... we'll have all-weather recreation centres, with swimming pools, discos, live bands, stand-up comedy, bingo ... we'll re-landscape the steeper hills – take the gradient down a bit, so that the more adventurous people can go for a walk ... In fact, and this is where it gets really clever – we replace every natural thing up on that moor with its cybernetic equivalent. Birds, animals, plants, everything will be man-made and indistinguishable from the real thing, except we can programme it all through the computers to behave exactly as we wish. We can kill, breed, move and mutate the whole ecosystem at the touch of a few buttons. You realise what this means? I, Obadiah Hardstaff will go down in history as the man who fulfilled God's pronouncement of man's purpose on earth to the letter, as written in the Book of Genesis – "Replenish the earth, and subdue it: and have dominion over the fish of the sea, and over the fowl of the air, and over every living thing that moveth upon the earth." Chapter one, verse twenty-eight. Come to think, there's no sea up there is there? We'll have to get one put in. Oh, and the other thing – we'll make a lot of money.'

Everyone was silent.

'Erm, Dad. I didn't think you believed in God.'

'What's that got to do with it? I'm going to become one.'

'Right, fine. That's great is that, Dad. Er, so basically

you're saying, tear up the Yorkshire Moors, and replace them with an identical replica of them with a roof over the top.'

'That's pretty much it, but of course, driven by the metaconcept.'

Jane looked as if she wasn't sure what a metaconcept was, but as if she knew exactly where she would like to put one if she got hold of it, and wondered what overpriced marketing seminar her father had been on to pick up the term in the first place.

'Will there be a golf course?' said Jeff.

Jane stared at her reflection in the fine old Louis Quinze dining table, jammed her feet hard down into the antique Persian carpet and forced herself to visualise Jeff naked and erect, all rippling muscle and inexhaustible stamina, thus restraining her desire to seize one of the solid silver candelabra and wrap it round his head.

'Golf courses? Of course. There will be seven. Each themed on different major philosophical systems of the world.'

Jeff now had the gall to nod silently for a full twenty seconds, as if he were considering other aspects of the facts and figures and conjectures that Obadiah had laid before them before concluding:

'I think it's a great idea. Totally cutting-edge.'

'Actually,' said Quintillia, 'I have something to tell you that might be of great commercial value in this enterprise.' They all turned, attentive. 'You might find this hard to believe, but . . .'

And then the doorbell rang.

'Who's that calling round during lunch?' said Quintillia. 'And there's no one to answer the door since Mrs Womersley's bizarre skateboarding accident.' She threw an acid glance at Joanna, who had that moment returned briefly from the bathroom to get another tape.

'It's OK, Grandma, I'll go,' said Joanna, springing on to her feet, suddenly ten years old again and bright and cheerful and helpful for an instant. It paid to keep them guessing, she calculated. Never let them work out whether one was unpredictable simply because one was a teenager wrestling with hormones and standard identity crisis, or whether it was part of a bigger subversive plan. Joanna wasn't entirely sure which it was herself: she wasn't that bothered as long as it left her in control. She was most definitely not in control when she opened the door though. She had been only two when Tony had left, only knew him through photographs; photographs she had found one Christmas while hunting in the attic and kept secretly, for Tony was a non-person in this family, and his likeness a potent symbol of rebellion and subversion. It would not take long, of course, for Joanna to discover her idol had feet of clay, but that was still in the future. He was standing there. A little more weatherbeaten, a little more serious in the eyes, but unmistakable.

'Uncle Tony?'

'Hello. You must be Joanna.'

'What are you doing here?'

'Good question. I'm not sure. Can I come in?'

'Of course you can.'

Joanna led Tony through to the dining room in a

state of high excitement, then gathered herself sufficiently to create the theatrical tension the moment demanded. Motioning Tony to wait out of sight, she opened the door and proclaimed to the room as casually as she could:

'Look who's here.'

Tony, hunched into his raincoat, stepped round the doorframe.

'Who is it? Bloody Columbo?'

'It's been a while, eh?' said Tony, and smiled feebly.

Four jaws dropped around the table, and seemed to gulp all the oxygen out of the room. Joanna was quivering with anticipation.

Tony's mother was the first to speak. 'You! After all these years!!'

'Oh my God . . .' Jane's voice trailed off as blood again began to trickle from her nostrils.

'Don't worry love, I've got a hankie. Tilt your head forward now, that's right . . .' said Jeff. 'Now look what you've done,' he added, staring accusingly at Tony.

'Well well,' said Obadiah, calmly.

Jane was now making a curious whining sound. Jeff poured a shot of Jack Daniels into her nostrils. Quintillia seemed to be finding it difficult to breathe.

'So, how is everyone?' asked Tony brightly.

Joanna stifled a snigger.

'Mind if I sit down?' trying to be as informal as possible. He smiled weakly. No one smiled back.

His mother stared at him, eyes bulging. All the blood had drained from her face.

'We thought you were dead,' she said, in a tone of utter disappointment.

'I'd been meaning to write . . . then I thought, why not just surprise them by turning up?'

'But of course you weren't,' hissed his mother. 'Life could never be that fair. You've never ever caused me anything but pain right from the time you threw up on me that New Year's Eve.'

'I was six months old.'

'Exactly. Malice right from the off. And now this . . . Oh, my heart . . . oh oh . . .'

Quintillia's body shuddered. Her legs jerked out, under the table and she hurled herself sprawling across the table to save herself from falling, scattering Meissen crockery and Sheffield silver plate cutlery in the process.

Her splaying collapse took Tony back to an afternoon in San Francisco when he had watched an aged sealion trying to climb on to the quayside at Fisherman's Wharf. Later that day he had gone to the City Lights bookshop, and then to Vesuvio's, the bar next door, where he had met two preppy Ivy League students pretending to be beat poets in their summer vacation, got very drunk on Martinis and slept with them after his gig. The memory ran through him with a warm glow and he was back there, reliving the whole period – the friends, the rehearsals that always started an hour late, lugging his conga drums in and out of beaten-up vans and pick-ups, the cafés and the crash-pads . . . the fact was, through all his maniacal practice he'd become a talented percussionist, but it had not occurred to him at the time. He had been enjoying himself, and that was always fatal; whenever he experienced contentment, it was swiftly followed by a feeling that somehow it was more than he deserved, that he had no right to set down roots and belong. Mixed with this restlessness was a fear that, if he surrendered to his sense of completeness, it would be a sign for the Gods of Providence to immediately start taking down their trousers and crap on him. Nevertheless, he was allowing himself to enjoy those happy memories of playing music in California when he was brought back to the present by a feral screaming which turned out to be his sister, who was being restrained by Joanna, Jeff and Obadiah from scratching his eyes from his face.

'Call a doctor! Get an ambulance! Look! The bastard's smiling!'

Tony was indeed smiling, for he was still in San Francisco. Once his sister had woken him up, however, it occurred to him almost immediately that this was not the most appropriate expression to wear while his mother writhed before him in the convulsive throes of a major heart attack. She was trying to speak.

'It's the shock . . . Tony – alive, it's too much.'

She tried to breathe as Joanna and Obadiah helped her on to a *chaise longue* which had once belonged to Kathy Kirby. 'But listen . . .' She fixed a greasy talon on to Obadiah's lapel. 'There's something very important I have to tell you . . .'

'It better not be something like "Obadiah, I've always loved you." Don't get soft just cos you're about to pop your clogs.'

'Shut up Dad!' said Jane, who had miraculously calmed

down and changed her priorities when she realised they were quite possibly within hours of a will-reading.

'No, it's not that . . .'

'Good. No need to get soppy just because you're about to breathe your last.'

'Shut up, Dad!'

'It's a secret . . . something of great commercial value . . .'

'What is it?'

'Ss . . . the . . . urgh.'

Quintillia's body suddenly stretched out, like a switchblade, thought Tony, and then lay rigid on the cushions.

Jane turned her face up and stared at Tony. Very calmly, she said,

'She's dead. She's dead. You've killed her. You've killed your mother.'

She paused, nodding at him busily. She looked quite pleased – in shock, but pleased – as if the best thing about her mother's heart attack was proving indisputably how disagreeable her brother was. 'Well, what have you got to say for yourself, eh? Away for fifteen years and then you come home and kill your mother.'

It was a tough one. Tony was stumped for a moment. 'Sorry?'

Obadiah stood by the fireplace, scowling. 'I'll tell you this lad, you've a bloody cheek, darkening my door and interrupting lunch with a bereavement.'

'Yes, I'm sorry about that. It is a bit of a bad start . . . but anyway, I was wondering if I could stay for a couple of days.'

'I'll have to think about it.'

'You'll think about it?' screeched Jane. 'He comes home and kills mother and you'll think about giving him house-room?'

'I'll remind you that I'm master in this house!' Obadiah's booming tone seemed to swell his body to a menacing size and Jane sat down and smouldered in a rocking chair that had been used on Val Doonican's biggest tour of Great Britain. 'Joanna, go and take your uncle for a walk in the garden.'

'Yes Grandad.'

As they stepped out onto the porch, Tony took a deep breath. 'The air's still good up here.'

'We're upwind of the chemical works. Well, you certainly know how to liven up the usual dull routine.'

Tony found himself objecting to Joanna's levity.

'She was your grandmother, Joanna.'

'She was your mother.' She turned and looked into his face. 'Don't tell me you're upset.'

'Well . . . I suppose I want to be.'

'You just feel you should be, that's all. It's social conditioning: we're brainwashed into believing we should naturally love our family no matter what. It's an insidious form of social control. Emotional fascism.'

'Is that right?'

'You're the one who left home fifteen years since without a word.'

'True.'

'And by the way, that's all from your diaries. I found them.'

'But they were—'

'—under the floorboards in your bedroom. I had an instinct.'

Tony now turned and looked at her. 'I'm not saying there's never a blood bond in the family,' she said. And he felt a thrill. 'So why have you come home?'

'I don't know yet. I just did. Anyway. Tell me about you.'

She looked at him with disappointment. ' "Tell me about you, young lady." "How are you doing at school?" "Are you working hard for your exams?" "My, how you've grown . . ." Maybe it was time you came home. You sound like you've turned into one of them.' He cringed inside. Was it really so easy to become uncool to teenagers?

'All right then . . .' he said with a sheepish bobbing of the head. 'How about . . . I know . . . I don't know. Have you taken any good drugs lately?'

'Trying too hard to cross the generation gap.'

'I still take drugs occasionally.'

'How many times do you ask your friends if they've taken any good ones recently?' She had skipped up on to the low wall which extended from the stone steps, dividing the ornamental lawns at the front of the house from the trees off to the right. The lawns sloped downwards as they moved away from the building and the wall, which was level, got higher and higher from the ground. Her feet were now at his shoulder height.

'OK. How long before you fly the nest and how can I help you?'

She stopped. 'That's better! Ready?' And she jumped. And he caught her.

A few yards on the wall tapered back down to nothing. They stepped over into the trees.

'So they're no better these days then?'

'Bunch of bastards. Look, a dead rook. The others gang up on one for no reason every once in a while.'

'I know.'

'They threatened to send me away to school.'

She looked at him, inviting a response.

'OK. So what happened?'

'I told them I'd burn it down.'

'I see.'

'I used to hack into the computer. Leak stuff about their investments to the papers. Grandad's got money in every disgusting regime in the world. They've upped security now. They still think it's just a phase I'm going through. Grandad was really impressed with how devious I was, and he reckons once I calm down I'll be an asset to the company.'

'So what are you going to do?'

'I'm going to get out. But not before I've got some money out of them.'

'Even though it's dirty?'

'Once it's mine I can clean it up, can't I?'

'Maybe.'

They walked on. She told him with glee about how furious her parents had been when she'd been arrested four times one summer at various ecological protests up and down the country, how she was seriously into yoga, and transcendental meditation and hypnotism, how the first step had been the simple one of becoming a vegetarian. She'd been amazed at how much upset this had caused, until a chance remark from her grandmother had revealed that Tony had done the same thing.

'You're my role model, so now you're here you'd better not let me down. Together we can smash them.'

Tony felt afraid. This felt a bit too much like commitment. He tried to change the subject.

'So you don't like living here then?' he said with stunning penetration.

'It's a shithole in the back of beyond, isn't it? Everyone's insane: look at your mate Dave and his pals. Survivalist Morrismen for heaven's sake!'

'I thought that was a secret.'

'I used to go out with one of them. A big strapping copper called Pete.'

He looked at her blue hair, her nose stud.

'You went out with a policeman?'

'He was very hunky. You know what the women are like in this family. Carnal desire overcomes character judgement every time. Look at my dad for example.'

'How old are you?'

'Seventeen.'

'How did you know I was mates with Big Dave?'

'I've got your diaries. So why have you come back?'

'I don't know.'

'You mean you don't want to tell me.'

'Actually, no, it's not that. I suppose I wanted to see if I could build some bridges.'

'Hmm. Well, killing me grandma's a good start.'

'You don't seem very upset.'

'Whereas you're devastated.'

'I wasn't thinking of the family – you know, the bridges thing.'

'Oh, Emily Earnshaw.'

'Yeah.'

'I know you and she were close, Uncle Tony, but . . .'

'That was ages ago for heaven's sake. I'm just asking.'

'The answer to the question you want ask is "No she's not married, and she still looks good." The answer to the question you ought to ask is, she's not a full shilling, Uncle Tony. And don't look like that. I'm just saying.'

'Maybe we ought to go back.'

'Maybe. Maybe you should never go back.'

'Well I'm here now.'

'I'm glad. Come on. It's getting cold.'

The doctor had formally pronounced Mrs Hardstaff dead some twenty minutes earlier. Her body was removed to the hospital mortuary prior to autopsy, and as the front door closed, everyone filed grimly back into the dining room. Tony walked in with Joanna to find the others all staring at him accusingly.

He attempted a weak smile. Joanna sprawled immodestly in an armchair and opened a magazine.

Jane had turned a very particular purple, the like of which Tony had only seen in natural history documentaries, on mandrills' bottoms. Jeff was standing by with a couple of pills and a glass of water, and he gently forced them both upon his wife as she made to lunge at Tony once again.

'Now now love, calm down . . .' He leant closer to her ear and whispered, though still audibly, 'You know when you get all fierce like this it reminds me of Mrs Thatcher in her prime . . . and . . . we're not at home . . . how am I going to burn off the excess energy?' Jane's body visibly became more relaxed. Jeff looked at his watch. 'Ooh, actually, talking of excess energy, that reminds me . . .' Transferring Jane into Joanna's arms, he walked towards the phone.

Tony fidgeted nervously. 'I was hoping we can let bygones be bygones and make a fresh start.'

'Pah!' said Jane, sitting down abruptly as the pills took full effect.

'Let bygones be bygones,' growled Obadiah . . . 'What were your last words to us when you left?'

'I can't remember.'

'"Hope I never see you alive again you hypocritical cryptofascist capitalist bastards – anything I've learnt about being human I never got from you."'

'Cool,' said Joanna under her breath.

'Well, you know, the impetuosity of youth . . .' said Tony pathetically, and they were back to silence. 'And if I remember correctly, what I actually said was "Some day I hope to see the error of my ways, come home and make it up . . . but for *now* I hope never to see you alive, etc, etc."'

He didn't need to look at Jane to know this had hit home.

On the other side of the room, Jeff was talking quietly into the phone.

'Hello Bill? It's Jeff. Yes, look I'm sorry, we've had a bit of a personal tragedy this afternoon and . . . well Jane's mother's just passed away . . .' He stared at Tony. 'Dropped dead over Sunday lunch . . . no, after the roast beef, but before the apple pie. So anyway as a result, there may be a problem with badminton this evening . . . can we make it eight rather than seven thirty? All right then, Bill. Bye.'

'See?' said Jane. 'Jeff's had to rearrange his badminton cos of you.'

Tony did not have the energy to defend himself. 'Sorry about that. So like I say, it'd be great if I could stay for a few days.'

There's more to this than meets the eye, thought Obadiah. He stared hard at Tony, who had to keep telling himself that his father's withering gaze was not capable of reading his mind.

'I suppose there's nothing wrong with you staying long enough to pay your respects.'

Jane was stunned into silence.

'Thanks Dad, I'd like that.'

In days to come, Tony would realise he should never have taken his father's charitable response at face value. It was only through luck that he survived.

Jane now tried to speak, but fell back in a faint, with blood issuing from her nose once more.

'Oh dear, Mum's head's exploded again.'

'Go and get the Jack Daniels will you, love?'

'OK. Just putting a record on.'

'How can you think of music at a time like this?'

'It's specially for Uncle Tony.'

And the sound of Peters and Lee singing 'Welcome Home' filled the room.

CHAPTER NINE

Joanna's choice of music didn't go down well.

Tony couldn't prevent a smirk, which didn't help Jane's mood when she caught it.

It took time for Jeff to register the song and Joanna's ironic intent. After that he simply stared in disbelief. Meanwhile Jane, nosebleed now staunchly cauterised by Jack Daniels (a tot up each nostril), had stormed across the room, torn the record from the deck and hurled it at Tony, who ducked. Joanna played the innocent with a wide-eyed 'What?'

'Oh dear, Jane, love, calm down. You've torn the wallpaper now, look, on top of everything else your dad's had to put up with today. I'll have to get out me *Barry Bucknell's Complete DIY Encyclopaedia* to search for a handy repair hint when we get home now.'

Jane punched him in the mouth.

Joanna sniggered, and was already ducking gracefully as Jane turned and swung at her.

'Perhaps it's time we went home,' said Jeff.

Tony was feeling very confused. Although he already knew his parents were deeply strange and distasteful people, discovering they had a Peters and Lee record was somehow a profoundly chilling and disturbing surprise.

'You're going nowhere till you've shown me how to work that microwave,' declared Obadiah. And then looking at Tony, he added: 'You realise I'll have to cook for myself now. And do my own washing.'

There was an awkward feel to the rest of the afternoon.

Obadiah dealt with the comings and goings of paramedics, lawyers, doctors and policemen, coldly calm and matter-of-fact with all of them.

Much as he had always enjoyed upsetting his sister, even Tony felt embarrassed as Joanna kept asking him questions about what he had been up to during his exile. Normally he would have enjoyed spinning yarns of his travels and experiences, had an automatic tendency to exploit any opportunity to impress and captivate any audience, but in this situation even he felt reluctant. Joanna was clearly genuinely interested, and Tony felt quite thrilled at how much of a mythic hero he had become to the teenager. But he could tell how Joanna's 'wows' and 'cools' and 'wickeds' were meant largely to irritate her mother. Jane was sitting in an armchair in the corner, now heavily sedated, with a glazed expression on her face, and Tony doubted that she could make much sense of anything around her. But Joanna was clearly operating on the assumption that even if there was only a slim chance of her mother understanding, she was not going to miss the opportunity of upsetting her.

Jeff perched on the arm of Jane's chair, periodically mopping her brow with baby wipes, tearing them off from the large plastic tub he held in the crook of his arm. Tony noticed that Jeff barely looked up from his golfing magazine while doing this. He had clearly done it before, many times.

Tony wasn't sure what he felt, but he was certain that the others should have been showing a little more concern or at least solemnity. He realised that although it had been a long shot, he had carried some small hope of getting to know them all again and maybe getting on with them, and realising that this was now clearly impossible with his mother filled him with some regret.

Suddenly Jeff looked at his watch, and stood up.

'We really ought to be going now or I'll be late for badminton.'

CHAPTER TEN

Tony thought it best to wait in the drawing room rather than see his sister's family to the car. He heard the front door slam and realised with rising panic he was only moments away from being alone with his father for the first time in fifteen years.

'So,' said Obadiah, entering the room. 'I take it you're in some kind of trouble.'

'What makes you say that?' said Tony, trying to remain relaxed.

'Why else would you come back here?'

'I wanted to try and make things up.'

'I bet you're bloody making things up.'

'Look, I know you planned for me to be your heir, to take over the business, and I know it upset you when I turned out to be an autonomous individual with my own mind, but I see how wrong that was now, and how you were right all along, and I hope that over the next little while, I'll be able to convince you how much I've changed.'

Tony was calculating that you couldn't ever flatter the delusions of tyrants to excess.

'You'll remember where your room is,' he said. 'We'll talk more in the morning.'

Left alone, Tony spent ten minutes or so surveying the bookshelves, the rows of leather-bound unopened novels and complete works of whoever's complete works were considered an indispensable wall covering by credit card companies and quality Sunday magazine advertisers, listened at the foot of the stairs to assure himself Obadiah had disappeared into his own rooms for the night, and quietly climbed the stairs. His room was empty, save for a bed. The walls were bare; there were no curtains. There was no evidence of his having lived there, not even under the loose floorboard now that Joanna had sussed his secret. He felt disappointed, a little hurt, as if subconsciously he'd thought they would have kept it the way it was when he left. He knew that was ridiculous, but he felt upset nonetheless. He also felt upset that he didn't feel upset about his mother. If he'd been thinking more clearly, he'd have asked himself why his father had agreed to let him stay.

Next morning Tony heard a car speed up the drive and brake very hard on the gravel. The door slammed aggressively and Tony knew it could only be Jane. He decided to lie low. Aside from anything else, his father had always hated him for lying in in the mornings, so it would be a statement that he was not going to be obsequious.

Downstairs in the kitchen, Jane was complaining.

'I've told you Jane, I have my reasons for letting him stay.'

'Well I demand to know what they are. Do you think he's a reformed character? The prodigal son returned? Well I'll tell you something, there'll be no fatted calves getting the chop round here if I've got anything to do with it.'

'No I don't think he's reformed. What do I do now?'

'You put the tea in the teapot. That's too much!' She grabbed the spoon from his hand. 'Just watch me.'

'I shall have to get a housekeeper.'

'So what is it? I've a right to know. I'm the one who's stopped here all my life working for the company while he's been poncing off seeing the world and God knows what and having fun . . .'

'All right, all right, I'll tell you. In fact you'll like it.'

'What then?'

'As you know, I've survived to a good age.'

'A hundred and eighty-three. It's incredible.'

'Aye well, it was just a question of willpower. Willpower fuelled by hatred, greed and bloody-mindedness. And I like being alive. But being realistic, I can't go on forever, especially now the competition's dropped off the perch . . . can you cook eggs in these microwaves?'

'I'll do it. Get on with the story.'

'I can't go on forever, not in this body. Oh marvellous, there's egg all over the floor now. Just call the dog, he'll lick it up. Here boy. You'll have to put a couple of handfuls of mince on it first though. And a bap. That's right. Look at him go.'

'What do you mean, not in this body?'

'It's only a few years off, according to my contacts in the Swiss clinics, before brain transplants are a distinct possibility. But you need a very compatible donor. Will you put those eggs down before you smash the lot?!'

Jane was trembling with delight. 'You don't mean . . .'

'If he's the same blood group, we could be in business. But we've got to keep him here for a few years yet. So be nice to him, OK?'

'Dad, I'm so proud of you.'

'All right, that's enough. And mind you don't be too nice, or he'll know summat's up.'

When Tony came into the kitchen twenty minutes later, he was surprised to see his sister rise up from the table and greet him with a smile.

'Did you sleep well, Tony? Cup of tea?'

'What's going on?'

'Nothing. I was just trying to make you feel at home.' Obadiah cleared his throat and Jane's tone hardened. 'You ungrateful bastard.' She hurled the cup at Tony, who had been ready to duck since he entered the room.

'Look, I said I was sorry about yesterday. If you don't mind I'd like to stay long enough to pay my respects, and then I'll be on my way again. Like I say, I know it wasn't the best of starts, but—'

'You must be in big trouble to come back here.'

Tony picked through his argument word by word like a stilt walker crossing slippery stepping stones.

'Not at all. I just thought that it would be nice if we could all get together as a family again, settle our differences . . . because despite everything, I've missed you.'

'Aye all right. That's settled then. Now, there's work to

be done. Do either of you know anything about communicating with the spirit world? No? Marvellous. I'll have to do it myself then. Elvis, come here. Sit.'

Obadiah dangled his pocket watch in front of the spaniel, who yawned, and, it became evident a few moments later, farted disgustingly.

'Come on boy – do your job, damn you.'

'What are you trying to do?'

'I'm trying to put it into a trance of course.'

'You're trying to put a cocker spaniel into a trance.'

'Don't take that tone with me! You walk in here, kill your mother, expect a bed for the night and then start with that tone first thing next morning! Well don't. I know it looks bloody daft, but your mother claims – claimed that this dog is a spirit guide. A medium. Your mother used him to talk to Mrs Womersley the housekeeper after Mrs Womersley skateboarded off the viaduct. Fetch boy! Fetch your mistress.'

'I didn't mean to be sarcastic. That's very touching.'

'What is?'

'That you miss Mother so much that you're trying to communicate with her like this. I'd never have thought you—'

'Miss her! How dare you sir! How dare you walk back into this house after fifteen years' absence and impute such effeminate metropolitan sensibilities to me! I am a Northerner sir, and a man, and you'll do well not to forget it. This is nowt to do with poncy stuff like feelings! You great Southern wuss. It's strictly business. Your mother was about to reveal a valuable secret pertaining to Elvis the Spaniel here; a secret of great commercial value, so she claimed.'

'Oh.'

'And just when she was about to tell us, you walked through the door and killed her,' added Jane.

'I've said I was sorry.'

Obadiah turned back to the dog.

'Fetch boy! Go fetch your mistress from the spirit world . . . You are feeling sleepy . . . Great Scot! His breath smells as if the dead of centuries reside in his very mouth! Speak, you legions of the damned! I want your words, not your noxious odours of decay! Listen you . . . dog! You will produce the shade of your beloved mistress immediately, or you've already had your last bowl of earthly Winalot! Do you understand? Do you? Ah . . . look – he's writhing; perhaps the spirit possesses him at last! Don't you know anything about this kind of stuff lad?'

'Sorry, no.'

The dog farted again, this time audibly. All three of them rushed back, towards the open back door, which slammed shut as they reached it. The dog began rolling on its back, and the microwave began flashing and bleeping hysterically. The dog flipped over again, stretching its back legs out behind it and a dark ball of vapour emanated from between them. It grew in size and gradually, to the gaping amazement of the Hardstaffs, materialised into the shape of their late departed Quintillia.

'Oh for goodness sake, Obadiah!' The two men recognised the voice but did not dare to trust their ears. For one brief moment, which revolted them both to the point of near-nausea, they were a pair, united by the common shock and their reaction to it. Both of them gaping and wide-eyed and slack-jawed. They turned simultaneously. In front of the ornate full-length mirror but unreflected in it, stood Mrs Hardstaff, tall, pale. Like a waxwork, but with the same disapproving look and a menacing new tweed suit. Her hair had been newly permed and set, and the faint cobalt-blue rinse in it seemed to glow slightly in an eerie and disconcerting way.

'Well isn't that sweet! What a touching family scene.' To their great horror, the three Hardstaffs noticed that they were clutching hold of each other, frozen in a pose of standard fear, as represented in a science fiction film by the first unfortunate victims of the monster, immediately prior to being eaten, paralysed with terror, vaporised or blown to bits according to the special-effects budget available to the director. But what chilled them more than the undeniable apparition before them was to discover that in their panic they had physically reached out to each other for comfort and support.

'That's enough. Leave the dog alone,' she said.

'Quintillia!'

'Mother!'

She took in Tony with the merest flicker of a head turn. 'So you're still here are you?' she said contemptuously.

'There's no need to be like that.'

'No. I suppose not. Being killed by her own first-born son is the kind of thing a mother should just take in her stride I suppose.'

'All I did was say hello to you. How do you think I

feel, knowing that setting eyes on me would be enough to kill you?'

Obadiah intervened. 'All right, all right, that's enough of this who killed who and who feels what bollocks: let's get down to business. Quintillia, what was the secret you were about to reveal to us?'

Tony couldn't take this in. 'My mother's ghost has appeared to us, three of us, we can all see her, and all you can say is "Let's get down to business?" What about the metaphysical ramifications? What it implies about life after death, about the existence of the soul outwith the body . . .'

'And what good would that do us, you great Southern wuss?'

A second figure seemed to be materialising next to Tony's mother. Short, stout, fearsome. At first Tony thought it was the Duchess from *Alice in Wonderland*. But as the shape filled out with colour and acquired more definition, Tony realised the yellow plastic house-coat and ankle-length furry boots, the gnarled fingers as strong as pliers, the blue eye-shadow could mean only one thing. Mrs Womersley the housekeeper, who could skin and gut a rabbit and box the ears of three small children in under a minute without losing the ash from the end of her cigarette.

'Oh that's very nice, isn't it Mrs Hardstaff? Not a word of asking how you are nor nothing. Just straight to what can give him personal gain. Oh and look who's there with him. The prodigal matricide himself.'

'Mrs Womersley?'

'Yes. Don't look so bloody stunned. I've served this

house loyally girl and woman for many a good year. I don't see why a little matter like death should divide me from my duties when I feel that way inclined.'

'Right. How are you?'

'As if you care one way or another. And don't put that mug straight down on the table; it'll leave a mark.'

Obadiah was getting impatient.

'All right all right; that's enough. Jane. Stop gaping like a goldfish! You heard your mother many a time say the spaniel was a spirit medium. Now you know she wasn't bonkers like we thought, so pull yourself together. There's work to be done. Quintillia. Just before you croaked yesterday you were about to impart a secret of great commercial value.'

'Yes.'

'Well you're back again, so get on with it.'

'I'll tell you when I'm good and ready. There's a few conditions need setting down first. My funeral had better be bloody spectacular. I want everyone to see what an important figure I was round these parts, understood? I want weeping crowds, throwing flowers. I want everyone to have a day off work. I want photographers. I want a mausoleum built on the island in the lake. I want you to think of stuff to surprise me with. I want it to be impressive, OK?'

'Yes,' said the mortals.

'Cos if you don't, the spaniel's secret stays with me. Understood?'

'Yes.'

'Tony, what are you all dressed up like that for? The funeral's not till Thursday.'

Tony shuffled his weight from foot to foot.

'Er, no. I thought I'd go and pay my respects to Emily Earnshaw.'

'Emily Earnshaw? What do you mean, pay your respects?'

'Her dad's just died, Dad.'

'I know that. I waited a hundred and sixty years to see it happen.'

'So? I don't imagine you'd be that upset if your dad died. You certainly don't seem that upset about me.'

'It doesn't surprise me he's off to the Earnshaws',' said Mrs Womersley. 'He always was a selfish little brat. Even when he was a baby. Two weeks old and it was nothing but sleeping and eating and crying and soiling his nappies.'

'Emily and I were very close at one time.'

'Oh I see. That's it,' said Obadiah. 'You're hoping to catch her while she's vulnerable and get your leg over.'

'Typical Hardstaff.'

'You know what, Mum, it wouldn't surprise me if you had that heart attack on purpose just to make me feel bad.'

'Still managing to blame other people for his own failings, Mrs Hardstaff. In all the time I was your housekeeper, he always had an excuse for everything. Nothing was ever his fault.'

'You're quite right, Mrs Womersley.'

'If you caught him crying – was it because he was a mewling self-pitying little softy? No; it was because you'd forgotten his birthday, or because you'd ripped his potato prints off the fridge because they were rubbish.'

'You've always had my best interests at heart, haven't

you. Like when you sent poison pen letters in my handwriting to my schoolfriends so they all ostracised me.'

'That was for your own good.'

'It was very upsetting to your mother, watching you having friends.'

'Yes. It was like a knife in my heart, seeing you wasting your time playing and laughing and having fun. There was none of that when I was a girl.'

Tony bit his lip and opened the back door. 'I'll see you later.'

Quintillia motioned for her husband to step into the hall.

'No offence, Jane love.'

'None taken.'

'I take it, Obadiah, you have your reasons for allowing your wife's killer to sleep under your roof.'

'Of course I do.'

'I know Jane's very upset about it.'

'Well there you are then. Don't you remember all the fun we had playing them off against each other when they were young?'

'Well it better hadn't affect her planning of my funeral, or you'll never hear the secret of Elvis.'

'Confound you! Of course it'll be a nice funeral, I give you my word. Don't you trust me?'

'Of course not. And think on – that spaniel has the power to pull more tourists to the new Holiday Centre than if you put on public executions with a free hamburger thrown in. So make sure nothing goes wrong.'

'Wait – before you go, I don't suppose you could arrange

a meeting for me with Jacob Earnshaw? I wish to taunt him over winning our bet.'

'He can't be doing with you,' Mrs Womersley chipped in. 'He's got higher things to think about.'

'Oh aye. Like what?'

'Like contemplating the essence of existence, and communing with the godhead.'

'Pah! It's all a load of mumbo jumbo.'

'It's all very interesting in its way, actually. We've already found out what really happened to Glenn Miller.'

'Well, we'd best be off. And mind you look after that dog. It's very important.'

'Surely you can leave me some shred of useful information?'

'I've got one. This whole place needs a good hoovering,' said Mrs Womersley.

'Ye Gods!' said Obadiah.

When he returned to the kitchen, Jane was still standing on the same spot, reflective.

'Is it just me, or was that a bit weird?'

'Who cares what it was,' said Obadiah. 'We know what we've got to to do now to discover the secret of the spaniel. So get home and get on with planning the funeral.'

'Yes Dad.'

When, over yet another bottle of tequila some weeks later, Tony finally told us the secret of Elvis the Spaniel, I was so shocked my mouth fell open. I am not easily shocked, so to find myself making even this relatively common and mild expression of surprise was such a great shock, that no sooner had I closed my mouth than shock caused it to fall open again. So shocked was I to sense this second physical expression of shock that my mouth fell open again and . . . well you get the idea. Unfortunately, one of a group of bees seeking a new place to swarm happened to alight on my lip at the moment of the imparting of knowledge, and as if in a hideous parody of affirmation of Pope's dictum that a little knowledge is a dangerous thing, I began involuntarily to chew the bee. Now is not the time to reveal the secret of Elvis the Spaniel, but I will say this: I can never since that day listen to 'Love Me Tender' – the King's version of course, for in my universe there is no other – without breaking out in painful empathetic swellings on my mouth and lips. But I digress . . .

CHAPTER ELEVEN

Jeff's morning routine consisted of lying in and watching *The Big Breakfast*; being the consort to such a powerful business magnate, he felt an obligation to keep his finger well and truly on the pulse of current affairs. He then got up and walked to his *en suite* gym, where he spent an hour and a half pumping iron and pounding the running machine and walking the stairmaster, admiring his glistening, sweating muscles in the mirrored walls, before entering the bathroom, where he spent half an hour showering and shaving and admiring his talced muscles in the mirrored walls.

When Jeff finally came downstairs, he found Jane in the office, furiously busy with both computers up and running. He stared at the new screensaver on the inactive one, which showed an image of Tony gradually dissolving in a vat of acid.

'Aversion therapy,' Jane explained with a nod of the head. 'I've not had one nosebleed all morning.'

'That's terrific, love. But should you be working today? You must be very upset. Why don't you put your feet up today?'

'Too much to do.'

'That's you all over, love – immersing yourself in work to kill the pain of bereavement.'

'Yeah yeah, whatever. Here's the copy for the new holiday centre. What do you think?'

'Experience first hand the romantic England of the Period Costume Period: the land of the Brontës, Jane Austen, Robin Hood and Emma Thompson – the Yorkshire Moors Experience – all the wildness and passionate beauty of the rugged hills contained in an air-conditioned luxury weatherdome, with shopping malls, sports centre, "Dig Your Own Coal from the Pitface" Facilities and much much more.' Yes, very nice start is that.'

'Of course, there is one small obstacle.'

'I know. Don't worry, it's all taken care of. I'm due on the first tee with Councillor Jeffries at eleven.'

'Good. The other thing that worries me is Joanna. With her going through this ecology phase of hers, it might be best not to mention to her any of the plans for building up on the moors. She might get upset.'

'Right.'

'Who might get upset?' said Joanna. She wore Levi's and a crop-top which would have looked small on a doll.

'Me – if you keep wearing clothes like that. Have you no shame?'

Jeff congratulated himself for so skilfully having changed the subject, then felt a dark foreboding that statistically he now stood very little chance of doing anything intelligent for the rest of the day.

'Anyway, I'll be late. Bye.'

Joanna opened her mouth but Jane jumped straight

in before she could speak. 'Joanna love, now you're up. I want you to give me a hand with the preparations for the funeral.'

'What's the big deal about a funeral? You just sling the stiff in a hole and they rot.'

'How dare you talk about my mother like that?'

'I'd talk about my mother like that. You don't really care about Grandma at all.'

'Yes I do. But we have to face up to reality. Life goes on, and her funeral is a great chance to promote the family company: Hardstaffs – the greatest Yorkshire-based multi-national in the world – and when they put one of their own to rest it's with all the pomp and circumstance of royalty. It puts us on the map. Listen kid, it's a dog-eat-dog world out there. You've got to seize your opportunities when they come along. And this funeral is an opportunity. So come on, there's lots of phone calls to make . . .'

'It's really important to you isn't it?'

'Important? Your grandma's funeral is going to be the greatest event this town has seen since Geoffrey Boycott used the gentlemen's toilet in the Red Lion. Now come on, there's loads to do. Here – have a look at the proposal.'

'Do you really think you'll get Elton John and the Welsh Guards who carried Princess Diana's coffin?'

'Money talks, love. We're not stinting on this one.'

'So I see. Barbara Cartland's personal make-up artist to lay her out . . . fly-past by the Red Arrows . . . that must be costing an arm and a leg for a start-off.'

'Like I say, money's no object.'

'Right. OK. Of course I'll help you.'

Jane was too preoccupied to notice the undertone of calculation in Joanna's voice.

They worked steadily through the morning, brainstorming, making phone calls. Joanna even came up with a brilliant suggestion: that Damien Hirst might be persuaded to convert the whole town into some kind of cutting-edge installation, a municipal twenty-first-century statement on the nature of death and bereavement. Jane was delighted by this, and said so.

'You're a very talented organiser when you put your mind to it love. You'd be a natural for running the company with a bit of experience.'

'Thank you.'

'I was just wondering – you don't really want to go travelling when you leave school do you? When you could go on day release to Business College in Dewsbury and learn to take over the reins?'

Joanna made her move.

'I'll think about it,' she said.

'Brilliant. You don't want to waste time poncing off round the world when you can control huge chunks of it from here. I've never regretted it.'

'Yeah right,' thought Joanna. 'Er, can I have the keys to the jeep?' she said.

'What, now?'

'I've got to go out.'

'But . . .'

'What are you? The secret police?'

'Where?'

'I'm meant to be meeting people for lunch. I know you can survive on adrenalin, but I need lettuce and mineral water. I'll only be half an hour.'

'Go on then.'

CHAPTER TWELVE

Tony had wanted to avoid the centre of town for fear of bumping into Dave or anyone else he knew, and had chosen instead to walk to the Earnshaw house the long way round, across the moor where he and Emily had conducted their adolescent love affair and he could think without distraction. He recognised the secret places where they had met all those years ago and adored each other and tenderly explored each other's minds and bodies and fallen in love. There was the ruined cottage in the dip where they had first kissed; there was the beck where they had stripped naked and made love in the freezing water; there was where they had lain in the shade until the midges had arrived with dusk and forced them finally to get dressed . . . they had given their own private names to every feature of the hillsides. It had been Emily's idea.

'It's like the aborigines do – map out the land with songs and secret names; this moor is no longer Ludolf Moor, it's Tony and Emily's Dreaming,' she had said one searing hot summer day, as they sunbathed naked on a warm flat patch of exposed limestone. She had stroked his body ever so gently with a twig of heather and kissed him on the mouth and he had opened his eyes to see there was not a single cloud in the whole big sky. He recalled how every night after they had taken leave of one another, he had got up in the middle of the night and covered the same route, to deliver by hand yet another love letter, and felt the same self-pitying thrill he had felt at the time imagining her delight next morning at finding these grandiose gestures of his love upon the mat.

'And then so strong was your love that you pissed off and left her for fifteen years,' commented Conchita, without looking up from her photo-essay on the contents of Marcello Mastroianni's garden shed.

Tony drew greedily on his cigarette and nodded meekly.

'Fair point. Fair point.'

The same stile was still there in the drystone wall which separated the grounds of the Earnshaw mansion from the sheep pastures. He hopped over it and then circled round to the drive. He decided that his first visit after so long demanded the formality of approaching from the front. The house was less extravagant than his parents' solid square eighteenth-century Yorkshire stone. As he approached the front door his stomach did a complicated back flip and he was pleased he had had no breakfast. It all felt and looked so familiar he wanted to believe that she would open the door and everything would be exactly the same, that fifteen years of absence could be forgotten and disregarded just because he wanted it so. As if she were his possession, kept in suspended animation until he deigned to reactivate her with the flick of a switch. The thought appalled him, and he stopped, about to turn away. If he was not entitled to be there, unworthy, then it should be Emily's choice to send him away. He owed her at least the opportunity to vent her anger upon him, to humiliate him and reject him just as he had done to her. Why had it taken him fifteen years to work this out? He knocked, trying to make it sound respectful and unassuming.

As the door opened, Tony's stomach decided to somersault round the asymmetric bars, and then Emily stood before him. She wore a black sweater and long black woollen dress, clearly out of respect for her recently departed father, but despite this, Tony could not help noticing how these mourning clothes clung tightly enough to her form to show a slender and arousing figure. She had hardly changed as far as he could see. The same straw-blonde hair, pale skin, the same blue eyes, refusing to betray any emotion. Perhaps she was more careworn; her skin seemed stretched a little tighter across the delicate bones of her face. But she was still beautiful. Tony didn't know what to say, and for once, said nothing. Breathing had suddenly become a conscious effort. He wanted the reassurance of seeing her mouth break into the warm wide smile he so often eulogised about in his more exuberant moments. Indeed, in his more wayward uncontrolled spells in the bar, he attempted many poems and songs, in both Spanish and English, in which he tried to express and capture the essence of Emily's smile. They are all of an appalling standard and will not be reproduced here. It is enough you know that he was obsessed with her smile, with her mouth.

Unsurprisingly, Emily did not smile at him.

'Tony? It's been a long time.' He could discern no feeling in her voice.

'Aye. Sorry to hear about your dad.'

'Well . . . you'd better come in.'

'Are you sure?'

'Well you'll be wanting a cup of tea, won't you?'

'That'd be nice.'

She led him through the stone-flagged hallway into the kitchen where, in a glass case, sat Jacob Earnshaw, embalmed, and dressed in his Sunday best. Tony watched Emily fill the kettle and set it on the Aga, assuming she would make the first reference to the corpse. None was forthcoming. Tony tried to be casual.

'Your dad's looking well, considering.'

'Yes, the taxidermists have done a wonderful job, don't you think?'

'Yes. When's the funeral?'

'There isn't one.'

'No funeral?'

'He left strict instructions.'

'Lovely glass case.'

'Yes. It lights up at night. Look.'

'Terrific.' He shifted involuntarily in his chair.

'That was my idea.'

'Right. Very classy.'

'Are you all right, Tony? You've gone very pale.'

'I'm fine. Fine. Could . . . could I have a glass of water please? . . . Thank you. So, where are you going to keep him?'

'Here.'

'In the kitchen?'

'Yes. Luckily, he transferred the house into my name years ago, so your father won't get his hands on it. Although everything else is his now. Including the moor.' She stifled a sob and then threw her head back haughtily, recovered her composure. 'Do you like his suit?'

'Splendid. Hangs really well.'

'Paul Smith. Traditional, but with subtle modern touches – the cut of the lapels for example. I think he'd have liked it. He may have been one of the most powerful industrial magnates in West Yorkshire for over a hundred years, but deep down all he ever wanted to be really was a male model. There just weren't the openings when he was a lad. In those days if you were born into the New Industrial Bourgeoisie it was one of two options – become an opium addict or oppress the masses for profit and sport. He wasn't a bad man, Tony; he was a victim of social forces.'

Her almost trance-like composure, which Tony had found rather unsettling, suddenly deserted her. And she wept. Tony was surprised to find his awkwardness disappear. He automatically embraced her. Her tears trickled down his neck and he felt as if he had a reason for being alive.

'Now now. There there. It's OK.'

He gently shifted their position so that he could prop himself against the great oak table and held her, stroked her head, rubbed her shoulders in an attempt to dissolve the shuddering grief and knew he was prepared to stay there as long as it took. He looked up and saw Jacob Earnshaw staring at him with an expression of thorough disapproval.

Emily gasped. 'The kettle!'

She broke away from him and made the tea.

'I'm sorry,' she sniffed, not looking at him.

'What for?' He did not want to force an answer from her, and hurried on, reaching into the carrier bag he had brought. 'I brought you some flowers.'

Her face brightened. 'Daffodils! My favourite! They're beautiful.' She buried her face in them, and Tony was disconcerted to hear a greedy munching sound. 'Mm, delicious too. Thank you. I'll put them in water and save the rest for later. Are you all right?'

Tony made a great effort to appear calm and unruffled, as if munching on a daffodil was a customary part of anyone's elevenses.

'Fine. It's good to see you again.'

She said nothing.

'I walked across the moor. Saw all our old places. It doesn't seem fifteen years.'

Emily reached up on tiptoe to get the sugar bowl from a high shelf and Tony tried to ignore the delicious glimpse of her pale slender waist which was revealed momentarily as her sweater lifted with the stretch of her arm. Unsuccessfully. 'It's silly, but I suddenly started thinking about us. How it used to be. Good times. But there's a lot of water under the bridge since then. Daft.'

'It's quite understandable. I mean here we are, drinking tea in the kitchen just like we used to, just the two of us, nervous of the lurking presence of my dad, whose embalmed corpse now sits in the corner reeking of formaldehyde . . . it's bound to give you a romantic tremble.'

'Yes. It was good, what we had.'

'Is that why you disappeared and sent not a single word then?' she said, without a trace of sarcasm.

'I meant to write. Really I did. I thought about you a lot. I just . . .'

'It's OK. I understand. You were too busy becoming a rock and roll star.'

'Emily . . .'

'Did you ever become rich and famous by the way? I kept looking out for you, but perhaps I was reading the wrong music papers.' He still couldn't tell if she was being sarcastic or not, and decided not to ask.

'So, what have you been doing with yourself?'

'Oh, looking after my father, ministering to the poor as befits my station, taking them pies, fish suppers, chocolate Yoyos, that kind of thing—'

'You always had a charitable streak.'

She tilted her head to an heroic angle and stared into the middle-distance. 'It's duty, that's all.'

'And what about your spare time?'

'I spend it in solitude, Tony, out on the moors, painting, composing verse, communing with the primal state of Nature.' She turned back to him and leant towards him across the table, excited. She was smiling. 'It's so wild and free on the moors! We should go up there later Tony, and be wild and free and unbound by the constraints of society. Milk?'

'Yes please. You're as beautiful as the day I left, Emily.' The thought escaped before he could close his mouth. 'Sorry, that sounded very corny.'

'No it didn't. Thank you.'

'I heard from the lads in the pub the other night that . . . you've never married.'

'From the lads in the pub? How long have you been back then?'

'Since Saturday. I would have come sooner but . . .'

'Don't apologise. I'm glad that you haven't lost your sense of priorities. It's not a true Yorkshireman who'd put his love-life before his ale.'

He smiled, then took in fully what she'd said.

'Love-life?'

'I knew you'd be back some day, Tony. Many's the night I've heard your voice carried to me by the wind across the moor. "Don't worry, Emily love, I'll come back for you some day . . . I'm off for a kebab just now but I'll be back some day . . ."'

'Oh aye?'

'Yes, and many a night I've dreamt I heard you outside, scratching on my window pane begging to be let in. I've always said you'd come back Tony, to anyone who's ever asked. And to quite a few that never did. "He'll come back to me," I'd say, stepping boldly up to a stranger in Morley's the Drapers. "He knows he's hurt me and one day he will return." And they say about me, "She's stark staring bonkers that Emily Earnshaw – ravishingly beautiful, with her blond ringlets, and her steely blue eyes and her lithe and handsome figure . . . ravishingly beautiful, but definitely several ferrets short of a trouserful, that Emily Earnshaw," but I vowed I'd prove them wrong. That you'd prove them wrong. Let's go into town now, Tony and show them!! Come on, I'll get me bus pass.'

'Emily, I think we should take this a bit more slowly . . . I mean it's great to see you again, and you are beautiful, more beautiful than ever, but . . .'

'What say we go for a walk on the moors this moment then, like the old days?'

'Why not? The fresh air might do you good . . . do us good, I mean.'

CHAPTER THIRTEEN

Although not blessed with an intellect much greater than that of the average front-row forward, Jeff was capable of being trained, like a laboratory animal, to perform apparently quite complex tasks. His special skill was doing business over golf. The opportunity to spend all day on the course was a huge incentive, and he had knuckled down and mastered the non-sporting elements of the exercise in a surprisingly short time.

Thus he was now standing halfway down the third hole of the Grimedale Golf course, prematurely congratulating his opponent on what turned out to be a very ordinary approach shot, largely due to Jeff applauding halfway through the downswing.

'Good shot Councillor! Difficult lie,' he added, as the ball scudded sixty yards along the ground from its perfect position in the middle of a gorgeously short and springy fairway.

Councillor Jeffries said nothing.

'Well, let's hop on the trolleys and scoot up the fairway.'

'I've never used one of these things before,' said the

Councillor as they buzzed along. 'They're quite snazzy, aren't they? By the way, sorry to hear about your mother-in-law.'

'Thank you. It was a terrible shock, but we're dealing with it as best we can.'

'I understand it was in the middle of Sunday lunch?'

'Yes.'

'Awful thing to happen at the best of times, but during Sunday lunch . . . well that seems additionally cruel somehow.'

'Well yes, it is. I think I'm safe in saying I think we all found it hard to sit back down and deal with the apple pie.'

'Oh well, at least she'd had her roast beef and Yorkshire then. I presume it was roast beef?'

'It was, yes.'

'Well, that's something I suppose. At least she died with a good square British meal inside her. Was it a heart attack?'

'Yes.'

'Sudden and unexpected, or had there been warning signs?'

'Right out of the blue.'

The Councillor dismounted and played his third shot.

'They say garlic and red wine are good for the blood.'

'Yes.'

'I suppose it's a bit late to say that now. Although frankly, garlic and red wine, it all sounds a bit too much Common Market for me. No, if I'm to thin my blood, bolstering the French economy will not be a side effect. I'll stick to rat poison thank you very much.'

'Very wise.'

'I hear your brother-in-law is home for the funeral?'

'Yes. In fact it was Tony's arrival that prompted the cardiac failure. They never really got on.'

'Oh. I didn't realise. Mind you, that's Mrs Hardstaff. Never hid what she thought of folk.'

'True.' Jeff stopped his cart and dismounted. 'Now, I think my ball went in the bushes somewhere here. Could you give me a hand, Councillor?'

'Surely. Hey, what's this?'

'Oh yes. It looks like one of those new state of the art digital televisions.'

'What's it doing out here, still in the box?'

'Who knows. Still, finders keepers. Lucky you, Councillor. I'll give you a hand to put it on the cart.'

'Er . . . right. Thanks.'

'So, how's things on the planning committee these days?' asked Jeff, nonchalantly.

CHAPTER FOURTEEN

Quintillia Hardstaff's body was lying in at Mill's the Undertakers. It was twelve thirty, and all the staff had gone down to the Boot and Tooth for a spot of lunch, leaving Eddie, the half-witted apprentice, to man the phones. Eddie was always happy to take the late lunch break on his own, as being left alone for an hour at the shop gave him the opportunity every day to drift off into his obsessive fantasy, which involved himself and the gorgeous Joanna Grimethwaite on a huge water bed with black satin sheets. Thus when he furtively pulled back the net window drapes and realised that it was none other than Joanna herself trying the bolted door, he was flabbergasted. He grabbed his top hat and fumbled at the bolt.

'Hello, Eddie.' She oozed past him into the reception area. 'Shut the door please.'

'Yes, Joanna.'

'That's Ms Grimethwaite to you. I'm well-bred gentry.'

'Oh aye? And that's what well-bred gentry girls do is it? Gyrate their bellies at apprentice morticians?'

'Concentrate on my navel stud.'

'I'll do me best,' said Eddie, in a stifled voice.

'You are feeling very sleepy ... you will remember nothing of this ... you will help me get my grandmother's corpse into the jeep, help me conceal it, and you will only wake up when your mates come back from the pub ...'

CHAPTER FIFTEEN

From the eighth tee, Jeff had expertly hooked his drive into the copse a hundred yards down the fairway.

'It's very kind of you to help me look for my ball again, Councillor.'

'You've lost a hatful this morning, Jeff. Not like you at all. Good heavens, what's this?'

'What's what, Councillor? . . . Oh yes. Looks like an envelope. I wonder what's inside?'

Jeff met the Councillor's quizzing turn of the head with an innocent smile.

'Two open return tickets to Barbados . . . in my name.'

'Well . . . It certainly is your lucky day, Councillor, what with the television and the fridge freezer and the microwave. Oh. Found my ball . . . !'

CHAPTER SIXTEEN

Jane and Joanna had been working furiously all afternoon on ideas for the funeral and were taking a
break to watch Leni Riefensthal's documentary of the
1934 Nuremberg Rally for inspiration on how to shoot
crowd scenes when the policeman knocked at the door.

He was short, rotund, with a red face and took off his
cap respectfully to reveal a head of wispy light brown
hair which he flattened quickly with a sweaty hand into
a fetching Bobby Charlton style.

'I'm really sorry to bother you at such a delicate time
Mrs Grimethwaite . . . but I've some bad news for you.'

Joanna suspected the officer had been chosen to deliver
the bad news to spare his colleagues briefly from his
appalling body odour.

'What is it?'

'Well, there's trouble at Mill's.'

'Trouble at mills? We don't own any mills; what's it got
to do with me?' Jane automatically went to the window
and opened it.

'No, I mean trouble at Mill's the Funeral Directors'. Your
mother's been . . . kidnapped.'

Joanna emitted the perfect little squeak of horrified disbelief she had practised all the way home in the jeep.

'Kidnapped? But she's dead.'

'Aye. But kidnapped nonetheless. We found a ransom note.'

The policeman moved towards Jane, who was still by the window.

'No, it's all right officer, let Joanna read it.'

Joanna, who had lit a cigarette to improve the quality of the air, took the sheet of paper from the policeman's quivering outstretched hand. 'We have your mother's corpse. She is being well looked after. But unless we get five hundred thousand pounds by this time tomorrow there will be no funeral and it will be the worse for her. Signed Burke and Hare.'

'So there's no need to worry,' said the policeman, confidently.

Joanna was indignant. 'No need to worry? That's my grandmother you're talking about!'

'They've given us a vital clue.' The policeman waited to see if the womenfolk had figured it out, before continuing, smugly. 'They've inadvertently told us exactly who they are – at the end there.' As the policeman moved towards Joanna and the letter, Joanna backed away and held the paper at arm's length. 'See – "signed, Burke and Hare". We'll have them nicked in no time. Even now we have our computer boys running through the databases. It'll only be a matter of time before they find a Burke and Hare who live in the same address, then bingo.'

'Burke and Hare were bodysnatchers in the eighteenth

century,' said Jane, grinding her teeth and fanning the window open and shut.

'Are you sure?' said the policeman, looking at the note as if it had just rewritten itself to embarrass him.

'Oh. I'd better tell them to stop trawling the database then. They'll be ever so disappointed. Have you any idea who might be behind it? Our other thought was that it might be someone who could do with an extra half million quid. We're running a check through the databases on that as well.'

'It must be someone who bears a grudge against our family.'

'That narrows it down,' said Joanna.

The policeman emitted a guttural laugh, fooled by Joanna's jocular tone.

'She's right there! Everyone hates your family round here, don't they.' Only now did he notice that Jane was not sharing the joke. 'When I say hate, I meant, resent. Pathetic I call it, the way some folk envy them who've got a few bob . . . I mean, I don't include myself in that . . . what I meant was . . .'

'Where do they want the money leaving?' snapped Jane.

'It doesn't say.'

'So they're going to get into contact again.'

'Ooh, it doesn't do to rely on that kind of speculation Mrs Grimethwaite, I know it's hard but you mustn't build up false hopes . . .'

'It's not speculation! If they want the money and they haven't said where to leave it, they're going to get back in touch again to tell us where to take it, aren't they?'

The policeman thought about this and then continued in an admiring tone. 'Have you been trained in police methods Mrs Grimethwaite?'

'No.'

'Well I tell you then, you're a natural for it. Well, I'll be in touch as soon as we hear anything. I can let myself out.'

'Wait. I can tell you who's behind this. My brother Tony. Find him, you'll find the body.'

'Mum, don't be ridiculous.'

'He'd stop at nothing to spite me.'

'Don't worry Mrs Grimethwaite, I'll put out an APB.'

'I've always wondered, officer,' asked Joanna innocently, 'what does APB actually stand for?'

The policeman beamed a condescending smile.

'APB stands for All Points Bulletin.'

'Oh right,' said Joanna, returning a smile. 'And what about BO?'

CHAPTER SEVENTEEN

Blissfully unaware he was now the prime suspect in his mother's post-mortal disappearance, Tony was watching Emily spinning round and round gleefully in the bracken on the slopes of Ludolf Pike.

'Oh Tony, it's grand up here, isn't it?'

'Anywhere's grand with you Emily,' he replied quietly.

'There's something so primal and elemental about the rushing wind and the cry of the curlew and the ancient splendour of the rocks and the pissing rain don't you think?'

'Aye Emily. There is.'

'But Tony, what's wrong? A frowning shadow of self doubt draws across your craggy features. What can worry you my love, now that we are united again, and communing with the elemental force which is the moor – a symbol of our untamed passion for each other?'

'Well, it's just that, you know, you can't live by communing alone. Weekends we could come up here all the time and be, unbridled and so on, but we need to make a living.'

'True enough. Such are the strictures of an industrialised

society that bends us out of shape whether we like it or no.'

'So what I'm trying to say is, what would you like to do – for a living – if you had the choice of anything at all? Or do you have enough capital for us both to live on forever without working?'

'Hardly. Your dad got to inherit my father's fortune, or had you forgotten?'

Tony dipped his head apologetically.

'What would I like to do? Like I say, commune with the primal forces of nature up here on the tops. That and run a fish shop.'

'A . . . fish shop.'

'Yeah, you know, a fish and chip shop. Not just fish and chips, but saveloys, pies, pop, pickled eggs. Conferring the bounties of nature on the indigenous population in a form they understand. For a modest profit, naturally. But it's more than that. Most of all I suppose I've always loved the smell of boiling chip fat.'

Start a fish and chip shop? Tony knew that this was the point at which he should have turned tail and run. This woman was beautiful, yes, but also stark staring bonkers. He still felt for her; it wasn't going to be easy; but it had to be done, or else he would be committing himself through pity, not love.

'Emily . . .'

'Yes Tony?'

He stared into her eyes: their blueness had the depth of oceans, the energy surging within them like a tidal wave of passion. Their mad, crazed stare said 'Run away! Bale out! Danger!'

'Emily . . .'

He paused. It was the big turning point of his life. He was about to speak, to make excuses, leave, when she gently took his hand.

'Feel my heart, Tony! Come, relax your hand. Feel it now? Beating like a caged bird, struggling to fly unbounded into the open sky of freedom which is your love?'

'Yeah yeah, I can. That's exactly what it feels like, yeah. God Emily, you look gorgeous in that cagoule.'

'Is it the way the wind wraps it fleetingly around the lissom contours of my nubile frame? The tantalising glimpse of a passionate, red-blooded, firm yet yielding female form, there for an instant and, in the next, replaced by a sagging billow of orange plastic?'

'Yeah, I suppose it is . . . Then that's what we'll do, Emily. We'll start a fish and chip shop, and commune with Nature every spare hour God sends.'

'Oh Tony, you make me so happy. But what about your dreams, your ambitions? Will it be enough for you, working in a chip shop when originally you'd set out to be the new Kajagoogoo?'

'Listen Emily, I've done some bad things in my time: betrayed all those who've trusted me, spent all my money on drink and gambling, failed to live up even to my own modest conceptions of human decency. But seeing you again Emily, makes me believe I have a chance of redemption. My dreams are to love you and make you happy, Emily. Everything else is so much ground chaff in the wind.'

'Oh Tony! You're not just saying that to get your leg over are you?'

'N-no. Course not.'

'Kiss me Tony. Kiss me.'

'Oh Emily . . .'

'Oh Tony . . . Take me Tony, take me . . . consummate our passion, now, here: this clump of damp bracken will be our bed . . . take me amongst the desolate beauty of the heather and the sheep droppings and the empty coke cans . . .'

'It's a bit chilly to get our kit off isn't it?'

'I've got my crotchless hiking trousers on.'

'In that case . . . oh Emily . . .'

They collapsed into the bracken.

'Oh yes, Tony, yes! But as I was saying about chip shops, the standard of fast food round here is scandalous. Oh yes! Yes! There! . . . Absolutely scandalous! Crappy chains, crappy standard of ingredients – it's shameful. Oh my love! Press a little harder! Oh Christ! . . . And my mission in life is to turn the tide and get takeaways round here back to what they should be . . . Never mind the rain, get your trousers off . . . and after, I'll take you into town and show you what I mean. Oh yes . . . like that, yes!!!'

CHAPTER EIGHTEEN

Jeff and the Councillor had reached the nineteenth just before the rain came down. Jeff returned to their table with two large whiskies.

'Well Councillor, cheers. You had a good round didn't you?'

'You beat me six and five.'

'Aye, but all the stuff you found – a telly, the tickets to Barbados, microwave, keys to that new BMW in the car park, insured in your name – every time I lost a ball in the bushes you seemed to get another free gift. Anyway, I was wondering if we could have a little chat sometime, about a business proposition . . .'

'Oh?'

'Yes. As you might know, my father-in-law has just inherited Ludolf Moor from the Earnshaws . . . and we were wondering what the exact position is about planning permission for an Area of Outstanding Natural Beauty . . .'

CHAPTER NINETEEN

As they drove up to the big house with the detectives, Jane had explained clearly to Joanna that they must break the news of Quintillia's disappearance to Obadiah very delicately, for fear of the effect on the old man's health. Joanna nodded obediently.

The huge door, deliberately made from tropical hardwood from unsustainable resources, creaked open.

'Grandad! Guess what!' exclaimed Joanna, taking Obadiah by the arm and leading him, perhaps a little too hurriedly, into the drawing room, 'Grandma's corpse has been stolen and the police can't find the kidnappers and the ransom's half a million pounds to be paid into a Swiss bank account tonight!'

'Joanna, what did I tell you?' Jane hissed.

'Sorry Mum, I'm just knocked sideways with the distress of it all.'

'Half a million quid? For a dead body? Stuff that.'

'But she's your wife.'

'So what? You called me away from playing the markets on the Internet for this? I could be causing economic collapse throughout the Congo Basin.'

'So what do you want to do?'

'I don't know. Just fill the coffin with spuds – no one'll be any the wiser.'

'But Grandad, if we did that, the kidnapper would simply reveal the whereabouts of the body and make us all look really bad,' Joanna exclaimed. 'Maybe,' she added, belatedly.

'She's got a point, Dad.'

The doorbell rang.

'That'll be Jeff,' said Obadiah. 'Let him in will you?'

'OK Grandad.'

Jeff said that the golf match had gone exactly according to plan, and was so pleased with himself for handling it all so well, that only desperate sign language from Jane prevented him from blowing the whole thing by going into detail about the moor in front of Joanna, who fortunately was distracted by her urgent desire to discuss the kidnap.

Obadiah grudgingly conceded that they had no option but to transfer the money. They all looked very solemn and grave, except for Joanna, who did her best to appear so.

CHAPTER TWENTY

Emily and Tony were sitting at a table in the Mechanically-Recovered Meat Emporium. The bright orange plastic chairs and bright blue plastic tables and bright pink walls were presumably designed to distract from the almost total lack of colour in the burgers.

'See what I mean, Tony, these burgers are terrible.'

'They certainly are.'

'Ninety per cent minced nostrils and Lord knows what the rest is. If you're not going to eat that, I'll have it. Don't give me that look! There's nothing like a good hump in the open air to get my appetite going . . . and look at this tomato sauce bottle. That mould round the cap is like a flap of damp velvet.'

'Yes.'

'Want some?'

'No thanks.'

'Taste these chips. You know what they were fried in? I'll tell you. Rancid tallow at least a month old.'

'Emily, you've convinced me. There's a gap in the market. But tell me, did we really have to bring your dad with us?'

She stared at him, affronted. 'He's as much right to a trip out as anyone.'

'But Emily, my love, he's dead.'

'So? One law for your family, one for everyone else, is it? Don't give me that blank stare Tony Hardstaff – that's your mother behind the counter isn't it?'

Tony was stunned. Emily was right. Propped up against the milkshake machine, wearing the uniform of the Mechanically-Recovered Meat Emporium, under the reluctant orange glow of the heat lamps, was his mother. He beckoned over a small, nervous boy in a similar staff uniform who was attempting to make the cigarette burns on one of the tables less conspicuous by burning some into all the other tables.

'Are you in charge here?'

'Well, sort of – I mean, I've got the key to the toilet, if that's what you're after. There's a fifty pence deposit. Paper extra.'

'No – look, do you realise there's a dead body propped up over there by the milkshake machine.'

'They're all dead bodies behind the counter. They've been here since the nurses' Christmas party.'

'What?'

'Aye. I phoned police when it happened like, and they said they'd be round when they could, but they're right stretched, you know, so bloke said to keep 'em in t'fridge, and fetch 'em out during day to see if anyone claimed them like. They're all right once you get to know them. One of them got promoted other week. You haven't to keep them in the same fridge as the salad though.'

'Well I'm claiming that one.'

'I don't recognise her. She must be new. Bloody hell: that means they've had another party at the nurses' home without inviting me.'

CHAPTER TWENTY-ONE

It was the strangest bus journey of Tony's life. More disturbing than having to carry two dead bodies on board was the way no one paid any attention. Emily's insistence that they sit on the top deck, for the view, had not improved his mood.

Today was the first time he could remember putting his arms around his mother, and instinctively he knew it would have been better if she'd been alive. Although, if she'd been alive of course, she would have resisted him with swift and bony elbows. He saw a little boy of about four sitting further up on the other side of the aisle and noticed with envy and regret that the little boy was also sitting next to his mother, but that his mother was alive and they were holding hands. He was distressed by all these feelings of wanting to feel affection and tenderness towards his parents. It didn't seem natural, and yet it was there. He needed a drink. In the double seat in front of him, Emily was chatting away merrily to her father, pointing out the sights, filling him in on recent local gossip. He tried to look on the bright side, tried to tell himself it showed what a close relationship Emily had clearly had with her father.

Inside, Tony was filling with panic. No matter how hard he tried, he could not deny that carrying the embalmed corpse of a parent around with you was taking it too far. No, be honest, it meant she was round the bend. As Joanna had said, so cruelly, but, he had to admit, accurately, Emily was not a full shilling. Just as he was contemplating leaping through the emergency exit and running off into the night, Emily turned round and with a radiant, beautiful smile that lit up her whole face, looked at him through tearful pale blue eyes and said:

'Tony, I love you so much. Even if you are a Hardstaff.'

Luckily by this time they were the only people on the bus. He smiled back, and kissed her. Maybe she was mad, but . . . 'But what?' said a voice in his head that sounded like his father. 'She's as mad as a hatter and that's the long and the short of it. Going to stay with her out of pity are you? Consign yourself to looking after a lunatic till the end of your days just because you feel bad about dumping her when she was sixteen? You can't look after everyone else in this world you know. Whatever else you do, look after number one.' Which of course, was exactly the creed that made Tony hate his family. The fact that in these circumstances it probably made perfect sense enraged him, and made him even more determined to defy it.

There was a stop directly opposite the gates of his parents' house. (Built in the old days for the convenience of their staff.)

They lugged the two dead parents down the stairs and began to march up the drive. Emily had a little folding set of wheels which she strapped to her father's feet. She executed the whole manoeuvre so expertly and unselfconsciously she had clearly done it many times before. Tony felt numb.

It was Jane who answered the door to find Tony standing there with their mother dressed in the uniform of a fast-food restaurant. The rest of the family and the three police officers left at their disposal by the deferential and slightly terrified chief constable came running to the door when they heard the stammering, high-pitched chicken noises which was as articulate as Jane could get.

Two of the policemen jumped on Tony, while chivalrously leaving their female colleague to deal with the body. Tony was handcuffed and frog-marched into the living room.

Jane had finally recovered her voice. 'Fancy kidnapping your own mother, and then having the effrontery to bring her back in person once the ransom was paid!' she yelled, and made a grab for the harpoon gun which Obadiah kept leaning by the French windows where it was handy for squirrels.

'Now now Jane, calm down,' said Jeff quietly as he restrained her. 'Remember all that trouble with the noisy carol singers last Christmas. We wouldn't stand much chance of getting away with two "tragic accidents" with the same weapon would we? Especially with four police officers as witnesses? So relax. Deep breaths. That's right.'

Joanna was relieved and horrified in equal measure: relieved to know the money was safe in a Swiss bank account, having seen her grandfather calling his lawyers and arranging the transfer, horrified to see Tony turn up with the body and be arrested: partly of course because she knew him to be innocent but also, she had to admit, because if he'd turned up an hour earlier, the money would have gone West.

Jeff had finally managed to get Jane to release her grip on the harpoon gun, but she continued her assault verbally.

'Thought we wouldn't press charges because of the scandal eh? Well you're wrong about that!'

'I keep telling you, we found her in the burger bar.'

'We?'

'Emily and I.'

'Oh. "Emily and I"? So you've taken up again with Miss Diaphanous Cranium 1983 have you?'

Emily was listening through the French windows. She had refused to set foot inside the house of her father's great rival, but hearing this, she stepped out of her hiding place in the rhododendrons and rapped on the glass. 'You're a wicked piece of work, Jane Hardstaff as was.'

'Oh she's here is she?' Jane was gleeful. 'That's right,' she said, tearing the French windows open. 'I am; and I could punch your lights out as soon as look at you, you . . . you . . . outpatient.'

Obadiah squinted into the shadows, momentarily alarmed. 'Who's that you've got with you, lurking in the bushes? Good grief – it's Jacob Earnshaw.'

'Aye, it's my father. And we take care of the dead in my family – look, that's quality embalming is that; and he's his own glass case at home, that lights up at night. And he's got his own bus pass.'

Jane giggled. 'Well Tony, I take it all back. I hope you'll be very happy, the three of you.'

'And what would you know about it, you blood-sucking robot?'

Obadiah came over all wistful.

Eee, it's just like old times, he thought to himself, watching the two of them tearing away at each other.

Blue lights and sirens were approaching from the valley below. The Black Maria was on its way.

A detective explained to Tony he was being arrested for kidnapping his mother's corpse, and then he was led out into the van.

Joanna had been sitting very quietly in the corner. Whenever Tony had caught her eye she had done her best to pretend to be innocent and twelve, as opposed to the seventeen-going-on-Lucrezia Borgia she had appeared in the garden the previous afternoon.

As they led Tony into the van, Emily could be seen in the pale spill of light from the house, halfway up the slope of the moor.

'I know you're innocent, Tony! I'll see the truth comes to light one day!'

Obadiah chuckled.

'And there she goes, off across the moors like a demented goat, with her embalmed father slung across her shoulder.'

'Yes, you have to say, she's very strong for such a slip of a girl,' observed Jeff.

'Don't worry Tony!' called Emily. 'I'll see the truth will out – I'll set you free. Look at me, Tony – remember me this way, silhouetted by the harvest moon, defiant and alone on Ludolf Crag, and don't forget, our love makes you free even now, even if you do spend the rest of your life banged up in a narrow cell with nary a glimpse of the light of day – for I will carry you with me in my heart across the broad moor every waking hour, and sleeping too, and I shall write poems to you and declaim your name to the open skies.'

'Yeah, that's all very nice love, but write to Paul Foot.'

A policeman pushed his head down and forced Tony into the van as the family watched from the porch.

Jane was concerned. 'Shouldn't we have had her banged up too?'

'No, no love. No need. If Emily Earnshaw runs the campaign to get him released, who's going to take it seriously?'

Up on the hill, Emily was overcome by the tenderness of Tony's parting remark. '"Mind your poor foot." Even in his hour of need, his first thought is for my verrucas. And I never even told him. He just knew. I love you Tony Hardstaff . . .'

Jeff and Joanna were dispatched inside to prepare drinks. Jane smiled. 'Well Dad, at least we know he's not going anywhere for a few years now. He should be out just in time for your brain-swap operation.'

'Aye. I wonder who actually did do the kidnapping?

Still, it's not important. Funny how things have a habit of working out all right in the end. Let's go and have that drink.'

CHAPTER TWENTY-TWO

And so it was that, in the days running up to his mother's funeral, Tony sat in a cell in Grimedale police station, refused bail on a charge of kidnapping her corpse.

It had to be said the cells were comparatively comfortable, and a plaque on the wall of the recreation area proudly announced that they were in fact winner of the *Homes and Interiors Magazine* award for *Best New Remand Prisoner Block In The Private Sector*.

They had been built at considerable expense, by a Hardstaff company, to compensate for some bad publicity concerning an internment camp for political refugees and asylum seekers which had turned out to be built on toxic landfill. Obadiah was himself confused as to why this had been such a terrible thing. He knew the Government considered the asylum seekers an expensive and embarrassing burden, and that they wished they would disappear altogether. But apparently they drew the line when this hidden agenda became incontrovertibly apparent when the unfortunate inmates, having contracted spectacular and distressingly unpleasant decaying diseases of the skin, began to die. It had all been cleared up in the end as a tragic mistake, that no one had known about the toxic material when the camp was built, even though a minister at the Home Office had specifically, though of course off the record, instructed Obadiah personally as to the exact location of the building. Apparently the terrible wasting sicknesses that preceded death had not been anticipated in the initial radical proposal.

Tony spent his time brooding and disillusioned, trying to come to terms with his situation. It seemed excessive behaviour, even by his family's standards, that they would let their own son go to prison for something he didn't do. Then, sadly, he thought about it a bit more and realised the only thing that was surprising about it was that he found it surprising.

He was pretty hopeful, however, that he would be acquitted at the trial, although his confidence was somewhat dented when he met his solicitor. He had qualified for legal aid, and only realised the parlous effects of the spending cuts on this area when introduced to his solicitor, a seventeen-year-old A-level law student with pimples and a worryingly vacant stare.

What had he done to deserve the terrible fate of being born into the Hardstaff family, with enough of their self-indulgent appetites to get him into constant trouble, and enough of a conscience to make him feel constantly guilty, and to restrain him from going the whole sociopathic hog into some kind of amoral, depraved but reasonably secure lifestyle?

The moment he got out of prison, he decided, he would

turn over a totally new leaf. Perhaps this cruel and unde-
served incarceration was a judgement on his life so far. He
would clean up his act. No indulgence of his major vices on
the basis that everyone deserves a little fun. They would
always lead him into trouble. He would henceforth listen
to his conscience in its sternest voice; he would forsake
all earthly pleasures, and seek atonement for all those he
had wronged; he would live in ascetic simplicity. He would
investigate all major religious systems and find the one
exclusive worldview that was right for him. He thought
about Emily, and reflected that Joanna was right: Emily was
mad, and if he elected to stay with her, it was for the wrong
reasons, a relationship based on pity and remorse, not love.

Joanna was sullen, trying to figure out how she could make
amends, without of course giving herself up. If he went to
trial, and was convicted, could she live with herself? She
would rather it didn't happen, of course, but as for standing
up and taking the rap? She knew the answer. She was a
Hardstaff. But on the other hand, it didn't necessarily need
to come to that . . . some clever plan was surely not beyond
her capability to devise? After all, again, she was a Hardstaff.
She owed it to Tony, not only because he was innocent but
because, over all these years, he had been her icon, ever since
she had realised they shared the same rogue gene, the same
ability to see what their family stood for, and hate them for it.
Without his example, she might have taken the easy option
and given in to the lifestyle of wealth and double-dealing that
was on offer. She was determined to find a way . . .

*　　*　　*

Tony was in his cell listening to a phone-in on the radio when the door was opened and Dave, wearing the dark green uniform of the 'Duck's Arse' Security Company came in.

'Now then Tony.'

'Dave!' He automatically looked around conspiratorially even though he had been alone in the cell for twelve hours, and lowered his voice. 'Is this an escape?'

Dave looked around too, then replied in the same whisper:

'No, I work here.' He resumed his normal speaking voice. 'Anyhow, I've fetched you summat to read.'

'Thanks.'

'Bit of porn, couple of music mags, and a novel.'

'*The Man in the Iron Mask*. Thanks.'

'It's great. About this bloke who spends virtually his whole life in prison even though he's innocent. Oh. I never thought. Want me to try and change it?'

'No, it's fine.'

'Sorry.'

'No problem.'

'Oh, and you've got a visitor. Put your shoes on and I'll take you down.'

Joanna was wearing a leopard-print minidress and a pair of tiger-striped Doc Marten's. Just the sight of her, a vibrant patch of eccentricity amidst the sad institutional monotones of the visiting hall was a refreshing fillip for Tony.

He sat down opposite her at the desk and pressed his palm against the plexiglass screen.

'Hi babe!'

She smiled weakly. 'How are you?'

'Not bad. My solicitor's applying for bail this afternoon.'

'Do you think you'll get it?' There was no optimism in her voice.

'Why not? It's all completely farcical isn't it? I've got alibis, witnesses – there's no case.'

'Well normally that would all be pretty good I suppose.'

'Of course it would.'

'They're going to frame you, Uncle Tony.'

'Oh come on, not even our family are that bad.'

'I've heard them talking.'

'Why?'

'Spite, amusement. They might even believe you did it.'

'But you don't. Do you?'

'No. In fact . . . I know for certain you didn't do it.'

She looked at him. Waited.

'You mean . . .'

'Yes. It was too good an opportunity to miss. A nice nest egg. I was planning to leave in a couple of weeks, once the dust had settled. Look, I'm really sorry you got mixed up in this. But I'm going to get you out, OK?'

'You could confess. Say it was a practical joke that got out of control or something.'

She knew that if all else failed, she would let him take the rap. But it was not easy to look someone in the eye and tell them that.

'It's too big a risk. Anyway, that doesn't mean they'd let you go. They'd probably say you put me up to it and you'd get extra for corrupting an innocent schoolgirl.'

She sat back, pleased with herself. It was a brilliant and plausible objection thought up on the spot.

'You've got a point I suppose. Do you have a plan?'

'I'll think of something. I promise.'

'Do they know you've come to see me?'

'Of course! It's really pissed my mum off. Her nose doesn't bleed any more when I mention your name though, which is a shame. Hey, the other night, Grandad didn't mention anything about Ludolf Moor to you did he?'

'No. Why?'

'I dunno. But there's something. I just know it – every time it comes up in conversation in front of me they get dead shifty and change the subject. What a bunch of bastards, our family, eh?'

'Yeah.'

'I know this might sound a bit callous, but I'd love to see the lot of them dead and gone like my grandma. I really would. That's terrible isn't it? To feel like that about your own flesh and blood.'

'Well, it's not our fault.'

'It's not, is it? But what really pisses me off is I still feel guilty.'

'I know. By the way, this is going to sound a bit weird, but your grandma's not gone.'

'How do you mean? She looked pretty gone last night.'

'Yesterday morning . . .'

He told her of the apparitions, and of Quintillia's insistence that she held a vital commercial secret concerning the spaniel.

'Uncle Tony, how are you getting on with the other prisoners?'

'Fine. Why?'

'Are they giving you drugs?'

'I'm not making this up, Joanna.'

'Right. Look, I'd better go. Oh, I grabbed a couple of books for you. There's *The Count of Monte Cristo* and *Kiss of the Spiderwoman*.'

'Thanks.'

He could always plead insanity, thought Joanna as she walked to the car.

Obadiah was in a foul mood. Jeff was patiently and unsuccessfully trying to show his father-in-law how to operate the microwave oven, and Obadiah was getting more and more angry that something so simple that a moron like Jeff could master it was beyond him. He had also just received the results of Tony's blood test. Tony had been told by the prison doctor that a blood test was nowadays standard procedure, as was donating a pint of blood to the local hospital. This served two purposes. Firstly, the prison authorities could sell the blood and thus keep costs down, and by taking it on a regular basis they kept the prisoners in a constant state of low energy, which made internal discipline much easier to maintain. Obadiah had been furious when he found out that Tony's blood group and his own were incompatible for any prospective transplants. That afternoon, to make the revelation even more frustrating, he had received a letter from his doctor in Switzerland announcing that the brain swap operation should be feasible within eighteen months. Of course, he would be able to find another suitable donor without too much trouble, but he had had his heart set on taking possession of Tony's body, both because of the poetic justice he saw it would have provided, and also because, physically, they were very similar. Both men had always found this fact very upsetting and Obadiah had been temporarily delighted when it seemed there had been a reason for it.

'So Tony's AB and you're A? That's interesting'. Jeff was trying to make soothing conversation. 'I'm A myself actually.' He had unwittingly succeeded.

'Are you now,' said Obadiah, as innocently as he could, noting Jane was out of earshot. 'That's interesting.' His failure to work the microwave suddenly seemed a minor thing.

Jane and Joanna worked all afternoon on the funeral arrangements. Jane took several calls from the lawyers in private, returning every time in a better and better mood. Joanna didn't need to be told that the fabricated case against Tony was improving by the hour. But how could she get him out?

When she arrived at the police station the next day to see Tony, Joanna saw Emily was already there. The remand prisoners were in fact allowed up to six visitors at a time, partly in acknowledgement that they were still technically not convicts, and partly because the authorities had introduced an entrance fee. Joanna paused to get a can from the soft-drinks machine in the lounge, and then noticed Emily, or rather heard her, declaiming poetry. She darted out of sight, assuming that it would not be fair to interrupt the lovers, and also because she feared some violent reaction from Emily, who probably did not discriminate in her loathing of the Hardstaff family.

Emily was reassuring Tony that she would move heaven and earth to get him released.

'I'll get you out of here somehow, Tony my love, don't you worry. Anyway, let me read you another poem.

'One day you'll be free, you hunky chunk of rebellious Yorkshire granite, and we can live out our dreams together . . .'

Tony shrivelled with embarrassment as everyone in the visitors' wing turned and looked.

'Yeah all right Emily, keep it down . . .'

'. . . Running across the wild moorland, barefoot and free,
And opening the quality chip shop we've always wanted.
We will be as one, whether following the flight of the skylark
Or skinning rock salmon to the sound of Radio Burnley.
I love you Tony, and love conquers all.'

'Keep it down, will you?' hissed Tony.

'What do you mean?' Emily was oblivious to the unwanted attention.

'Emily, please . . .'

'Speak up, I can't hear you.'

'I said, keep it down. Your language, it's a bit flowery . . .'

'It's poetry.'

Tony grimaced.

'You didn't object when we were up on the moors together, Tony Hardstaff, with the wind wrapping my Arctic cagoule tight around my comely contours.'

'No, well . . . that was different. We were on our own.'

'You're embarrassed by my public expression of emotion?'

'No, no, I'm not, honest. Anyway, I ought to be getting back to my cell.'

The security guards, who could not help but hear all of Emily's side of the conversation, were looking uneasy, shifting from foot to foot and some even colouring at the public display of intimacy that they were being forced to endure. Suddenly Joanna saw a plan coming into shape.

'My darling, my love, my other cleft half of apple . . . do I shame you?'

'No, Emily, not at all, of course not. I've just got a bit of a headache. I suppose I've got to go back to my cell now,' he called to the passing security guard.

'No, you've still got ten minutes.'

Emily was hurt. 'Tony! Are you saying you'd rather be locked up alone than hear me read you love poems? Tony! Have you buried your feelings so deep?'

The security guard could take no more. He placed a firm hand on Emily's shoulder.

'Now then lass, get a grip on yourself. This is Yorkshire. We'll have none of that kind of talk in my police station. What you crying for? Oh come off it. It's not as if he's good-looking or owt.'

A few minutes later, a tearful Emily emerged into the car

park. Joanna was waiting.

'Emily . . .'

'Oh, a Hardstaff, come to gloat at the pain you've caused me and Tony, I presume,' she said, proudly, trying to quell her tears.

'No, I've got an idea, to get Tony released. Please, let me give you a lift home, and I'll explain.'

'And why should I trust a Hardstaff?'

'No reason, but I don't see what you have to lose.'

'I do. My pride.'

'Oh shut up you dizzy mare, and get in the motor. Just listen to me at least.'

Up at the big house, Quintillia was throwing a wobbly, and lots of furniture.

'For pity's sake,' cried Obadiah, dodging a low-flying table, 'will you please stop hurling the furniture around like some common poltergeist?

'What are you so angry for?'

'I saw you shaking your head while you were writing the cheques. I heard you say you could just fill the coffin with spuds. I heard you telling Jane to haggle with caterers and the suppliers!'

'But she talked me out of it. It really is absolutely no expense spared! Tell her, Jane!'

'Mum, it's going to be a wonderful ceremony. We've got helicopters spraying the whole town black as a mark of respect—'

'There's a whole host of celebrities coming, from Kenny Lynch to Melinda Messinger . . .'

'And here's a photo of the coffin . . .'

'. . . sponsored by Nirex . . .'

'The slogan on the side was my idea . . .' said Obadiah. '"Nobody buries better than Nirex."'

'There you are – can't accuse me of doing nothing for your big day now, can you?'

'All right Dad . . . now listen – here's the icing on the cake: Mum, you'll love this: I've just had confirmation – Princess Fergie is coming. Imagine that! A princess paying her respects at your grave.'

'So, Mum, are you happy?'

'Maybe.'

Obadiah was impatient. 'So can you see your way to revealing the secret of the spaniel, and its great commercial value?'

'After the ceremony. If I'm happy then, I will give a sign, and you will assemble the family in the office.'

'And what will the sign be?'

Quintillia's malicious grin grew wider. 'The sign will be . . . the sign, Obadiah, will be when the spaniel starts humping your leg.'

Obadiah bit his lip.

On the day of the funeral, Tony had mixed feelings. He couldn't help feeling a little guilty, as without doubt his return had been the cause of Quintillia's heart-attack. He also remained convinced that she might have induced it somehow purely in order to make him feel bad. Whatever the truth of it all, he couldn't deny that she had rejected him utterly and, to his great annoyance, he felt sad about it.

Then, Tony's cell door opened. Dave was standing there, in his security guard's uniform.

'Come on Tony, you've got compassionate leave.'

'I don't want compassionate leave. I don't want to go to my mother's funeral.'

'It's got nowt to do with your mother's funeral. Yon batty bird of thine has chained herself to the desk sergeant and she's been reciting love poetry all morning. We can't take it, so you've twelve hours leave to quieten her down. Come on.'

Dave led Tony to the desk, where the sergeant, festooned in large metal chains, was on his knees pleading with Emily.

'Please love, give it a rest . . .'

'I shall be heard!!!' she declaimed.

'This one is called "Shall I compare thee to a racing pigeon?"

'Shall I compare thee to a racing pigeon?
Like that fearless bird once you were blown off course,
But now you have returned to the safety
Of my loft . . .'

'Emily,' said Tony softly. 'They're letting me go for a few hours.'

'*Yyyes*!' She shook her fist in the sergeant's face. 'Never more will they scoff in this town when I speak of the power of poetry. Oh Tony . . .'

She embraced him, causing the desk sergeant to be jerked off his feet.

'P'raps you'd better unchain yourself from the desk sergeant first, love . . .'

The sergeant was still shaking and blushing as they filled in the requisite forms. 'You've got twelve hours to persuade her not to come in here doing that again, OK?'

'OK.'

'You'll be handcuffed to this security officer the whole while, so no monkey business, OK?'

'OK.'

They got outside. 'I expect you fancy a pint, Tony,' said Dave, and then turned to see the two lovers kissing desperately like a pair of drunken Christian Students. Dave took a deep breath. It was going to be a long day.

The pub was relatively quiet for lunchtime; the funeral procession had attracted large crowds. Everyone in Grimedale liked to see a dead Hardstaff. It was a long time since there'd been one. They all had to conceal their enjoyment however: security guards and policemen lined the route, looking grim and clearly expecting everyone else to do likewise. Early on they made an example of two men they caught singing 'Perfect Day': they were pulled over the crush-barrier, slung in the back of a van and later charged and fined on a charge of 'Being Inappropriately Jocular'.

The hearse was drawn by four black horses, people applauded as it went past – an equivocal gesture – the family followed on in limousines with dark glass windows; a dirigible balloon floated in the drizzle, bearing the company name. Flares of black smoke were set off around the church and after a sudden change in the direction of the wind, filled it, causing the service to be cut a little short. No one really minded; they hadn't been joining in with any conviction, and the bonus was, in Jane's opinion, that the local news cameras would have lots of dramatic shots of mourners coming out of the church with tears streaming down their faces.

The procession then made its way back to the House of the Spirit Levels for the wake, where minor celebrities rubbed shoulders with the great and the good of the county, lifting canapés and glasses from the trays of scurrying flunkeys, and then, as soon as was courteously possible, made their excuses, expressed their hollow condolences and went home.

Jeff's assessment of the day was positive, as usual. He did hope his enthusiasm would rub off on Jane. Life was so much easier when she wasn't boiling up with anger and vengeance over something or other.

'Well Jane love,' said Jeff, 'what a fantastic ceremony. Your mother's bound to be made up. I tell you, if Princess Diana was watching, I wouldn't mind betting she felt a twinge of jealousy.'

He had clearly hit the right chord. Jane almost melted.

'Oh Jeff, do you really mean that?'

'Of course I do love. It was a lovely ceremony. Especially when Fergie collapsed distraught across the coffin.'

'A shame she couldn't stay for the wake.'

'Well, she'd three supermarkets to open this afternoon and then she was off to Manchester for a recording of Celebrity Donors.'

'She works very hard that woman. I can't see why everyone knocks her.'

'You're right Jane; I mean, she cried so hard you'd virtually believe she knew Mrs Hardstaff personally. Did that cost extra by the way, the keening?'

'Yes, it did. I hope it was all worth it.'

'Oh, it was a lovely send-off. Your mother would have loved it.'

'I just hope the old bitch is happy enough to cough up the commercial secret.'

Dave and Tony's fourth pints had been downed for twenty minutes and Dave, still of course handcuffed to Tony, was unable to get to the bar for a refill as the two lovers were still wrapped around each other and attached at the mouth like two hideously mutated conger eels. Dave mopped his brow and tried once more to make his presence felt. He hit on something he was sure would get their attention. 'Right, time's up. Let's get back to the cells.'

Finally, Tony and Emily released their grip on each other.

'Dave, you can't . . . you can't send him back to that dank dark cell, and leave me to walk the moors, pining and forlorn, frail and unprotected, like an asphodel in a wind tunnel . . .'

'It's OK Emily,' said Dave.

'Look, Emily, I know you're upset . . . but you're going to have to be strong . . .'

'I'm not just upset. I'm swooning with grief, Tony.'

'Well do you want to get us a last round in while you're at it?'

'Of course. Wait! I feel another poem coming on.'

The two men smiled feebly.

'I bought my love a final pint,

And felt inside
Just like the foamy liquid in the glass—
Heady, ready for a man;
And bitter.'

'Terrific. Have you got money?'

Dave leant in confidentially now that Emily had finally moved to the bar.

'Now listen Tony pal, if I undo the handcuffs, they'll know I've helped you, and I'll lose my job. I mean, in a perfect world I'd be able to ply my professional trade and have me own shamanic drumming workshop. But life's not like that.'

'But there must be a way.'

'Hold your horses . . . There is a way. You don't think it was coincidence it's me you're handcuffed to do you? Joanna and I worked on her old boyfriend to get the shift rotas changed. It was Joanna's idea to get Emily to read the poems. Only we didn't tell Emily it was part of a plan – she'd have blown it. No offence Tony, she's sweet as a nut . . . well, she is a nut . . . well anyway, the point is, you can chop me hand off and slip the cuffs that way.'

Tony gaped.

'No, it's OK, really. There's this backstreet organ cloner in Heckmondwike. Only takes a couple of weeks to grow back.'

'But . . .'

'It's no bother – one time I had both hands took off, for a fancy dress party. Went as a Saudi Arabian shoplifter. Thought I was bound to win first prize, but some bugger came as John Wayne Bobbit. Any road, you whop it off, it'll look like you attacked me and I'll be all right. So, come on, let's get off to the Glue Boilers'. I keep a meat-cleaver behind the bar in there . . .'

At the House of the Spirit Levels, the final mourners had made their goodbyes, offered their condolences and tried their best to sound sincere, and disappeared. Only the immediate family and the caterers remained.

There was a scratching and whining at the front door. Jeff opened it and the spaniel rushed in and, with a joyful bark, clamped itself to Obadiah's leg.

Joanna caught a brief but urgent look from Jane to Obadiah who immediately regained his composure – as much as one can be composed with a spaniel clamped to one's leg.

'Er well, Joanna, Jeff, perhaps we should attend to those final documents. They're in the office. Follow me.'

'Right Dad. Er Joanna, perhaps you could do me a favour and . . . take these cases of wine over to our house would you? We've got some final documents to attend to and then we'll be back in a little while.'

'Sure Mum. Bye Grandad. I'm so sorry.'

'Thanks love. You've been a great help so your mother tells me.'

'Well, what else could I do?'

She ran to the jeep, hurrying the caterers to get the wine into the boot, shot off down the drive, pulled up into the opening of a farm track a hundred yards down the road and ran as fast as she could back across the grounds of the house, and sneaked up to the window of Obadiah's office. Fortunately there was a small gap in the curtains.

Her grandmother's ghost stood imperiously by the fireplace, a couple of feet off the ground for effect.

She was reviewing the funeral.

'I particularly liked the flowers, and the ode by Pam Ayres. I was a little disappointed that Fergie did a book-signing outside the church, but I'll let that go.

'I have decided you are worthy of learning the secret of Elvis the Spaniel. Jane, go to the Hoshaki AD2000 total music system please.'

Jane looked disconcerted, but did as instructed.

'And now, put on the *Karaoke Elvis Presley* CD.'

'Is this really the time—'

'Just do it.'

'Any particular track?'

'Just play it.'

As the first chopping guitar licks of 'Mystery Train' came over the speaker, the spaniel began beating its tail in rhythm, then suddenly sprang upon its hind legs, gyrating, somewhat shakily but impressively nonetheless, before bursting into the lyrics in a stunningly accurate impression of the King himself.

When the song faded out, the spaniel sat down calmly and wagged its tail. No one spoke for a moment.

'All right, so the dog can do an Elvis impression. Where's the big money in that?' said Obadiah.

'Not an impression – he's a reincarnation, aren't you Elvis.'

The dog hopped into an armchair and sprawled back in

it. 'That's right sir. Never made it to England during my career, always wanted to see it, so here I am. The name's Elvis Presley. Pleased to meet you.'

The family were silent. They all looked at the dog, at each other, at Quintillia, at the dog, at each other.

'You're Elvis Presley?' said Jane, a tad sceptically.

Mrs Womersley, who had appeared next to Quintillia in a flounced fifties bobby-soxer's dress (frankly an ill-advised fashion choice in her case) was incandescent. 'Isn't that voice, those gyrating hips proof enough in themselves?' She smiled coyly at the spaniel. 'I wore this dress first time I went to see *Jailhouse Rock*.' Then she turned back and scowled at Jane. 'How can you be so disrespectful to the King as to doubt his identity when you've just seen him do "Mystery Train" live for the first time in more than twenty years?'

Elvis himself, lying in front of the fire and munching on a deep-fried banana and peanut butter sandwich, was more conciliatory. 'It's OK honey, it's a fair point. Let me explain a little more,' he said, and explained how he had chosen to inhabit the spaniel's body. Mrs Womersley, always a huge Elvis fan, had been charged with looking after the dog from when it was a puppy. She fed it on a diet of burgers and deep-fried peanut butter sandwiches. One day, Elvis's spirit had been cruising the astral plane and, tempted by the attractive meal laid out before the dog, had entered the spaniel's body. After a while his visits became more and more frequent, and finally he had complimented her on her cooking, but asked if he might have more ketchup and mustard. He had been torn between his desire for anonymity and his craving for a little more mayo. Mrs Womersley had known for some time that the dog was capable of providing a conduit to the spirit world. Several of her departed acquaintances had spoken to her from time to time. They could give no explanation as to why this particular animal was such a good medium, and as Mrs Womersley put it, 'You don't need to know how a television works to turn it on.' Even so, knowing that the King himself was using the dog was something else. When Elvis had proposed taking up virtually permanent residence, Mrs Womersely was so excited she had taken a small sherry to celebrate.

Obadiah was outraged when he realised the two women had known about the dog's true identity for so long. Quintillia had justified her secrecy by needing to keep the revelation back for an opportune time when she needed leverage.

'Ma'am, could I trouble you for some more peanut butter please?'

'Yes of course.'

Suddenly he leapt off the couch and on to the floor, alert and inquisitive, running up to the French windows and pressing his nose against the glass. 'Did a squirrel just go up that tree? It did. It did. Let me out, I got to get at him. There! There! There he goes!'

Obadiah was impatient. 'Elvis! Sit! Sit down I mean. Please, carry on with your story.'

'OK. Excuse me.' He turned and trotted back to the sofa. 'There he is again!' He bounded back to the windows. 'Please, let me have a go at him. Just for five minutes. Please?'

'We'd better do as he says,' muttered Obadiah. Jane

opened the French windows and Elvis Presley, yapping and barking, chased a squirrel up a tree.

Obadiah was now recovering from the shock and assessing the situation through his usual frame, the balance sheet. He paced the room excitedly, went to the tantalus and poured a large cut-glass tumbler of whisky, gesticulated with uncontainable delight.

'By God, don't you see? When the Americans hear that Elvis Presley is reincarnated as a dog on the Yorkshire Moors, there'll be no stopping the flood of tourists . . . this must be the greatest licence to print money since the privatisation of the monarchy.'

Jane looked as if a huge weight had slid from her shoulders.

'Well now that's sorted, perhaps we should go and get some brochures printed.'

'Excuse me . . . don't the words "Thank You Quintillia" spring to mind?'

They muttered perfunctory gratitude and scuttled for the door. It wouldn't open. Mrs Womersley's huge frame materialised before it.

'Is that all you've got to say? To your own dead mother?'

'Er, yes – because I'm so upset. We'd better go – I'm sure you and Dad will want a private moment.'

Obadiah paled.

'No! Please . . .'

But he was now alone with his wife.

'You look nervous, Obadiah.'

'Nervous? Me? Pah! Can we assume that now you'll be

leaving us in peace – that now you'll be leaving us for ever, my dear?'

'Yes, Obadiah, you can.'

'In that case, well, Quintillia, I've never been good at goodbyes, but you and me, you and me, we . . . well . . . how can I put it . . . If ever I liked anyone – which I never have – but if I had, it would have been you . . . probably. Right, well; that'll do; I don't want to go completely over the top. Bye.'

And he smiled and left the room.

'You can assume that I'll be leaving you in peace, Obadiah. But it doesn't mean it's going to happen.' And she swirled up the chimney.

The amputation was swift. They walked into the snug at the Glue Boiler's, Dave tipped the nod to the barman who produced a meat-cleaver from under the counter, knocked back a double whisky and whacked down on the wrist that bore the handcuff. As instructed, Emily was ready to immediately spray some WD40 on the stump before applying the bandage. Dave knocked back another large whisky. 'Right, better not hang about.'

'Don't you want the hand back?'

'No, that tattoo was a mistake anyway. Paper Lace have been rubbish for ages. Keep it as a souvenir if you want.'

Tony dropped the severed hand into the ashtray.

'Is this hand dead?' the barmaid politely enquired, before sweeping it into her dustpan with the empty crisp packets and fag ends without batting an eye.

'Dave, I owe you one . . .'

'Come on, Dave's right – this is no time for male bonding:

we should make our escape – they'll be looking for you soon. We'll have to go into hiding, up on the moor . . .'

'She's right. Listen, I know a place. Here, let me draw you a map. Damn. Should have drawn the map before we got rid of the handcuffs.'

'OK Dave, I don't know how to thank you.'

'I do! Dave, first chance I get, I'll be round your house with a basketful of nutritious comestibles – milk puddings, broth, quince jam and herbal infusions to ward off the ague.'

'Great, yeah.' Dave could never work out if Emily was taking the piss.

Emily swooned and grabbed Dave by the arm.

'And not only that, I'm going to immortalise your self-sacrifice in an ode. An ode to friendship.'

'Well take your time – you know, make it a masterpiece.'

Joanna had brought the jeep back to the house, screeching to a halt with a handbrake turn which sent a hail of gravel rattling against the door which she then kicked open and stormed through.

'Whatever is the matter with you, young lady?' said Jeff.

'You can't build on the moor – it's an area of outstanding natural beauty.'

'Were you eavesdropping on us?'

'Never you mind. You can't build on the moor.'

'Just watch us lass. It'll be a new wonder of the world. The Obadiah Hardstaff Yorkshire Heritage Memorial Dome – Featuring Elvis Presley.'

'Well I'll just say this. You've got a fight on your hands.'

*   *   *

Tony and Emily were on the moor, Tony picking his way carefully in the gloom to avoid a twisted ankle.

Emily was quivering with joy and skipping up the hill ahead of him, finding her footing effortlessly.

'Eeh Tony, this is exciting isn't it – the two of us tramping across the moors together, in total darkness, heading towards the secret nuclear fallout shelter built by your friend Dave and his pals in the Morris Dancing Neo-Fascist Survivalist Militia at the foot of the ash grove they held to be sacred to the Norse God Odin . . . Just think, if it weren't for their collective paranoid delusions about the nature of international politics, we'd have nowhere at all to hide.'

She gasped for breath.

'Steep hill, eh?' said Tony.

'It's not the terrain Tony, it's the effort of getting all that exposition out in one sentence. I do feel bad though, leaving my dad in the house alone.'

'Emily, he'll be fine—'

'Are you sure.'

'Of course I'm sure. He's dead; he's embalmed; he's in a glass case.'

'But that glass case lights up at night, and there'll be no one there to switch it on.'

'Emily. I need you more than he does.'

'You're right. And I will look after you. Just think, you might be a fugitive for the rest of your life.'

'I don't really want to think about that.'

'A hunted man, living permanently underground, and me carrying food up to you every day. It'd be like having a pet hamster again. I could get you a little wheel to exercise on. Bigger than what a hamster would use, obviously. Would you like that?'

'Emily, please . . . we must be realistic.'

'You're right. I'd never get an eight-foot wrought-iron wheel up this hill.'

'Shall we sit down and have a rest?'

'Good idea. I could soothe you with some of my poetry.'

'On second thoughts, we ought to keep going.'

'Don't you want to hear my poetry?'

'Of course I do . . . The acoustics will be better in the shelter, that's all.' He smiled and stroked her cheek.

'You think of everything, don't you?'

'No. Actually, I only think of one thing, Emily. You.'

'Do you really love me, Tony?'

'Of course I do.'

'Why?'

'Because, well, I just do.'

'That's good. I was worried it was because you felt obliged to look after me because I'm unbalanced and batty and no one else would put up with me.'

'Emily, don't be daft.'

'But I *am* daft, don't you see?'

'Well, anyway, why do you love me?'

'That's easy—'

'Is it? Sometimes I look at myself and think no one could. No one in their right mind.'

'Well there you are then.'

They had reached the clump of ash trees, which lay in a

small hollow above the general tree line. 'Come on, Tony, I think I can see the entrance.'

Joanna was still trying to reason with Jane and Obadiah, but they were not prepared to listen.

'Right, that's it.'

'Where do you think you're going?'

'Away. And you can't stop me.'

'Jeff, grab her.'

Joanna dodged away from Jeff's lunging hands and, continuing her turn, delivered a fearsome spinning back-kick into his jaw.

He fell backwards, and moaned dismally, almost drowning out the delicate tic-tac-toc sound of the full lower set of his teeth scattering on the parquet floor.

Joanna ran down the marbled hallways like the wind, pausing for only a moment to pluck her father's front incisors from the instep of her thirty-six-eye handpainted Fun Lovin' Criminals Doctor Marten boots, burst out through the ecologically-unsound mahogany double doors of her grandfather's house, leaving behind her family and all it stood for. Helter-skelter across her grandfather's hallowed croquet lawn she hurtled, hacking indelible heel marks of anger and outrage as she ran, like a hound of hell, hurdled the ha-ha in a single bound, and did not stop until she stood astride the summit of the moor, where she turned towards the house and hurled out loud the single thought that flowed throughout her young and defiant frame:

'Vengeance!'

Emily and Tony found the underground shelter quite comfortable, if a little gothic in its décor. Posters of heavy metal bands and garish murals of Norse deities crowded the walls, interspersed with the odd centrefold calendar and runic device. There were two largish dormitories, each containing about twenty camp-beds, a kitchen and dining area with a couple of trestle tables and benches, and three or four old armchairs and a tattered sofa in one corner. There was a stereo system, and a huge collection of CDs. There must have been over two thousand. They were all heavy metal. Tony sprawled out on the sofa and clasped a mug of tea to his chest. Emily sat in one of the armchairs, also holding a cup of tea and smiling. He had never seen her look so happy. Nor, it occurred to him, had he seen such a calm look in her eyes. There was no trace of her usual derangement, and Tony wondered if perhaps this could be the start of a new phase in their relationship. Maybe the unbalanced side of her nature was all caused by stress; maybe it would work out after all.

'Are you all right, Emily?'

'Never better, Tony. I feel a huge weight has slipped from my shoulders.'

'Me too.'

'You're free!'

'I know. Maybe we can finally start a life together.'

'Yes. I've been really crazy the last few weeks. I've been under so much stress. But it's past now, and I'm sorry.'

'It's totally understandable. We'll have to try and get out of the country.'

'Yes. It won't be easy, but where there's a will . . .'

'Exactly.'

'The hardest thing is going to be getting my dad shipped out without setting anyone on our trail. I love you, Tony.'

Tony smiled his feeble smile, closed his eyes and sighed. He was going to have to bite the bullet at some point, and there was never going to be a good time.

He had dozed off, awakened by the piercing ringing of the doorbell, which was incredibly shrill and loud. Emily ran to the entrance, slid open the spy hole, and then unlocked the massive lead-lined door to admit Dave, who was carrying two rucksacks full of provisions.

He smiled and waved his bandaged stump in friendly greeting. 'How you doing?'

'I'm all right. You've not been to the organ cloner yet then?'

'Hadn't had time. Wanted to fetch you some ale and a couple of takeaways. Have you found the microwave?'

'I'm not convinced they're a safe way of cooking food Dave, without wanting to sound disrespectful. I think they're unhealthy. Could you not have found room for even a small deep fat frier?'

'Sorry Emily love, you'll have to make do.'

There was another piercing burst from the doorbell.

'Bloody hell, that's loud intit?' said Dave. 'We thought about having a soft two-tone chime affair, but consensus was it would be a bit wussy, given this is the hiding place of the fearless warriors of Odin. But now I've heard the alternative I'll resubmit it to the committee.'

It was Joanna, breathless and agitated. She accepted

everyone's congratulations at the brilliance of her plan for springing Tony, but waved them into silence.

'This is really important.' And she filled them in on the nefarious plan to build over the moor.

'They'll have a fight on their hands,' said Dave.

'Is there anywhere I can plug in this laptop?' said Joanna. Dave proudly showed her the phone points, and within minutes she was on the Net, sending messages to her comrade eco-warriors all over the country.

Dave had gone back into town. Fortuitously it was the night of the weekly meeting of the Morrismen, and he was back within two hours with the full membership, armed to the teeth and jangling rather incongruously.

Pouring another glass of tequila, I remarked that Tony's niece Joanna seemed a proud and fearless young woman.

'That she was, Señor García, until I broke her heart.'

'And how did this come about?'

'Through malign fate and the destiny of my blood. Nothing less! Despite what the priest tries to tell us of paradise and redemption there is nothing but malign fate and the void! Bring me more tequila please. I'm sorry, Señor García. It was just the terrible memory of it all. Let's talk about something else. Have you never married?'

'There once was a woman I loved, Tony, but it was long ago. I am married to my work. My calling is like the priesthood; it requires celibacy. I suppose Conchita and I are man and wife through the medium of the bar, and the customers are our children, whom we nourish and delight with our food and in whom we encourage controlled bouts of infantile behaviour and innocence through the oblivion of drunkenness. As for my physical needs, well, once every few months I travel to the city to take confession, and pleasure myself in the bordellos.'

'With whores?'

'Yes. I admire them for the way they . . . how shall I put it – draw my venom – every so often, and demand no emotional commitment in return. Magnificent creatures, the sisters of mercy.'

'And do you wish for nothing more?'

'To live within one's expectations brings peace of mind.'

Tony paused and pondered for a moment, watching the red phosphorescent tracks of a fire beetle spiralling around in the gloom.

'Don't take this the wrong way, Señor García, but you're more screwed up than I am, aren't you?'

'Perhaps I might be, if I paid it any mind. But there is too much to do.'

'Does that mean you want me to shut up?'

I assured him that, far from it, I found his tale fascinating, and that he must do as he saw fit. And besides, it was an excellent way of being diverted from my own concerns. By now his impromptu tellings of the story had become more frequent, and begun to keep quite large numbers of people in the bar until late. At first I must admit I objected to doing the bulk of the serving while the man who was officially my bar-man sat on a stool and did nothing but talk. But then I real-ised he had become an attraction and I reassessed the situa-tion. In fact I even cancelled the lavish bar-room adornment I had ordered to pull in the crowds when there was no football on TV. For what need had I now of the Quesada brothers and their life-size statue of Princess Diana carved in sugar crystal?

Messalina and Ramón looked in frequently to monitor Tony's progress, and I must give credit to Messalina, for she seemed genuinely pleased at the improvement in Tony's condition, even though his increasing energy, his new-found lust for life and delight in the company and attention all suggested that the priest, rather than she, would be the winner of their bet. Nor did Ramón gloat at all in his apparent victory. That said, no one would ever risk gloating at or mocking Messalina since Coronado the chicken merchant had ill-advisedly let slip one day how he had once tricked her over the price of a consignment. One day while delivering an order to the Asylum of St John the Hallucinogenic Over-Indulger he declared he was a hen, clucked proudly, did the Birdie Dance and pecked the ground for worms. He was only released when he started to lay perfect size A eggs on a regular basis. (He was sold at market and the proceeds went towards the Asylum Christmas Party.) Curiously, I realise that this unlikely incident leads us smoothly into the next episode of Tony's story.

The next morning, Obadiah, Jeff and Jane found Elvis in a businesslike mood over his burger and Winalot.

'OK, now before we go any further with this live concert idea, there's some serious negotiations to be done,' said Elvis. 'If you wouldn't mind stepping this way, I'd like to introduce you to my manager, Colonel Tom Parker.'

'Colonel Tom Parker? Here?' said Jeff. 'But he's dead too.'

'Let me show you.' He gambolled up the lawn.

They all followed, and after another brief diversion when Elvis spotted a rabbit, chased it into the hedgerow at the end of the lawn and spent ten minutes or so snuffling around in the bushes before finally accepting, reluctantly, that it had escaped, were led by the spaniel to the chicken coop. The Rhode Island Red cockerel was perched on the water trough, drumming its claws impatiently and surveying the visiting party with a supercilious eye.

'Come on Elvis, you know the rules, business before pleasure,' said the cockerel.

'Sorry Colonel. I really thought I was gonna catch that one.'

'Hmm. Now, if you folks want to let me out, we can go and talk turkey.'

Once they had reconvened in Obadiah's office, Jane, by way of ice-breaking chit-chat, addressed the issue of Colonel Parker's being a chicken and why he had chosen to be reincarnated in such a form.

'Weren't no choice involved at all,' said the Colonel, bitterly. 'It's some kind of karmic debt I owe on account of me having started out in showbusiness with chickens dancing on a hotplate. Damn that fat-assed Buddha.'

'Anyhow, sit down, Mr Hardstaff,' said the rooster. 'We need to do some negotiating.'

Obadiah was a little below his best at first. It was difficult to take your opponent seriously when he was a chicken. But pretty soon he got over it. The Colonel was tough, even if he did have feathers. Within a week, the principal clauses of the contract were all drafted. There just remained various subsidiary riders.

Elvis insisted on a pink Cadillac, customised for him to drive, and a kennel in the shape of Graceland to be built in the garden near the rabbit warrens.

It was difficult to concentrate through these meetings when every so often Colonel Parker would crap on the carpet, emit an ear-piercing cock-a-doodle-doo or hop up on to the top of a cupboard. One time they reconvened after lunch to find Elvis fervently humping a sofa cushion. He desisted almost immediately, apologising to Jane. 'Sorry honey, it's the beast in me.'

'He's still got it,' leered Mrs Womersley's disembodied voice.

Despite everything that had happened, Obadiah still remained unconvinced about the existence of the spirit world. He preferred to think of it as a mass hallucination, or perhaps something in the water supply. But as long as there was a clear opportunity for making money, he was happy to go along with anything. He also felt uneasy about the idea of immortality, apart from his own, as again, if the spirit world did exist, then it did undermine the purpose of material greed, so he preferred to ignore or disbelieve the elements that did not serve his own personal purpose. He and Quintillia would often have huge rows about her insistence that material things were pointless. 'That's because you've no need for them any more.'

Quintillia agreed, but always maintained she had transcended them. Obadiah refused to accept her argument. 'You'd love a chip butty if you had a gob you could stuff it in.' She pointed out she could always come back like Elvis had done if she wanted to, or spend all her time on the other side.

'Then why don't you bugger off completely?'

'Because I like annoying you.'

The Hardstaffs were too busy planning their great scheme to hunt too much for Joanna, who, now eighteen, was legally entitled to do what she wanted anyway.

The camp on Ludolf Moor grew by the day, spreading out organically from its hub at the fallout shelter in the sacred grove. All shades of environmental protester, from tweedy widows with labradors to hard-core crusties with didgeridoos and ex-army ambulances and mutts on strings appeared in dribs and drabs and huge jovial body-pierced columns.

Aerial runways and platforms were built in the trees, tents and bivouacs and benders sprang up amongst the rocks and brush, gun-hides were roofed with plastic sheets and bracken thatch. Guitars and ghetto blasters and a cosmopolitan orchestra of curious ethnic instruments from all over the Third World, home-made in Notting Hill and Plymouth and Ullapool and Galway, provided a constant soundtrack, giving a common if cacophonous voice to the heterogenous gathering.

The sheep, initially scared away to the highest slopes or even down into the outskirts of the town, gradually returned, began to graze closer and closer amongst the tents, perhaps feeling an affinity with the new humans, so many of whom seemed to have fleeces as tangled and hardy as their own. Both sheep and protesters were equally suspicious of the newspaper reporters and TV crews who periodically picked their way through the tribal encampment seeking out the most spectacular and eccentric-looking protesters for interviews and profile pieces. They would be sounded out at distance until their intentions and credentials could be ascertained, and they were either shooed away or granted initially cagey soundbites.

Joanna was one of the ones the media homed in on. Tall and striking looking, with her long green hair and body jewellery, she was exceptionally weird, and being exceptionally weird was just the kind of person the media people wanted to hold up as a typical-looking eco-protester. In front of a microphone or a camera she showed a natural talent. She was witty and articulate, fearlessly dismissing the more ludicrous or banal questions while expressing the environmental case concisely and convincingly. She was asked to appear on TV panel shows, offered a recording contract, a modelling contract, all of which she rejected charmingly, sarcastically, contemptuously. She was profiled in a dozen articles as the woman the media could not buy at any price. She inspired a 'look'. All over the country, hairdressers were running out of green dye.

Dave and his Morrismen wanted to march directly on the Hardstaff mansion and burn it to the ground when they heard that the ash grove was endangered by the plans. But Joanna was persuasive in her arguments that violence was counterproductive and should not be used while there was still a chance of finding another way. Once the motley and vibrant group of ecoprotesters had arrived, with

coloured hair, strange clothes, musical instruments and recreational drugs and demonstrated it was possible to have
an excellent party while they fought to save the planet,
the Morrismen were quite happy to let it take as long as
it took and enjoy the festive atmosphere forever, if need
be.

Emily was in her element, cooking on a frier that had
been donated by a fish and chip shop in Hull and carried
triumphantly the last four hundred yards from the nearest
point the van could reach by a dozen of Dave's musclebound
Morrismen comrades.

Differing shades of ecoradicalism exchanged ideas and
opinions round campfires in solemn academic debate, rag-
ing argument, patient proselytizing, over beers and cider
and mushrooms and Hackney home-grown and Dutch garage and Nepalese temple balls, in poems, songs, stand-up
comedy, wood-carving, face-painting, dancing, tantric sex.
Oracles were consulted from runes and tarot cards and the
I-Ching, birth charts were compiled, palms were read, spirits
and gods were communed with and evoked, from Christ and
Buddha and Manitou and Odin to Bilbo Baggins. People
practised Tai Chi and yoga, meditated, chanted, shared food
and drink and joints, sat in sweat lodges, had sex, built
latrines, practised locking themselves together in trees and
sealing themselves in dark tunnels, attended workshops
on how to react when arrested, how to stay sitting down
in front of a bulldozer without losing your bottle, how
to charm security guards and bailiffs, how to undermine
their resolve and persuade them to defect, how to freak
them out with unusual behaviour, such as handing them

flowers, hurling ancient Celtic curses at them, engaging in homosexual kissing, cross-dressing, challenging them to beer-drinking competitions and soccer matches.

Tony considered this the happiest period of his relationship with Emily. But he realised later this was largely because the common purpose that united them meant they spent very little time alone together. Private relationships were subsumed by the intense social activity. At the same time he was not completely free of that terrible feeling that his contentment and sense of belonging were only the prelude to something going horribly wrong. He knew he should be completely happy, but found himself wondering about all the other lives he could have led, the other paths he could have taken.

Of course there were hardly any security guards to threaten the security of the camp, as each and every one for a hundred miles around turned out be a member of Dave's Survivalist Morris Dancers, so were already on the side of the angels.

This had, to put it mildly, annoyed Jane and Obadiah. They were sitting at home, trying to make the best of things. There was lots of planning that could be done on paper, and although Elvis was willing to perform once the venue was built, he had added more demands. He wanted all the original Jordanaires reincarnated and on stage with him, plus tailor-made spaniel tasselled jump-suits, while Colonel Parker objected, feeling he should go back to his original rough-diamond image of Levi's and Blue Suede Shoes. Jane tried to argue that he didn't need to wear anything at all. She was even worried about the quiff, which everyone else saw as essential.

Jane was apoplectic at Joanna's media-stardom, and the articulate way she publicly shredded everything the family stood for. She blamed Tony, of course, for corrupting his niece, and in between fainting fits and nosebleeds, she took out her anger on Jeff, and plotted her vengeance. She kept telling herself it was just a matter of time, but she had to take a lot of tranquillisers.

CHAPTER TWENTY-THREE

Above the door of the Red Lion Hotel in Grimedale stands a blue plaque which reads as follows:

One day the great, gritty, taciturn and peerless Yorkshire and England batsman Geoffrey Boycott, en route from the hallowed turf of Headingley to his home in the heart of what was once the South Yorkshire Coalfield, felt the need to relieve himself, and indicated as much to his driver in a characteristically taciturn, gritty and indeed peerless manner. Thus it was that ten minutes later Geoff Boycott's chauffeur-driven Jaguar (custom-built to do 0–100 in two days) pulled up in front of the Red Lion Public House, and the gritty and taciturn Peerless One walked into the gentlemen's conveniences and dignified them simultaneously by his presence and excrescence.

'Or in other words,' the plaque concludes: 'Geoff Boycott Pissed Here.'

The pub is now a place of pilgrimage for true believers

as far away as Guisley and Brough, and every year, on the anniversary of the event, the town of Grimedale celebrates this proudest moment in its history with a whole carnival devoted to the Boycott Cult, and celebration of the traditional Yorkshire qualities of grittiness, taciturnity and peerlessness. But more of this later.

In the House of the Spirit Levels, Obadiah stood shaving, as he had done every day since his twelfth birthday, with a bowl of steaming water on a wrought iron stand and a cut-throat razor.

'Not a bad looking face staring back at you from that mirror, Obadiah Hardstaff . . . not a bad looking face at all, for a man of 183. I'm a testament to the virtue of naked avarice – living to this age just to win a bet . . . and a hand still steady enough to wield a cut-throat razor! By God! Was there ever such a man as me?! Immortal, that's what I am! Defying the laws of nature through the force of my own willpower! Immortal!'

The razor slipped and made a painful yet harmless incision in his neck.

'Stop talking bollocks, Obadiah,' said his wife, materialising behind him. 'That cut is two millimetres from your carotid artery – so stop getting ideas above your station. Immortal? Give it a rest. Next you'll be spouting all that rubbish about how you can make love all night and you're hung like a horse when you know as well as I do you're only as power-crazed as you are because you've got a penis the size of a thunderfly.'

'Hell's teeth woman! What do you mean by sneaking up on me like that?'

'Oh stop moaning. And tell me this. If you're so all-powerful how come Ludolf Moor is still covered in curlews and sheep dung without so much as a single slab of prefabricated concrete in sight.'

'We've had some problems.'

'Good business is about anticipating problems.'

'Anticipating? How could I anticipate Joanna – my own granddaughter – would tip off every damned environmental protester in the country about our plans? Not to mention our damned son Tony and his batty Emily Earnshaw up there stirring it too? And how could I possibly anticipate that every last building worker and security guard for a hundred miles around would be a member of a Morris Dancing survivalist Pagan cult, prepared to resist to the last our land development because it threatens an ash grove they believe is sacred to the Norse God Odin?'

'Always got an answer, hasn't he?'

'Always has, Mrs Womersley. Why haven't you cleared them off?'

'Well, our South African mercenaries have had problems getting through customs – apparently they didn't have the right work permits. But I've got them readmitted, posing as the Johannesburg Chapter of the William Wordsworth Appreciation Society – a coach party of seven hundred ostensibly en route for the Lake District.'

'Well you'd better get a move on. I've spent the last four days planting rumours with some of the most influential psychics in North America to the effect that Elvis Presley is reincarnated and living here in Grimedale. Word has reached the headquarters of the Church of Elvis, who have dispatched a delegation to investigate the veracity of the claim.'

'Excellent. You haven't told them he's reincarnated as a cocker spaniel?'

'No. I thought that might put them off. Anyway, the delegation will be here any day now. So you'd better spruce the place up a bit. And perhaps give the dog a bath. And stop whimpering – it's only a superficial cut.'

'He always was an attention seeker, Mrs H.'

'That he was, Mrs Womersley.'

'Attention seeker, Mrs Womersley? In fifty years here as housekeeper, you never so much as acknowledged my presence except when your mistress ordered you to.'

'Did somebody say something?' said Mrs Womersley.

'To hell with you, you old sorceress!!! Now, do you have anything else of use to convey, or are you hanging around just to vex me?'

'We have a word of warning.'

'What?'

'Well, perhaps when you finally do get round to building the leisure complex, you ought to think about including a shrine to the Virgin Mary.'

'The Virgin Mary?'

'Yes. She happened to catch me talking to the psychics last Monday – we always have a game of bingo Monday afternoon and I was running a bit late, and anyway, she got a bit vexed. She's not at all happy about all the attention that Elvis Presley has been getting over the years. Apparently she feels usurped.'

'Very jealous at Elvis having his own church.'

'The Mother of God feels threatened by a mere rock star? Preposterous.'

'Well quite. Personally, I think it's more to do with her being miffed that Elvis is spending much more time with Princess Diana than he is with her.'

'But I thought Elvis lived in our spaniel?'

'He can come and go as he pleases.'

'And who can blame him with Lady Di hanging on his every word,' said Mrs Womersley. 'She's looking lovely again now you know.'

'I don't suppose there's any chance of getting her to turn up for the opening night is there?' asked Obadiah.

'First things first, Obadiah. She's in a right paddy at the moment. Like I say, maybe you should rig up a shrine or sell some snow-scenes of her in the gift shop or something. Maybe even convert to Catholicism.'

'Me? Acknowledge the existence of a higher power?'

'You wouldn't want her fouling things up.'

'Do you realise how much this project is costing me already?'

'She spent all last night hurling thunderbolts at a video of *Jailhouse Rock*.'

'Begone, you foul demons – back to your celestial driers for a pink rinse and a surreptitious scan of the problem page in *Marie Claire* while you're waiting for your highlights to set. Now will you leave me alone to shave in peace?'

When Jeff was told by Jane about the imminent arrival of the South African mercenaries, he defied the laws of Nature by having an original and unselfish thought.

'What about Joanna?' he said simply.

Jane was brutally dismissive. 'She's made her bed, she can die in it. Lie in it I mean.'

But that night Jane could not sleep, lay in bed in a cold sweat, wracked with concern, a concern which, she could barely bring herself to acknowledge, was generated by maternal instinct. She was disgusted with herself, but next morning watched herself get up early, pull on her boots and walk across the moor. She had contacted Joanna on her mobile phone, and after a formal period of mutual abuse, had persuaded her to meet up on neutral territory. The place they had agreed on was a small gully where once the family had gone on picnics when Joanna was little, in happier days when Jane had still been able to see her daughter as an entertaining and completely dependent possession who provided delightful distraction from the pressures of work.

As arranged, Jane stood on the stepping stones in the middle of the stream on the gully floor and waited.

Joanna appeared from behind a rock some eighty feet above her.

'What do you want?'

'Joanna love . . .'

'Stay where you are. I can hear you.'

'But . . .'

'Come any closer and I split. Say what you have to say.'

'Look love, I'm very impressed with what you've done, in a way . . . you've shown marvellous organisational skills, even if it hasn't been for what I consider a good cause, but it takes a lot of gumption to do what . . .'

'Cut the crap. Have you come to negotiate?'

Jane's rage swelled up, neutralising the tranquillisers she had purposely taken to stop herself losing it.

'No I bloody well haven't come to negotiate. I've come to tell you it's about to get serious. You might have had a good time laughing at us and playing the bloody fool with your hippy layabout friends and thinking you're oh so clever going on telly with your green hair and your bloody Gaia theory! Well you won't feel so clever when eight hundred South African mercenaries turn up and start kicking seven kinds of shit out of you next week!'

'Oh really. That's interesting. Very interesting.'

'Joanna, please love, come home. I don't want you to get hurt.'

'Don't worry. I won't. Anything else you wanted to say?'

'Joanna, please . . .'

'See you.'

Jane was furious with herself. In a moment of weakness, she'd succumbed to maternal instinct and, in so doing, forewarned the enemy.

She got home to find Obadiah explaining yet another disaster to Quintillia.

'It's not my fault! What were the chances of a coach party of South African Mercenaries, posing as William Wordsworth aficionados, running into a coach party of WB Yeats fanatics at Scratchwood Services and getting deported for rioting? A bad streak like that can't last forever.'

Back at the camp, Tony and Emily were enjoying the view.

'Eeh Tony, makes you feel good to be alive up here

on the tops, amongst Nature in its purest form, doesn't it?'

'Yes love, it does.'

'What better way to live than out here, encamped on the moor, fighting to protect its elemental timeless beauty from the bulldozers of greed.'

'I tell you what Tony, Emily here will make you a wonderful wife.'

'She certainly will, Dave.'

'Dave, Tony, would you like to share the last saveloy? There's one left at the back of the warming shelf. It'll only be lukewarm like, but the batter's gone lovely and flaky.'

'Right, I won't be a minute.'

'She's a good 'un, that, you know, Tony. You don't find many women round here with a private fortune and their own portable catering-size deep-fat frier.'

'You're not wrong there, Dave.'

'What's up?'

'Well, I'm just thinking . . . we hold out here for a while, but it'll only be a matter of time before my dad sends in the heavy mob and clears us off to make way for the bulldozers.'

'Now then, we'll have none of that kind of talk round here. The worshippers of Odin will fight to the last man to preserve this sacred ash grove.'

'Do you think it has to come down to violence?'

'Not if your dad backs down.'

Joanna, returning from the meeting with her mother, had approached unseen over the brow of the hill behind them, and Tony later speculated she must have overheard their conversation, for she quietly took Dave by the arm and asked if she might speak to him privately. They shut themselves in the computer room and did not come out for twelve hours.

Emily was talking Tony through her latest sketch drawings for a state of the art fish shop when Dave and Joanna emerged, looking grave and concerned.

'Hello there!' said Emily brightly. 'Did you have a good hump?'

Dave and Joanna looked appalled.

'Don't worry, we couldn't hear you.'

'We've not been shagging,' said Dave, 'but since the subject's come up, Joanna, if you ever fancy it you've only to say the word.'

Joanna offered the insincerest smile outside a day-time TV studio.

'We've been working,' Dave continued. 'Events are coming to a head.'

'This is strictly confidential,' said Joanna. 'Uncle Tony, you speak Russian, don't you?'

'Yes.' (I have often reflected on the irony that Tony, who had a huge talent for languages, and could communicate articulately and entertainingly in many, was capable of truly expressing himself in none. But I digress.)

'We may need your help as an interpreter.'

Tony said what Joanna then told them made his hair curl. (Pepe was confused, and pointed out that he understood Tony's hair always to have been curly. There was then a long and irritating digression while we explained to Pepe that Tony was using a figure of speech; a digression that was only brought to an end when Conchita slapped Pepe round the head and told him to shut up.)

Swearing them to secrecy, Joanna explained about the imminent arrival of the mercenaries, and how she and Dave had decided they needed a deterrent. That they had trawled the Internet, investigating numerous website addresses advertised in the back of Dave's collection of military hardware magazines, and had contacted a bunch of Russian businessmen who were willing and able to supply the ecoprotesters with a Russian navy-surplus nuclear submarine complete with on-board missile.

'We can sail it up the Ouse as far as Goole and then if my mum and me grandad don't back down, we blow them to bits.'

Tony was unnerved by the enthusiasm this proposal met with from the others. 'Isn't that . . . a little drastic.'

'Sounds great to me,' said Dave.

Emily concurred. 'It's the only language your father understands. Fishcake, Dave? Look at the golden sheen on those breadcrumbs!'

'Lovely.'

'But . . . he'll call our bluff.'

'We won't be bluffing. As warriors of Odin we are ready at all times for Ragnarok.'

'What's Ragnarok?' asked Joanna.

'The prophesied final battle between good and evil when the world will be consumed by fire, leading to Twilight of t'Gods.'

'Cool.'

'So let me get this straight. You're prepared to launch a

thermonuclear attack on my dad's house if he sends in the mercenaries,' said Tony.

'That's the long and the short of it, Uncle Tony.'

'Even if we all get destroyed?'

'One out, all out. That's solidarity. We've got to make a big symbolic gesture that those of us who are determined to save the planet are no longer prepared to be pushed around and go no further than acts of civil disobedience,' replied Joanna.

'Hear hear,' said Dave.

'Even if it means exploding a nuclear missile?'

'The means justify the ends. Desperate measures for desperate times.'

'But Joanna . . .'

'Besides. There'll be room here in the fallout shelter for some of us. We send everyone else home the day before we press the button.'

'What about the people in the town?'

'We warn them as well.'

'It's insane.'

'We won't have to fire it. We just have to make my grandad believe we will.'

Tony tried again.

'Look, I know this is going to sound selfish, and I know that the sacred ash grove is very special to all you Morrismen, but, the thing is, Emily and I are in love, and frankly although I'd sooner see the moor stay the way it is, if it's a choice between the holiday centre being built and nuking the North of England, then I choose building the holiday centre.'

Emily threw her oven gloves to the floor, outraged.

'Nay Tony! Much as you may love me remember you are a Yorkshireman! There's scrapping to be done and grudges to be settled. Unless you knuckle down and stop acting like a Southerner, you'll not see the inside of my drawers again.'

'Well said Emily. Spoken like a true daughter of Yorkshire,' said Dave, looking at Tony in a way that suggested Tony had forgotten where he was born.

'So that's settled then.'

'Wait a minute,' said Tony. 'How much is this going to cost?'

'A million pounds. I've got five hundred thousand, as you know, Uncle Tony—'

'Five hundred grand?' Dave gaped.

'A windfall. So we only have to raise another half million, and we're laughing.'

'How long have we got?'

'We need to move as fast as we can. I suggested to the Russians they came on the day of the Geoff Boycott festival. Visitors will be less conspicuous. They'll have it off the coast near Hull. We give them the cash, zap down the M62, take possession, I tell my bankers in Switzerland to transfer the balance, we're home and dry. That gives us two weeks.'

Tony was relieved. It was an impossible task.

'Two weeks to raise half a million? We're going to need a lot of lottery tickets.'

'No we won't!' exclaimed Emily. 'There's exactly half a million pounds in cash in my house, concealed about my father's person. I hid it there to keep it from the evil clutches of Obadiah Hardstaff.' She gazed vacantly into the middle distance. 'How strange: I don't know how, but I had a hunch that it might come in useful some day.'

'Well then, we're sorted! Destiny is smiling upon us! Let's break out a few ales!' said Dave.

'So like I say, Tony, we'll need you as our interpreter. Just to make sure there's no monkey business . . .'

As Tony put it, a wave of fear ran though him, crashing against the breakwater of his soul and susurrating out along the beach of his anxiety: what if the Russian gangsters turned out to be those he had met while he lived in St Petersburg? A little backwash of trepidation demolished the sandcastle of his forlorn hope as it ran back into the ocean of his terror. But that surely would be a coincidence too far?

The day of the Boycott Festival arrived. By six in the morning, the town was transformed. The pubs were bedecked with bunting of every hue, their cellars stuffed to the gunnels with kegs of bitter; beer tankers were on emergency stand-by at every brewery within a two-hundred-mile radius, all pint glasses had been carefully locked away and replaced by plastic ones; the recruitment of temporary bar staff had cut unemployment in the county to zero. Burger vans and hot-dog stands lined the streets nose to tail. Huge vats of mushy peas bubbled away on every corner. Giant video screens played the master batsman's greatest innings over and over on a loop: the 1966 Gillette Cup Final, the hundredth hundred against the Australians at Headingley, the ninety-nine in the West Indies where he was run out coming back for the run that would have given him the ton in both innings. Cricket nets had been erected in the market place, and the massed ranks of Boycott impersonators were warming up in front of the stumps, already playing the first of the many thousands of niggardly forward defensive shots they would play that day before dusk fell. The turnstiles had been erected in the gents at the Red Lion, the rubber masks in the likeness of not only Boycott but the whole pantheon of great Yorkshire cricketers were being hawked by small children at a fiver a shot. The station car park was full of coaches and the first merrymakers were filing up the hill into town to take their place in the beer queues that already snaked round and round every pub in the town even though opening time was still four hours away.

Up at the camp, Dave had ascertained through the Net that the Russians would be in the Whippet and Woodbine at midday.

Joanna gave everyone their final orders.

'Uncle Tony and Emily are going to pick up the money, then Emily and I will go and give my grandad his last chance to back down; meantime, Tony will meet you and the Russians at the Whippet and Woodbine with the dough.'

Dave suggested that they should have protection, but Joanna dissuaded him.

'It's nothing personal, but I still couldn't bear to be seen in public with a bunch of Morris Dancers.'

'OK then,' said Dave meekly. 'I'll wear civvies.'

And so, unsuspecting of his approaching Nemesis, Tony, with Emily, Dave and Joanna, all three disguised behind Freddie Truman masks, make their way cautiously down from the moor and wend their way through Grimedale, over the drystone wall at the stile behind the Mechanically Recovered Meat Emporium, and down into the market place, where the stallholders and hucksters, mountebanks, strolling players and confidence tricksters are swelling the festive throng.

In former days Emily and Tony would have stopped at every stall, here to sample a hard-boiled cricket ball in liquorice, there to put a pound in the hand-cranked zoetrope machine to see ancient, time-damaged footage of the last time England won the Ashes, but not today. Today they march on, looking neither left nor right, eyes glued to the hard-trodden patina of compacted fast-food containers, sweet-wrappers and discarded flyers for pawn-shops and fortune-tellers that form the uppermost layer of the pavement. For they are on a mission that can brook no distraction: to recover half a million pounds from its hiding place in the mummified corpse of Emily's father.

Dave directed Tony's attention to a sight that brought back happy memories.

'Hey Tony! Look! The Smell Their Weight stand!'

Tony swayed on his barstool, repeated the phrase in a horri-fied whisper that chilled us all despite the heat. Conchita and Yankee John moved to steady him as he swayed again.

'By Christ, the bugger's off his face!' screeched Hamish from the rafters.

'Take another cigarillo *hombre*, it will steady your nerves,' advised the doctor solicitously. Pepe lit one and handed it to the now shivering Gringo.

'Here Tony, inhale deep. That's better. Now, please tell us, what is the Smell Their Weight stand?'

The crowd (for there were now usually upwards of thirty or forty people in the bar each time Tony was in the mood to speak) waited expectantly, watching Tony's face contort with pain.

'The Smell Their Weight stand? It was my nemesis.'

He looked at us melodramatically. 'More prosaically, it is this.' He paused, indulging his recent habit of milking every moment a little too much. 'You pay your money, get given an article of clothing worn by a famous Yorkshire cricketer in a famous match. You have to identify the cricketer, the match, and the weight of that cricketer at stumps on the second day. As a child, I was unbeatable at it! I used to win every year and Dave and I would go and get pissed in Cleethorpes for the Easter Weekend with the winnings. Happy days . . . Well, that's enough for tonight. I must go to bed.'

The gathering sighed a collective objection, but Tony had already finished his tequila and was on the way to his hut.

'The boy's developing a real sense of the theatrical.' said Yankee John to himself, and we began clearing up.

Next morning Tony was in a morose mood as he set up the bar.

We sat down for breakfast, Conchita, Tony and myself, but Tony pushed his plate away and lit a cigarette.

'We entered the kitchen of Emily's little cottage . . .'

Conchita put her fingers to her mouth and emitted a shrill whistle. Within minutes dozens of people were running to the bar, recognising the signal that Tony was embarking on the next episode. For all his apparent pain and the impression he gave of needing to let whatever terrible secret troubled his soul gush out unhindered as if he could not control when and where the spirit moved him, I could not help but notice that Tony waited patiently for everyone to settle down before he continued his story, from the point where he, Emily and Joanna entered the kitchen of Emily's house.

'Hello Dad, how are you?'

Joanna was a little unsettled. 'But Emily, he's embalmed . . . in a glass case,' she said gently.

'He can still hear me. Sorry to leave you on your own in the house, but it's no place for a man your age up on the moor – you'd catch your death. Any road, we'll be back together soon.'

She asked me to lift off the glass case and sit her father on the table. Next she opened a little lid in the wooden base and pulled out an attaché case. It was full of fifty-pound notes. She seized a fistful and waved it triumphantly.

'Excellent. When we sail that nuclear submarine up the Humber, it'll make your evil father think twice before he desecrates the moor with a holiday centre. And to think that I, Emily Earnshaw, daughter of his fiercest rival, should finance the means of his humiliation!' She laughed like a maniac.

'It's a lot of money. Yeah . . . I've been thinking . . . Perhaps we should put Grimedale behind us though – make a fresh start somewhere else. It's not as if we need to run a fish shop for the money.'

'You don't understand, Tony – it's not the money: there's something deep inside me which is only nourished by the smell of the fat, the fierce sizzling of a bucketload of freshly-sliced Maris Pipers slipping under the bubbling surface, the gentle swaying of a Saturday night drunk at the counter as his barely-functioning nervous system sacrifices balance to contemplation as he wonders if he can cope with a pickled egg on top of his one of each . . . the pale yellow formica surfaces, the plastic overall . . . I was born for it, Tony.'

'Emily, it's not that I don't care . . . it's just that, I'm not sure about this nuking idea. It seems a bit extreme to me.'

Joanna was appalled. 'Uncle Tony, don't soften now! You know better than anyone what we're up against. We have to fight fire with fire.'

She stared at Tony, disgusted and staggered at his suggestion of compromise.

'I'm sorry. I don't know what came over me.'

'They'll back down, Uncle Tony. But not if we start losing our bottle.'

'Of course, you're right.'

'You OK now?'

'Yeah.'

'OK. Now take the money out of the briefcase and put it in your bag. It's less conspicuous. We'll see you in the Whippet and Woodbine.'

And Emily and Joanna took the short cut across the moor to the Hardstaff Mansion to give Obadiah the final ultimatum. Tony meanwhile, headed for his rendezvous with Dave and the Russian nuclear weapons salesmen. And then it was that he looked up, distracted for a moment by the sound of a plummeting microwave, hurled from the Billy Bremner Memorial Clock Tower by a bunch of high-spirited ruddy-faced alcopop-crazed choirboys; then it was that Fate's fickle finger wrapped itself round Tony's goolies . . . for when he looked up . . . well, for the time being we leave him, looking up . . .

'Look, Joanna!' cried Emily. 'Look! coming across the moor in their green wellingtons – striding dark and satanic across Yorkshire's green and pleasant moorland like some hideous animation of Blake's great work. It's your mother and father . . .'

'Oh ace . . .'

Jane was getting fed up with looking after Elvis. 'Ever since that flamin' dog was revealed as the reincarnation of Elvis Presley, it hasn't stopped singing.'

Jeff was more enthusiastic. 'It gives you a chance to relearn the words. He's doing the *Blue Hawaii* soundtrack at the moment. I don't think I ever did know the third verse of "Hula Hula Baby".'

'It's driving me mad.'

'But love, have some respect! It's the King!'

'He's giving me a headache.'

'But it's Elvis! Elvis Presley lives in our house! Fetches sticks for us! Eats our gourmet dogfood. OK, the hip swivelling is perhaps not quite as impressive these days but it's pretty good considering he's a spaniel.'

'Who cares?'

'Have you no soul?'

'No I don't. The concept of the eternal soul is just a fiction designed by the feckless and the lazy to try and make hardworking people feel guilty for oppressing the rest of society.'

'How can you say that when you've met your mother's ghost?'

'I hope you're not going soft, Jeff.'

'Of course not, no. It's just that you can't help wondering . . . if the soul is immortal, then maybe . . .'

'Listen Jeff, if you're going to get all ethereal, if you want to live like a hermit in a cave on nuts and berries with a crystal pendant and no deodorant, fine – just see how long it is before you come crawling home for a jacuzzi and a microwaved TV dinner. That flaming dog is more trouble than he's worth. I hate the sight of him.'

'Well then why did you come with me when I said I'd take him for a walk on the moor? Was it in the hope of seeing Joanna?'

'No.'

'Hello Mum.'

'Joanna! Come here immediately!!'

'Get stuffed.'

'Now love, don't talk to your mother like that.'

'Well said, Joanna.'

'Shut it, Emily Earnshaw – you great . . . cuttlefish.'

'This is my family now. They care about me.'

'Oh really? You'll come running home soon enough when the next series of *Friends* starts. And you needn't think I'm going to tape *Eurotrash* every week for you either.'

'I spit on your mass-media electronic culture.'

'Just you wait! Those South African mercenaries will get here one day. And they don't muck about. They've been longing to get stuck into a bunch of white liberals ever since President Botha went soft and became a Communist.'

'You talk a good fight, Jane Hardstaff as was.'

'Yeah. In twenty-four hours, we'll have nuclear capability.'

'Yes. Our chance meeting has saved us a walk. Even now, Tony will be handing over the money to the Russian entrepreneur who will be furnishing us with a Soviet navy-surplus submarine.'

'Yeah, so you'd best go back and tell my grandad: respect the integrity of the wild moor, or see the sky turn to fire and Grimedale turn to ash.'

'I don't know, Joanna, this really is overstepping the bounds of acceptable teenage rebellion.'

'Just make sure he gets the message.'

'Joanna . . . Jeff, come on. Call the dog.'

'. . . sky turn to fire . . .'

'What are you doing?'

'I'm just writing the message down love. Seems quite important to get it right.'

'Oh don't be daft. Call the dog.'

'Elvis, come on.'

Meanwhile Tony still stands, looking up; he looks down and is transfixed . . . for he is somehow back at the Smell Their Weight stall! Nostalgia and adrenalin sweep through him as he recalls those heady carefree days of childhood . . . he must play the game just once more, to feel some trace of innocence within him, beneath the betrayals and venalities that have plagued his adult life . . . not to mention the chance of doubling his money . . .

'Five hundred thousand pounds.'

If the stallholder was excited, he didn't show it. 'Right. Pick a garment.'

Trembling, Tony hands over the contents of his *Return of the Jedi* Rerelease Memorial Holdall, reaches into the air-sealed tub, and grasps a size six sock . . . inhales the aroma of grass stain, embrocation and sweat.

'Wilf Rhodes . . . versus Australia at Lords, 1924 . . . Eight stone . . . seven.'

'Eight stone nine. Better luck next time.'

Tony stands, shattered.

At the same time, Obadiah had answered the door and received the delegation from the Church of Elvis. Three sullen skinny men with quiffs and bad tattoos wearing Levi's who looked like Nicholas Cage at various different ages and who could have been father, son, uncle, brother or cousins to each other (or indeed, Obadiah surmised, all of the above) and a comely though wan blonde woman in a stetson and white jumpsuit bedecked with rhinestones, reminiscent of the one worn by the King in the Comeback Concert of 1968. He had led them into the parlour, offered them bourbon and coke, and watched their faces as they tried to come to terms with the fact that they had just heard and seen a cocker spaniel claiming to be Elvis Presley sing 'In the Ghetto'.

The woman, who had introduced herself as Sarah Mae, was listening to the spaniel explain the circumstances of his reincarnation while Colonel Parker, roosting on a hat stand that had once graced Matt Munro's vestibule, chipped in with the odd pertinent comment and involuntary ear-piercing cock-a-doodle doo.

'Well,' said Sarah Mae, 'it's kind of weird, but brother Zeke has the finest ears in the business, and if he says that was the King singing, then you're the King. There's no denying these tears running down my cheeks, and it's only the King's voice can do that to me with "In the Ghetto".'

She then looked over to the flickering computer, suddenly noticing the screensaver.

'I know this man!'

'You know him? He's my son.'

'Your son! Well no offence sir, but he is a no good son of a bitch. Figuratively speaking.'

'I agree with you there, love. We hate him round here. That's why his face is slowly dissolving in acid on the screensaver.'

Jane, who had been sitting quietly in the corner, sat up on the edge of her chair.

'You know Tony?'

'I was married to the no good rat. He ran out on me in Vegas and left me and my sisters with no means of makin' a living ... wait a minute! Do you know where I can find him?'

'I can do better than that,' said Jane gleefully, 'I can take you right to him.'

'All right! Let's go!'

'Well Sarah Mae, I never thought I'd say this about someone with such bad judgement that they'd marry my brother, but I think you and I are going to get on very well. Come on. Dad, I'll see you later.'

'Come on boys . . .'

'But Sarah Mae, we have found the Lord . . .'

'Religion can wait. There's going to be a lynching.' They rushed from the room, and Obadiah turned to Quintillia, who had immediately materialised in the corner.

'I'd love to be around to watch that.'

'Well love, sit down and put your feet up. I can beam it all into the telly.'

Natasha and Kropotkin sat in the snug of the Whippet and Woodbine, waiting for the rendezvous. Natasha was not happy.

'I find it intolerable that I, Nastassia Fillipovna Karamazov, am forced to travel to a dingy English ghost town and to sit waiting in a dingy bar where the dingy customers are so broken on the wheel of life they do not so much as even turn their heads when I, Nastassia Fillipovna Karamazov, the most beautiful woman in the world and the pride of all the Russias, strut in volupt uously and adorn their cheap reproduction furniture with my goddess-like yet all-too human frame.'

'They probably cannot believe that you are real, so stunning is your beauty. I sometimes doubt it myself.'

'You do? Oh Peter, you say the nicest things.'

'I only tell the truth, my darling. Now, would you like

another drink, my angel from another sphere of being, my delicate seraph from a higher plane?'

'A pint of mild, with a little paper umbrella and a pickled onion.'

As Kropotkin moved to the bar, Dave, who had been watching all new arrivals from a quiet corner, slid up and stood alongside him.

'We don't get that many Russians at the Geoff Boycott festival,' he said in a stilted delivery.

'Oh yes,' said Kropotkin in the same wooden style. 'His fame has spread even to the shores of Muscovy.'

Dave held out a massive hand.

'I'm Dave Riley, Mr Kropotkin. You may check my tattoos.'

'Let's see – *Paradise Lost* round one bicep, *Paradise Regained* round the other. OK. I am satisfied. Let us sit down and . . .'

Tony was still standing in a daze, deciding the best way he could run, when Emily and Joanna found him wandering in the street. Assuming he needed a pint of bitter, they took him by the arm and led him to the Whippet and Woodbine. There was no escape. Even before he walked through the door, he somehow knew now his worst fears would be confirmed. Sure enough, there sat Natasha and Kropotkin in conversation with Dave.

'You!!!!!!!!!!!' cried Natasha.

Tony tried to adopt a casual tone.

'Hello Natasha. Fancy seeing you here.'

'You dare to speak to me? You, the only man I have

ever truly loved, who deserted me when I risked my life for you?'

'Loved? Deserted? I don't understand,' whimpered Emily.

Kropotkin looked up and took a deep breath.

'So . . . Mr Hardstaff. Well well well . . . Fate brings us together again. And as I recall, we have unfinished business. A small matter of you seducing my beloved Natasha in a Petersburg hotel.'

'I can explain.'

'Tony, tell me this isn't true . . .' Emily's eyes glistened with panic and the pain of betrayal. She swooned a well-practised classical mid-Victorian lady's swoon and gracefully slumped to the floor, to the delight of Jane, who at that very moment had forced her way into the crowded boozer with the Americans and let out a delighted cackle.

'Oh, dear! Somebody pick Miss Batty Drawers out of the sawdust and give her some smelling salts. Hello Tony. Drinks all round please, landlord. A celebration is in order.'

Dave briefly assumed this meant the Hardstaffs had surrendered.

'So you've come to your senses, have you?'

'You're not going to build on the moor?'

'Oh we'll be building on the moor all right, Joanna. No, the celebration is that an old friend of Tony's has turned up from America.'

It was not a surprise to Tony to see his estranged wife. Everything was going so wrong it was the only logical next step.

'You owe me six rattlesnakes, punk.'

Emily, coming round, gazed up at the rhinestones and the stetson and cowboy boots. 'You're not from round here are you?'

'No. I am Sarah Mae Hardstaff, of the Holy Church of Elvis. And Tony Hardstaff is my legal husband.'

Emily climbed to her feet. 'Tony. Tell me this isn't happening. Dave, hand me that steak knife.'

'Get me one too,' hissed Natasha.

Jane was so happy she let the barman keep the change. 'I'm going to enjoy this. My brother about to be torn apart by three angry women! That's where your smooth-talking charm and your exciting, interesting life have got you, Tony Hardstaff, poncing off round the world while I was here in the rainy North building a business. Ha ha ha!'

At this moment, with the women closing upon Tony, the stallholder from the Smell Their Weight stall staggered across to them, stinking of whisky, and interrupted.

'Now now, there looks to be a lot of animosity at this section of the bar, and I'll have none of it. This is a very happy day. Everyone will have a drink to help celebrate my retirement. About twenty minutes ago, this fine gentleman here,' he put his arm round Tony's shoulder, 'came to my stall and lost half a million quid in one throw.'

Everyone stared at Tony once more.

'You spent our deposit on the Smell Their Weight stall?' said Dave, very slowly, standing up and moving towards Tony.

'Stop! None of you will touch one hair of my brother's head . . .' cried Jane . . . 'until I've got the camcorder out of me handbag. OK. Carry on.'

'Wait!' Tony was pleading. 'Please, just give me a chance to put my side of the story. Please . . . I'm sorry, I really am. Losing the money, I don't know what to say. I've never lost at the Smell Their Weight before in my life, and I just wanted to swell our coffers, make it a nice surprise for you all . . . as for hurting these three women here . . . what can I say? . . . You're all very dear to me . . . I . . . just want one last chance to make it up to everyone . . . look, how about if I get a round in and we sort it out in a civilised way over a pint? I can change, honest I can. I just want—'

'One last chance,' the massed ranks of those he had betrayed chorused sarcastically, and closed in an extra pace towards him.

Jane was smiling smugly. 'Not going very well, is it, Tony?'

'Let's kill him and get it over with.'

With his many would-be murderers vying for the coup de grace, it seemed as if only divine intervention could save him from his fate. And at that moment, there was a burst of bright blue light across the optics, a fizzing explosion and a squeal as the barman ran to plunge his smouldering toupee into the ice-bucket. The blue light coalesced, thickened and turned into the figure of a glowing woman, hovering above the bar.

'So, finally I track them down, the Elders of the Church of Elvis. You blasphemous heretics! Idolators! You dare to challenge my supremacy with your bloated white trash minstrel? Cop this!!!'

And from the hands of the mysterious stranger shot a

salvo of thunderbolts, smashing all the glass behind the bar
– optics, mirrors, clocks, the Waterford crystal figurines of the
Nolan Sisters, bringing down the lights, igniting the sawdust
on the floor, throwing tables, pints, ashtrays, half-eaten bags
of pork scratchings and uninhibited loving couples high into
the air, upending the spittoon which had stood unemptied
for three-hundred years, shattering the fruit machines, and
even catching the attention of the rest of the customers when
one went through the television and put paid to live coverage
of the Two Thirty from Haydock.

In the confusion, Tony seized his chance, and ran. Somehow, he ended up out on the street, where the Geoff Boycott Festival was now in full swing. Imagine the scene –
thousands upon thousands of simple Yorkshire folk, dressed
in cricket whites and Geoffrey Boycott masks, others in
panamas and blazers, kneeling over patches of dog-fouled,
thin-worn grass, digging keys into the soil and declaring to
an imaginary camera: 'This is the worst test match wicket
I've ever seen in me life.' Nonconformists in Freddie Truman
masks, with eyebrows made of cotton wool blackened in
boot polish, phalanxes of them, chanting 'Bloody Boycott
– only ever bloody played for himself' with the rhythm
and menace of a Zulu *impi*. Stand-up comedians telling
the joke about Boycott, the Pope and the Archbishop of
Canterbury out fishing in the boat together, the crowd joyously joining in on the punchline – 'What stepping stones?'
Coachloads of troublemakers from Burnley and Rochdale
chanting 'Lancysheer, la la la!' and pelting the natives with
red roses. The natives responding by pelting the intruders
with clenched fists: finally the day's festivities were fully

underway. This was the scene that met Tony's pursuers when they finally emerged from the debris of the Whippet and Woodbine. And Tony had vanished into the crowd.

Father Ramón was beside himself with excitement.

'You mean to say the Holy Virgin intervened to save your life! Surely this means for certain that you are destined to repay your weakness and treachery in some way before your time is come, my son. There must be a plan within this bizarre and unlikely tale. Did you get a chance to speak with her? I mean, what's she really like?'

Tony shrugged his shoulders.

'I was too busy running for my life. Anyway, I made it to the other side of town, hoping to hitch a lift. I had no idea what my next step should be, only that I needed to get as much distance between me and Grimedale as quickly as I could.'

'And this would be because so many people wished to kill you?' said Pepe hesitantly.

'That's right.'

I always admired Tony's patience with Pepe.

'I'm following everything quite well now, don't you think?' said Pepe.

We nodded encouragingly.

'Incredibly, a car stopped almost right away.'

'You'd best get in, Tony lad.'

'Dad?'

'Aye. Don't sound so surprised.'

'My life is in danger. Dad . . .'

'Aye I know. Your mother was beaming the whole Woodbine and Whippet episode across to our television. I might add she's none too impressed that I've resolved to help you.'

'You . . . help me?'

'Beggars can't be choosers. Now where do you want to go?'

And so it was that Tony was magicked out of town and to the airport by the one person no one suspected would ever help him – his own father.

'I don't know what to say, Dad. I never thought you were capable of something like this.'

'Like what?'

'Well, I'm your son, and you're saving my life . . .'

'Hmm.'

They drove on in silence. When they reached the terminal, Obadiah handed Tony an envelope full of cash.

'Right lad, *bon voyage*.'

'I don't know how to thank you, Dad.'

'Don't thank me, son.'

'But, saving my life – putting yourself out on a limb when everyone else in town is after my blood.'

'It was nothing.'

'No, seriously. I've always thought you were completely amoral and selfish and ruthless . . .'

'Now's not the time for compliments. What are you planning to do?'

'I don't know. Get on the first plane, wherever it's going, and make a fresh start somewhere. Wipe the slate clean and start again.'

'Fat chance.'

'What do you mean?'

'You're a Hardstaff – genetically programmed for self-seeking and treachery. You've no more chance of reforming than Pete Stringfellow has of presenting *Songs of Praise*.'

'Actually, there's an idea in that,' said Yankee John, and made a note.

'Well, I'll be sorry to see you go, son.'

'Thank you Dad, that means a lot.'

'It won't be the same having only your sister Jane around again.'

'Well, I'll keep in touch.'

'You see, the only reason your mother and I had two kids was so we could play one off against the other.'

'Eh?'

'There's nowt like treating two kids unevenly, treating one then suddenly changing your favour for no reason. They don't know whether they're coming or going.'

'Right. It certainly hurt me a lot.'

'Aye.'

'But I see now you were only doing it to make us see how cruel and random life can be. To make us more prepared for the real world.'

'Well, maybe in part. But basically I just like upsetting people. You know how when you're depressed, people tell you to count your blessings, to think of all the people who are worse off than you?'

'Yeah.'

'Well then, it stands to reason that the more people who are worse off than you, the happier you are. I've made sure I can make as many people as I can worse off than me, so therefore I'm dead happy.'

'That is sick.'

'You see, if they'd have caught up with you and killed you, that would have been it. All your suffering over in seconds. Whereas, by saving your skin, I guarantee you years of pain and self-loathing, dwelling on all your treachery. I haven't done this for you, I've done it for me. Don't you see? I win. I finally got you to trust me . . .'

'I see. Well, I'll be off then.'

But his father was in full flow.

'. . . Yes, better to let you waste away in self-loathing than have it blotted out at a stroke. You see, I know you haven't the capacity to end it yourself, because there's just enough of a gleam of hope within you to keep believing that one day you really can turn over a new leaf . . . and I know you'll always fail. Have a nice flight. Oh, and by the way, I would have had you killed by now if we'd shared a blood group. I've been looking for a host body for my brain transplant. But you hadn't even the grace to be that much use to me. Anyway, don't forget to write.'

As Obadiah watched Tony walk away, Quintillia materialised beside her husband and put her arms around his waist.

'Obadiah, I'm sorry I doubted you earlier on. That was magnificent.'

Whenever he related this episode, Tony would always say

how, if there was any justice in the world, he would have been able to conclude the scene with a pithy phrase or action that left his father coming off second-best. But he could not, and instead, turned, and walked away, devastated; then, recalling Sophocles' account of the meeting between Oedipus and Laius, he turned back, and kicked his father right in the knackers.

'Such, Señor García, are the benefits of a classical education.'

And so, when Tony boarded the first plane out of the country, a broken, guilt-ridden shell of a human being . . . he had betrayed all that he held dear; he had failed in his ambition to defy the treachery encoded in his genes. He had nothing to look forward to but self-loathing, contemplation, and death. But, as ever, there is a silver lining: once he'd settled down to life in Mondongo, boy, was he in a mood to drink!

PART THREE

Mondongo once more

CHAPTER TWENTY-FOUR

Over the months, as Tony unloaded chunk after chunk of his story upon us, his mental condition seemed to improve. His reputation spread down the river and across the towns and villages of the forest, and the bar would fill up earlier and earlier each day with people hopeful of catching him in the mood to convey the next instalment. I must say, I was not the only one who became more and more sceptical about how much of his tale one could believe. He appeared to relish the attention of the crowds, who hung on his every word, and I do not doubt he embellished and embroidered the bare facts with outrageous invention in order to satisfy his ever-growing appetite for adulation. Where once he would sit at the bar, staring forlornly into his glass, head in hands, forcing his narrative out with regret and shame, like a particularly embarrassing confession, now he had begun to declaim more and more confidently, making eye-contact, mastering the dramatic pause, acting out scenes, playing the different characters, doing the various accents, basking in the applause and the free drinks and the adulation. His performances had even pushed football matches into second place as a crowd puller.

He owed a great debt initially to Conchita and Yankee John, who between them would translate into Spanish, working in shifts, and often asking him to repeat the more outrageous claims of his story so they could be sure his words had been correctly understood. But in an amazingly short time he had learnt enough Spanish to dispense with them almost completely. I think his growing delight in the limelight and reluctance to share it with anyone acted as a spur in his study of the language.

Yankee John became more and more involved with Tony's performances from the sidelines, giving him advice, talking about stagecraft and image and 'hitting the moments'. A change came over him, which was perhaps even greater than Tony's. He bought a mobile phone. He talked of Tony's career prospects, spoke of future projects, of networking. At Yankee John's urging, we made certain investments. We installed a low stage and rigged a couple of small spotlights. On the verandah of his little hut, where once Che Guevara had made entries in his diary and begun to develop his vision of liberating Latin America from despotic capitalism, Tony wrote and rewrote drafts of what had once been the casual and spontaneous outpourings of his soul and honed them into slick routines under Yankee John's relentless scrutiny.

Working from pencil sketches supplied by Tony, Pepe the postman, who is a moderately talented painter, painted on an old canvas sheet an expressionistic map of Grimedale and Ludolf Moor, which was suspended from a rafter and hung as a backdrop during performances. When not in use it was rolled up into the roof and tied up tight with a brightly patterned woven band which had been presented to Tony one evening by the local Indians, and whose design symbolised their god Torqnbllx, the deity responsible for Staving Off the Boredom of Earthly Existence with Inherently Pointless but Engaging Distractions. In the evenings, the unfurling of the backdrop prompted a collective cheer from the bar which then subsided into a low, expectant murmur. Tony would take the stage and tie the sacred band around his neck; the crowd would cheer and applaud; Tony would raise his hands out wide to secure absolute silence and then begin the next instalment. Often, he would first recap the story so far, and add whole chunks of new material, claiming he had only just remembered it. We suspected it was more likely that he was giving more rein to his imagination than his memory.

Father Ramón was pleased to see Tony recovering his appetite for life, even if a little concerned to see how much this was driven by vanity.

'But let us look on the bright side, Señor García; vanity is merely a venal sin, whereas when he first arrived here he was in danger of committing the mortal one of suicide.'

'Nevertheless, Father, it is still a sin,' I said, watching Tony over at the corner table basking in the flirtatious attentions of three young mulatta students who had hitchhiked all the way from Venezuela to see him.

'So is envy, Señor García,' said Conchita, pinching my bottom. And giving me a sly wink.

We assumed Messalina would be less happy with Tony's condition. She was in danger of losing the bet to her husband, after all. But astonishingly, she appeared quite unworried, and was generally one of the first to gather round Tony at the end of his 'sets' (as Tony was by now describing them), hanging on his every word as he dissected the nuances of his performance in minute and (to the disinterested observer) quite unnecessary detail.

Messalina had been making him presents of *ayahuasca*, the sacred drug of the Indian shamans, which enable them to assume the forms of different animals and to commune with departed spirits. Yankee John defended her arguable abuse of a religious sacrament, claiming it was merely to enhance his storytelling by giving him access to channels which could give his mundane confessional stories 'a more cosmic dimension'.

Ramón gently accused her of infringing their agreement that neither one would interfere in any way with Tony's progress, but she insisted she was only administering it to Tony in recreational amounts, whatever that means. And she added that the better he told his story, the more likely it was Tony would purge himself through his confessions, and that Ramón would be the winner of the bet.

Ramón became irritated. 'Yes, but if he wins the bet with the aid of pagan sacraments, it's hardly a watertight endorsement of the Christian worldview, is it?'

'Oh, I hadn't thought of that,' replied Messalina innocently. 'Still, if you're really more interested in the integrity of the creed than the well-being of the person, of course I'll stop.'

Ramón was lost for a reply as Messalina got up from her barstool and crossed the square with her casual and easy gait.

'Insidiously cunning, your wife, Father,' observed Doctor Herradura.

Tony and Yankee John made a trip to Miami to buy clothes. Yankee John was insistent that Tony needed a 'sharper stage image'. Then one morning, shortly after he had had his goatee beard woven with coloured beads by his adoring *indios* handmaidens, Tony sat down at our usual breakfast table, took off his Tommy Hilfiger ski-shades and said:

'Señor García, we need to talk. I think it's time I was paid a fee.'

He argued that his stage appearances were bringing in huge numbers of punters, and that he was entitled to 'a piece of the action'. I immediately realised who had put him up to this, and my suspicions were confirmed.

'I don't think it's unreasonable Señor García, but if you have a problem with that, then I have to tell you that Yankee John has been talking to the landlord at El Gato y Violón [the cantina in the next village] and they've made us a very good offer.'

I had no choice, although I felt hard done by. It's not that I resented Tony's happiness, or his success, his new-found celebrity status, or his right to be rewarded for his endeavours, it's just that . . . well I don't know exactly but there was nothing selfish about my resentment, that's all.

I have to confess that Tony had not entirely lost all objectivity to his renewed self-belief. He still had the strength to acknowledge his mistakes, although only reluctantly. For example, his decision to hire a mariachi band and break up the performance with a selection of 'show tunes and torch songs with a Latin flavour' was not succesful. However, it was only a combination of the audience's politely muted but palpable disappointment and Yankee John's forthright trashing of his abilities as a singer that forced him to drop the music from the act. Some nights his performances could be terrible all on their own. When over-confident on *ayahuasca* he would lapse into meandering infinitesimal dissections of the meaning behind his experiences, reminiscent of Lenny Bruce's later tragic performances where he was obsessed with the minutiae of his legal battles. Indeed, one night a furious debate broke out amongst the Indians about whether Tony might be after all an incarnation not of Torqnbllx, but of Zzz, God of Sleep. One advantage of Tony's bad nights was that the miasmic atmosphere he created was so powerful it worked its way into the very fabric of the building and became an excellent if eccentric method of pest control: even the cockroaches would run outside on such evenings, and lie on their backs like drunken acrobats in a decrepit one-ring circus, begging the iguanas to put them out of their misery. But at his best, the telling of his suffering and misfortunes gave great entertainment and welcome respite from the daily toil and tribulations of my customers.

The pain and guilt which had gnawed at him so voraciously and patently when he first arrived had not disappeared completely. It may have been less prominent, largely anaesthetised by the enthusiasm with which he threw himself into his work, but it was still there in his eyes. It was Pepe who perhaps triggered the suppressed suffering within the Gringo to rise and effect the final tragic climax.

'Tell me señor, have you heard anything from home?

Whether the holiday complex was built, and if so if Elvis the spaniel who is a reincarnation of Elvis Presley attracts thousands of gross American tourists; or whether the Morrismen saved the holy grove of Odin from desecration; whether indeed the Morrismen carried out their threat of nuclear destruction; what happened to Joanna your niece; what happened to Emily?'

'I have no idea, Pepe. Excuse me, I must take my siesta.'

'It still pains you then?'

'Of course not, Señor García. It's all behind me now. Excuse me. I must take my siesta.'

'I did not mean to upset you in any way.'

It was a fateful siesta. That evening he came into the bar in a state of intense agitation.

'Please Señor García, a tequila.'

Yankee John looked extremely concerned. 'What's wrong, Tony boy?'

'Nothing.'

He stepped on stage to the customary applause. But there was none of his peacock posturing and cocky jack-the-lad walk. He was shambling, head down, hesitant at first, laden.

He stood silently for a full thirty seconds, gaunt and distant on the edge of the spotlight, his eyes hidden in deep shadows, frozen. Here and there a nervous giggle from his loyal audience, then a low murmuring.

He leant forward and reached for the microphone. The spotlight reflected in his glazed eyes, and as he drew breath to speak, a cock crowed by the river. The darkness around us seemed deeper now and the bar was silent once more.

'This afternoon, I'm taking my siesta. And my mother's ghost visited me while I slept.'

He proceeded, and there was an eerie feel to the performance. For although alone on stage, he spoke in many voices, and it seemed for all the world that, when he did so, it was not mere impersonation, but rather as if another spirit inhabited his body: his voice and physical movement changed completely; it was impossible not to know immediately which character was speaking at any moment.

'Enjoying your siesta are you, Tony? Enjoying your siesta and your cheroot in the shade are you?'

'Mother?'

'Who else? I've been watching you, my lad. Drinking less day by day, integrating yourself into the life of the community ... herding the goats, having a laugh with people, don't think I didn't notice you the other day helping the rest of the villagers put up that barn – who do you think you are – Harrison Ford?'

'That's none of your business.'

'Haven't you been wondering what's happening back home since you left, Tony?'

'No, no I haven't. It means nothing to me now! Here is where I belong. Now go away. We're watching *The Return of the Jedi* this afternoon.'

'Ooh,' cooed Mrs Womersley. 'On video?'

'No, laser disc. And it's the twentieth-anniversary cut.'

'Crikey ...'

'Mrs Womersley! Be quiet!'

'Sorry.'

'So you never wonder what happened to Emily?'

'N . . . no.'

His mother laughed. 'Come on Tony, I've something to show you.'

'She took me up into the clouds. I saw the village and the volcano disappearing, smaller and smaller as we rose . . . and then . . . and then we were back!'

He hesitated.

'Back where?' came an impatient voice from the crowd.

He could barely voice the word. 'Home,' he said.

A vulture strutted along the ridgepole of the outside toilet and shook its wings.

She took me back in time: I saw myself boarding the plane that brought me here, and then she ran the whole scene backwards: me, travelling from the airport with my father until I saw myself running backwards into the Whippet and Woodbine as the Virgin Mary was reconstructing the damaged interior by absorbing thunderbolts into her fingers.

Then Quintillia jumped the action forwards again, but we stayed inside the pub, observing. The Virgin hurled her thunderbolts out again.

I saw all the people who wanted to kill me stop in their tracks, the pub being smashed to pieces . . .

As the smoke cleared, Dave and the militiamen gaped in awe at the devastation. Then one of them said 'Bugger Odin, that's what I call a seriously hard deity.' And then they knelt before her. The Virgin pointed at Kropotkin and incinerated him. Possibly the only example ever of a religious figure carrying out an unequivocally good act on behalf of mankind. I saw Natasha greedily admiring Dave's huge biceps before collapsing into his arms in a calculated faint. I hope they're happy . . . Next we followed the Virgin as she left the pub. She made a beeline for the Graceland Kennel Mansion, and arranged a meeting with my father and Elvis and Colonel Parker, the rooster.

'And she struck them down with thunderbolts for their blasphemy?' asked Conchita, excitedly.

'No, she cut a deal.'

'Cut a deal?'

'Two solo numbers in the middle of Elvis's show when it starts, equal representation in the souvenir shops.'

Then it was the next day, at the camp on the moor. There was Jane, at a distance, flanked by Elvis and the Madonna, shouting out details of the deal through a megaphone. And the Morrismen . . . the Morrismen filed out and took the job that was offered to them – providing security for the new development and substantial reductions on their time in purgatory if they signed a no-strike agreement.

The other protesters stayed a little longer, but their muscle was gone, not to mention their morale.

We skipped forwards to the next day. The militiamen had all decided to convert to Catholicism in deference to the Virgin's destructive powers, and were filing solemnly up the hill that led to the Priory of the Holy Brothers of the Blessed Distillery.

'And look, Tony, look who that is being shown out of the back door.'

It was Obadiah, who was shaking hands with the prior.

Tony stepped to the side of the stage, vomited, took another glass of water and continued.

The prior is beaming. Pleased as Punch. 'Nice to see you again, Mr Hardstaff, and what a generous donation. I'm sure the brothers here will enjoy spreading the gospel all the more in their brand new Lamborghinis.'

'Always a pleasure, Prior Paisley.'

'Now is there anything I can do for you?'

'Well now that you come to mention it, there is. In about half an hour, six hundred burly Morrismen will arrive here to convert to Catholicism, Father Paisley. When they take confession, perhaps you could see your way to telling them to work for me by way of a penance.'

'No problem.'

'Lovely. If you could suggest they did it for low wages, I'm sure I could arrange to take care of that coach trip to Madam Jojos you've been saving up for.'

'Consider it done, you wily protestant heretic you.'

'Then she took me forward several months, showed me Ludolf Moor, covered in a huge plastic dome. An opening ceremony, with brass bands, limousines, male strippers in hard hats . . . men in suits with mobile phones . . . hundreds of adoring Elvis fans from all four corners of the globe . . . get me some water please.'

He drank copiously and it was some minutes before he could continue.

'The natural heritage exhibition – a huge replica of a

Yorkshire moor made in the latest space age hard-wearing plastics ... several golf courses themed on the spiritual precepts of the world's major religions. A huge statue of my father bestriding the entrance hall. There were hotels, monorails, theme parks, all staffed by workers who had signed no-strike deals with management. And a huge concert hall, where Elvis the Spaniel performed to a star-studded celebrity audience ... I saw my father's bank accounts filling with money, electronic figures with the noughts whizzing up and up. Noughts and commas filling up whole mainframe computers ...'

He paused again.

'Then I was listening to my sister and my father, in a different location, possibly the House. They were sitting back in huge leather armchairs, sipping brandy from huge balloons and smiling.

'You know what makes me happiest in a way, Dad,' said Jane.

'What?'

'What we did to Tony's secret trysting place down there by the beck, where he and that batty Emily Earnshaw whiled away the summer afternoons, making love and dreaming of opening a high quality chip shop: if he ever came back and saw we'd built a branch of the Mechanically-Recovered Meat Emporium on it, it'd kill him.'

'Aye. Never let it be said I'm not alive to sentiment, and how to stamp it into pieces,' smiled Obadiah.

And the worst thing of all? It was my father, my father's voice, my father's mannerisms, except physically, it wasn't my father, it was Jeff, my brother-in-law, but it was my father . . . gloating and pleased with himself. He had succeeded with the brain transplant. How did Jeff disappear? Again my mother changed the scene, taking us back in time to show me the crucial moment. It's a few months before. There's been an accident up on the moor. A couple of the protesters are in hospital; they've fallen out of a tree platform; they're in hospital with broken bones, and one of them has lost a lot of blood. Landed on an upturned didgeridoo apparently and she shows me – my mother this is – she shows Obadiah, my father, this must be a few days earlier, they're in the office together, and Obadiah says to Jeff it might be a good idea for public relations, a good photo-opportunity, if he gave blood for this guy, just to show that, although they're on different sides of an ecological dispute, they still respect each other as human beings. So Jeff agrees, naturally, but once he's in the hospital they give him a sedative, and cart him off to Switzerland in a crate. Next day my dad announces he has to go to Switzerland on business. Tells my sister Jeff's gone on ahead. Three weeks later, he comes back, on his own. Or rather he comes back on his own, in Jeff's body.

Jane meets him at the airport. Naturally, she says, 'Where's my dad?'

And Jeff smiles, except it's not his smile, it's my dad's. And Jane clocks this right away. She stands there. She remembers. Then she starts screaming.

'Now now, Jane . . . you'll get another one. It's for the good of the firm. Now come on, there's work to be done.' And he leads her off to the car.

Tony stared at the audience, letting it sink in. 'That's the kind of family I come from. My father is Dr Frankenstein and the fucking monster rolled into one.

'And my sister stops screaming and takes it all in her stride.'

'But Joanna. She's not given up? Surely she's still keeping the flame?' called a voice from the darkness.

Tony smiled sardonically.

'Oh yes. Joanna . . . she showed me Joanna.'

The scene changed once more. We were now in a television studio, packed to the gunnels with drunken, extrovert teenagers. Joanna was in front of a camera, asking a famous young footballer his opinions on female circumcision while smearing him in baby oil on a huge four-poster bed.

'Yes,' said Quintillia. 'She's become a Late Night Yoof TV Presenter.'

'Stop!' begged Tony. 'I don't want to see any more.'

'I can make you appear to her now if you'd like – look, it's four thirty in the morning and she's locked in the bathroom of her Holland Park maisonette, gripped in a cocaine-induced paranoia, cramming quaaludes in by the fistful and trying to recognise the person in the mirror while her boyfriend's in the lounge trying to get his leg over with her best friend amongst the pizza boxes and the empty vodka bottles . . . There – she thinks you're a hallucination.'

'Joanna . . .'

'Uncle Tony? Oh God – is that really you? Look at me Uncle Tony – look at the state of me. And it's all your fault! You betrayed us all – I thought you were a role model, and you turned into just another Hardstaff. If there was no hope for you, there was no hope for me . . . With my rebellious streak and my passion for rock and roll and John Hegley, I could have been the next Patti Smith, but you disillusioned me – I lost all self-respect . . . and sold out to the junk end of popular culture. Look at me now – nothing matters but money and fame, and I'm coining it, notorious for flashing my navel stud on telly and flirting with Jack Nicholson and being incapable of reading an autocue.'

'No!!!'

'I'm going out with someone from an Australian soap opera . . .'

'No!!!!!'

'He's got blond streaks . . . and we're going to do a musical together.'

'No no.'

'Here I am in the *Daily Mirror* promoting Bingo cards.'

'And look – here's her first photo-spread in *Loaded* – showing her breasts in the sincere belief that it's empowering in a post-feminist ironic kind of way.'

'And what of Emily?' we cried.

'That's all for tonight,' said Tony abruptly. 'I will conclude tomorrow.' And he left the stage.

Two hours later, when the audience had all left, feeling cheated but resigned to having to wait twenty-four hours for the next episode, the regulars sat round Tony at the bar. He was drinking tequila so hard that Dr Herradura offered to administer it by intravenous drip – to reduce the flow.

'It's time for me to go. I can't bear it – all my good intentions gone so horribly wrong . . . Only one thing could bring me back now – Emily's forgiveness. I threw away her love, and there is nothing left for me now.'

'But Tony, there is always hope,' said the priest.

'Oh really? Well unless she comes running out of that jungle and says she forgives me, nothing will stop me.'

Tony cancelled the next evening's performance, and it was only by hastily booking the acclaimed Lap Dancing Sloths of Estremadura that we avoided a full-scale riot from the disappointed punters.

The next few days, Tony's condition deteriorated badly. He spent more and more time drinking heavily, running up to the volcano, ranting, beating himself.

Messalina took him up the mountain to try an old Inca cure for depression, carrying stones to drop on the Cairn of Discarded Cares, where Pacamama the Earth Mother takes away our earthly woes and absorbs them into the rocks. It did not seem to work, although Yankee John seemed to think there was some potential in marketing the idea in Los Angeles and began researching franchising laws on the Internet.

On the days when he would cut down on his drinking and eat sensibly, it was no better – he was still like a man possessed, and he would spend hours sketching plans for fish and chip shops, which Pepe would then convert into more technical drawings.

'What is the purpose of this unusual alcove between the counter and the cold cupboard?' asked the postman.

'Oh, that's where Emily's embalmed father would sit in the place of honour.'

'You don't think perhaps that an embalmed corpse by the counter would affect the sale of pickled eggs?'

'Perhaps, but it would have made Emily happy. And that's more important.'

'And did your mother show you Emily?'

'Worst of all she showed me Emily.' He paused, staring straight out ahead. It seemed as if he felt the utter darkness of the forest as if its immense black silence reflected his state of mind.

'It is as if the immense black silence of the forest reflects my state of mind,' he said, slowly.

Somewhere in the canopy a mammal howled abruptly.

Reflexively we all sipped our drinks, saying nothing.

Then an expression of curiosity broke out across Pepe's face, heralding one of his ingenuous and fatuous questions.

'So if the darkness of the forest reflects your inner mood, what did the scream of that creature represent?'

'No, no, fair question,' said Tony, noticing the rest of us rolling our eyes to heaven. 'That would be the terrible pain I feel at the vision of Emily my mother showed me: she has been driven into poverty and forced into working in the Mechanically-Recovered Meat Emporium, serving chips.' He hung his head, and did not speak again for four days.

Pepe on the other hand was very excited at the deduction he had made of a connection between the life of the forest and Tony's mind, and continually inferred the mood of the latter from the activity of the former. He would stand outside the bar, watching the trees, making notes at each and every cry, call, shaking of branches, and then stroll across to give us his findings.

Every morning we would find Tony on the floor of his hut, comatose upon the Inca rug that some say still bears the imprints of the feet of Che, and drag him down to the waterfall to revive in the freezing water. Yankee John was beside himself, trying to get Tony back together.

'Come on Tony, you can't afford this kind of substance abuse until after we've landed the movie deal.'

Father Ramón remonstrated with Messalina, accusing her of giving Tony the *ayahuasca* in a deliberate attempt to destabilise his mind.

Yankee John threatened to sue her. She pointed out it had been his idea.

One morning, on a day when Tony had disappeared on walkabout, a handsome, waif-like blonde girl walked into the bar. She sat at a quiet table all through the morning, reading a paperback or gazing absently into the distance, avoiding all eye-contact. When periodically she gestured me over to order another drink, I attempted to engage her in conversation, but she was reticent. I politely enquired if she was English, which she admitted, at which point I casually remarked we had an Englishman living in the village. For an instant she betrayed an excited interest, and then returned to her book.

I had a hunch . . . could this be Emily? Apart from being blonde and attractive, she bore no resemblance to Tony's description of her, which made me all the more certain I could be right. Then Conchita began frying chips on the range, and the newcomer was captivated by a more than passing interest.

'Forgive me señorita, but is your name Emily Earnshaw?'

She looked at me, obviously staggered. 'What?'

'It was the way you were watching those chips being fried.'

'I don't know what you mean.'

'I do not wish to pry, señorita. All I will say is that if your name is Emily Earnshaw, then I believe you have come to the place you seek.'

Yankee John came into the bar, saw Emily and dropped his mobile phone. 'Emily Earnshaw!! You're an absolute ringer for Tony's description. I don't believe this. This is so wild. Señor García, do you realise who this is?'

'John, please, the lady does not wish to be disturbed.'

But John was not to be denied. He sat Emily down, bade me bring them two beers, smiled at her and said:

'I just want to say this. In the Andes there are six thousand different types of potato.'

She gave the look of someone who had never heard this particular fact used to begin a conversation.

'What I'm saying is, think of all the opportunities for research and development in the deep fried potato area! I think you could be very happy here.'

He told her that Tony was living here, that he still loved her, and that all he lived for was the cathartic moments he spent on stage telling his terrible story in an effort to rid himself of his guilt and pain.

'But he does have a real talent for holding the stage, you

know? Once the catharsis thing is worked out, I'm planning to take him a bit more mainstream. May I assume you're here to make him crave and beg forgiveness?'

'You can assume that.'

'Great, great. Great! The power of love to redeem us. It's beautiful. The perfect third act. He has a great future, if we can just stop him from killing himself – which right now is not a small problem, not a small problem. I have to tell you, he's going through a very bad patch right now. But that's the price you pay for that talent, right? And when I say talent, and mainstream, I'm not talking totally showbiz you understand, moms and dads, primetime, absolutely not, don't get me wrong, just a little more accessible is what I'm saying. Still hip, but less full-on confessional. I see a one-man show, the Village, San Francisco, Europe. Places the audience still has an attention span. I see movies, given the right role. I'm trying to get someone from William Morris to come down here, but you know what they're like. Or maybe you don't. They won't travel to see a show in the Valley, let alone in the middle of the South American jungle.

'But, I do have some friends of mine coming to shoot the show next week – super sixteen, just a demo you know. Cos he's flying at the moment, flying. Some of the stuff he's told us about you, so moving . . . he loves you, believe me, he loves you.'

Emily betrayed no reaction.

Yankee John was too excited to notice. 'But you know what could be great – the fact you're here . . . it's just too beautiful . . . I would love you to – you're here to see him right? If you came out tonight when he was on stage . . . I mean you're a cult figure round here, a cult figure, baby, that's what you are: your story, you know, it moves people . . . the idea of the reconciliation happening on stage . . . it would be – you remember when Marley is on stage in Jamaica during the elections – you remember, or maybe you don't – OK, April 1978 it was, that election campaign, it's intense. Intense! There's people actually shooting each other in the streets of West Kingston, so Marley plays a gig at the National Stadium as a plea for peace, and he brings the two candidates – Malcolm Manley and Edward Seaga – on stage . . . it's dusk and as he joins their hands above his head – at the very moment he brings their hands together, there's a clap of thunder and a bolt of lightning: that's what it would be like with you and Tony on stage together . . . bigger maybe . . . what do you say?'

'I'm tired, it's been a long journey. I must rest. Please don't tell Tony I'm here.'

'Are you kidding? I can't wait to see the look of surprise on his face when you step out there and tell him you love him. I'm crying, I'm crying. This is too beautiful. A happy ending, just like in the movies.'

'I will consider what you have told me,' she replied simply. 'Señor García, I believe you said you had a room?'

'Conchita will show you, señorita.'

That night, the bar began to fill very early.

John had been busy leafleting the outlying settlements, and we were offering a three-for-one drink happy hour from six until eight. (Tony generally came on stage about ten.)

The film crew had been setting up all afternoon, and as the sun set and oozed suddenly into the sea their extra lights cast the stage with an eerie detached focus, as if it belonged somewhere else.

By seven thirty, John was getting nervous. He had been making frantic phone calls all afternoon, and was reasonably confident of negotiating an *Oprah* special featuring just Tony and Emily: My Girlfriend Tried To Kill Me When I Stopped Her Killing My Family With a Nuclear Missile.

'They're sending a researcher down tomorrow. But I'm calling Rikki Lake's people too. Always have a fall-back position.'

The only problem was, Tony was nowhere to be found. We called on the priest and Messalina to see if they could help.

'Last time I saw him was this morning.'

We found him on the summit of the volcano, staring into the void.

Our approach disturbed the vultures who were watching him with professional interest from the ruined temple fifty metres or so to our left, and they bounced and swore off in an untidy token gesture of flight to a slightly more distant vantage point. He turned round to face us.

'It's a long way down. Is it OK if I don't throw myself in?' His voice on the further side of tears, empty.

Yankee John was concerned. For his business future.

'Of course it's OK, buddy. Why would you want to throw yourself in a volcano? Come on now, we love you, ain't that right, García?'

'Er, yes.' I am uncomfortable with the way these Gringos throw that word around, especially to other men.

'Now come on Tony, let's go back down to the village and get you in a nice cold shower.'

Tony began that evening's show with a recap of the *ayahuasca* dream where his mother visited him, and then moved on.

'So, I was up on the volcano this afternoon, thinking about throwing myself in. The vultures are watching me, and I'm making a list in my head: reasons for not throwing myself in the volcano, reasons to throw myself in the volcano. The "kill myself" list was pretty long—' he counted them off on his fingers: 'addiction to gambling over my loved ones; betrayal of loved ones by acquiring other loved ones; betrayal of old friends, ruining their lives; allowing the forces of greed and darkness to conquer the forces of light; failure to reform no matter how many chances I had; and then all the smaller reasons – tendency to get drunk and bore people; tendency to think my problems are greater than anyone else's because I can relate them in an entertaining way . . . or maybe worse – maybe it's why I make them entertaining, it's a competitive thing. Listen to me, never mind his shit, look at mine! I've coiled mine into interesting shapes! Mine doesn't stink! I've done all these terrible things but you can still love me because I can confess it in an entertaining way? It makes it OK because there's a laugh on the end? Presentation is more important than substance?'

The crowd were losing their tolerance. At the bar, John could feel it. 'Come on buddy, cut to the chase!'

'So there's the Throw Myself In list, and on the Go Back Down list is . . . I'm scared it will hurt.

'So Throw Myself In is out of sight in the lead you know, and I'm hesitating, there's no rational argument should be keeping me on the edge, and these vultures are staring at me and they say to me – cos that's the great thing about *ayahuasca*, I'm a regular Doctor Doolittle now – that and the flying obviously. Which is really good, being able to see everything from a hundred feet up, it's great cos in the tourist season you can see which beaches the day-trippers are filling up – this vulture says to me, all sympathetic and caring, "Hey Tony, don't throw yourself in the volcano, man, don't do it."

'I'm getting sympathy from a vulture here, that's like a big deal, right? Because you know, they're not noted for it, so I'm thinking maybe I'm not as worthless as I think I am, even the vultures like me.

'No?'

'"No! You throw yourself in the volcano, how we going to eat you? You always thinking of yourself. It's my little girl's birthday tomorrow. I promised her a nice gobbet of Gringo intestines, poor little chick's been on nothing but dead dog for weeks now. Have a heart. At least until I can get my beak into it."

'So I came down from the mountain, without throwing myself into the crater, which I realise may not be immediately obvious from my appearance, and halfway down I'm thinking "why" and . . . all I could come up with was, well, at least I pissed off some vultures. Jesus. By the time Alexander the Great was my age he'd conquered the known world – and was dead. My achievement? I have pissed off some vultures. Temporarily. But you know, at least it adds to the list. Now I have two reasons for staying alive – scared of dying (which is really original) and . . . pissing off vultures.

'I think every woman I've ever had a relationship with I'm thinking, is this woman good enough to be the mother of my children? And the answer is no. Not if she's prepared to let me be the father.'

He reached inside his jacket for a cigarette, flipping it into his mouth from the packet in a practised move. He paused, parody of cool yet cool enough to take the applause.

'You know, people always say, "Quit smoking, you'll live longer." Like that's an incentive? I kind of like the idea. Smokers are suicides who don't have the guts to do it in one go. It's like inviting a homicidal maniac to live in your house, but you don't know when he's going to strike. He's affable, polite, helps you through moments of stress, helps prolong the post-coital glow, really freeze-frames the moment, but one day, he's going to come into your bedroom and chop you into small bits. But there's a thrill to it. Maybe you'll be one of the ones that he likes. Well, enough about me . . .' He paused to light the cigarette.

'Yes, enough about you, Tony Hardstaff!' Emily was walking through the crowd towards the stage. John was frantically signalling to the follow-spot operator to pick her up.

Tony had clearly recognised the voice. He was frozen in mid-light, thumb still maintaining the flame. Then he saw her.

'Emily?'

A gasp from the audience. They had obviously recognised her too.

Yankee John was buzzing with delight, and frantically describing the action into his mobile phone.

'Steven, just listen now! This is dynamite. I see Winona Ryder and . . . Tom Hanks . . . just listen: . . .'

He held his phone towards the stage.

'Tony, thank God I've found you. I just couldn't rest until I'd sought you out . . .'

She was on the stage now.

'How did you find me?'

'Your mother appeared to me in a precognitive dream.' We all heard the sound of a woman sniggering in the darkness somewhere. Even Messalina shivered.

'And . . . You're going to tell me you understand, that you forgive me, that you love me?'

'Dream on, cockroach.' The crowd gasps. 'You were the only man I ever loved – but you betrayed me with another – in fact two anothers! You gamble away half a million pounds of my money on a single throw, chicken out of threatening your family with nuclear weapons and leave me to try and run a fish and chip shop on my own, trample on my dreams. Think what we could have had – a thriving traditional business and one of each every night free. But no – you threw it all away because you're rotten to the core, because you're a Hardstaff. I've come here for one thing and one thing only. Vengeance! To tell you I hate you.'

Silence. Tony staggers back, sways, almost falls.

'You've come all this way, across the swamps and through the jungle, just to tell me that.'

'That's how much I hate you, Tony Hardstaff – this humid atmosphere wreaks havoc with my ringlets, but I've happily sacrificed them to drive a dagger through your heart!'

Suddenly Tony collapsed.

'No, not this . . . Emily . . . please.'

'That's right,' cried the delighted Emily. 'Writhe! Writhe in your death throes . . . writhe like an eel cast into the boiling fat of a Satterthwaite State of the Art Organic Deep-Fat Frier . . . until you lie as still as a two-day-old black pudding in flaky batter. Yes! Venegeance is mine!'

Tony fell to his knees, breathing with difficulty. He reached into the back pocket of his tailor-cut Levi's (a sartorial idiosyncrasy he had adopted in homage to Lenny Bruce) and took out a piece of paper which he held out towards Emily with a trembling hand, then collapsed face-forward as she spat at him.

The crowd gasped again. Some applauded Emily's passionate tirade. The doctor ran to Tony and attempted to revive him. Yankee John dropped his mobile phone. The priest joined Doctor Herradura on the stage and knelt beside him.

Pepe cocked an ear to the forest to try and deduce what correspondence in the natural world reflected this seizure. Conchita slapped him round the head.

The doctor felt for vital signs, looked up at the priest grimly and shook his head.

Emily stepped forward and snatched the piece of paper from the weakening fist.

The priest had ignored the doctor's solemn gesture that Tony was beyond help, and had turned the lifeless body gently on to its back, pressed his hands on to the dead man's chest.

Yankee John was banging his head against a pillar and cursing.

'Shit, shit, shit . . .'

I was moved by John's fellow feeling, if disappointed with the crudity of its expression. 'Just when he was starting to take off.'

Unfolding the paper and reading it, Emily had staggered backwards across the stage, trembling.

'"Plans for the chip shop that Emily and I never had" . . . he's even designed an alcove by the cold cupboard for the embalmed corpse of my father to preside over the whole queue . . . and property deeds for a site in Brighouse . . . in my name. He did love me. Oh, woe is me . . .'

Now our attention was pulled to the other side of the stage – where Tony was stirring.

Pepe was still attempting to decipher the language of the forest, swinging his head back to see what was happening on stage. 'An owl . . . that must mean . . . writhing . . . no . . . resurrection!' He scribbled another hasty note.

The priest was helping Tony to his feet. The crowd were amazed, as were we all. He was disorientated, in a daze, but clearly alive. Yankee John was beside himself, deliriously happy at the revival of his dear friend who had been snatched back from the jaws of death, and furiously punching numbers on his mobile phone.

'Get me Spielberg! I don't care what time it is. Tell him I have the screenplay to end all screenplays!'

At the other side of the stage, Emily moaned horribly.

'He did love me after all. And I have killed him. Woe, woe is me.' And she collapsed in a heap on the floor. The doctor ran to her, checked for life, found no signs. The priest did a double take, left Messalina supporting the swooning Tony, ran to Emily, pulling the doctor away. He laid on the hands as before.

Tony was recovering his senses. 'Where am I? Have I died?'

'No Tony, you live . . .' said Messalina.

'Where is Emily?'

'Over there!' cried the crowd, pointing. Tony looked, saw the doctor shaking his head . . .

'Is she . . .'

'I'm afraid so. But the priest . . .'

Tony collapsed.

There was an enormous cry of '*Olé*' from the crowd. Emily had risen.

'Where am I?'

'Alive, señorita.'

'But Tony . . . he's dead.'

'Just wait a second, I'll see what I can do—'

But the sight of Tony's prostrate body was too much, and she collapsed once more.

Well you get the general idea. The priest rushed over to Tony, revived him, only for him to collapse when he saw Emily lying dead beside him. Then the process was reversed, Emily collapsing with grief at the sight of the dead Tony.

Neither of them could be sustained for long enough to listen and hang on for the other to be revived. Each raising from the dead was greeted by a huge cheer from the crowd. The process continued for some time – three days in fact, until finally the priest collapsed from exhaustion and the crowd erupted into spontaneous applause.

We discussed the paradox that Ramón had performed a miracle, bringing two people back from the dead hundreds of times, outdoing the Lazarus incident by a huge factor, but all ultimately to no avail.

'I tried the best I could.'

'Perhaps they have now found peace.'

Throughout the multiple resurrection, drinks flowed freely as you may imagine, and I made a tidy profit. My customers had much sport with side bets: whether the couple would end up dead or alive, how many times they would be resurrected in total, whether Yankee John would batter himself unconscious against the wooden pillar . . . It was Conchita who predicted the correct number of multiple miracles – seven thousand two hundred and eighty-nine synchronised revivals from the dead. Come to think of it, she slipped the priest a particularly large glass of tequila just before he finally collapsed. Whether this was intended to revive him or to knock him out at the opportune moment we will never know. I have to believe it was pure coincidence rather than malice aforethought on Conchita's part. I have to. She cooks my meals.

After the funeral this morning, as we sat in the bar and drank away the afternoon, the mourners drifted away and the mood became more and more sombre. The priest, who had been silent for some hours, began to try and extract the meaning in all that had happened.

'Why seek a meaning, my love,' said Messalina. 'It just happened.'

'But if it just happened, how come I brought them back from the dead? There must have been a reason I was given this miraculous power.'

'Why?' asked Messalina.

'Because why else would I be given the power to overcome the laws of science? There must be a sign, a message, a reason in it somewhere.'

'If you look hard enough you'll find one I suppose. But it doesn't necessarily mean it was there in the first place. Just because something happens doesn't mean it has to make sense.'

'Here's the sense of it Ramón, baby: I keep telling you, I got it all on tape,' said Yankee John. 'Ever thought of moving to California? Think of it – a resurrection therapist, with video evidence? We could make a lot of money.'

The priest thought for a moment.

'You're saying God put the power of life into my body so that I could move to Los Angeles and help Yankees live longer?'

'Why else was I able to shoot the promo? It's God's way of telling us to coin it.'

Messalina took Ramón by the arm.

'Is that what you want?'

'There must have been a reason.'

'It was just one of those things. Now let's go home and go to bed.'

'What do you think, García?'

I said I didn't know. Of course, we only had the doctor's word that they were dead at all before the priest revived them, but he is one of my best customers, and in the conflict of profound metaphysical enquiry and good customer relations, I feel safer embracing the latter.

Of course, word spread throughout the region, and almost every day the priest was called out to attempt the laying on of hands for all manner of deceased. Most were recent, but some were not. Some were human, but many were farm animals, household pets. Some people even asked him to lay his hands on their video recorders and other broken household appliances. He never succeeded again, and gradually lost all authority. He was accused of racism, on the grounds that he would only carry out miracle-work on white Europeans. The priest was distraught and shattered that his briefly-held ability to act as such an incredible conduit of God's power (as he interpreted it) had brought him only ignomy and contempt from the people he loved best.

Then one day our President died. A man who had pocketed most of the country's gross national product for eighteen years and made us the world leaders in corruption. The President who had turned our country into the most feared military power in . . . inside its own borders, and the most ridiculed economy in the whole of Latin America. We had been quietly celebrating, when next day, a huge twin-rotor helicopter thundered over the hills and landed on the football pitch. Men in dark suits and sunglasses with bulging breast pockets fanned out around the aircraft. The tail door was lowered, and an enormous stretch limousine backed out down it on to the turf. From the back of the limousine, the Archbishop emerged. He was immediately recognisable from the pictures of him that had been taken in a Panamanian brothel and printed in many magazines and newspapers throughout the continent. He strode to the bar, surrounded by men in dark suits and a few token clergy. A state television crew started setting up in the bar, clearing customers out of the way as if they owned the place. One of the men in dark glasses asked me where he could find Father Ramón Gutierrez. I could not but tell them, as the barrel of a gun is a persuasive tool in gaining accurate directions. Other men in dark glasses were dispatched to the presbytery and returned some moments later with the priest and took him out to the limousine. The President's corpse was wheeled out in a fridge and the priest was told to lay on the hands. The priest had no choice. He laid on the hands, and of course, this time it worked. The priest brought the President back to life. The Archbishop was on hand to explain the significance of the event, which was why the TV cameras were there. The President's revival, explained the Archbishop, demonstrated the divine right of his rule that he and his policies were blessed from on high. The President, still a little blue but almost completely thawed, appeared beside him and announced there would be a three-day national holiday. Then they all got back into the helicopter and went away again.

Ramón was gutted. Now he had the reputation for being

the man who had not only saved the life of the maddest despot ever to rule us, but he had made his position even stronger to boot.

That night in the bar the priest sat drinking, downing glass after glass in quiet desperation. The Doctor, Messalina, Pepe, Yankee John and myself kept him silent company, while Conchita periodically tried in vain to force food upon him.

Ramón raised his eyes to the heavens, or more accurately, to the rafters.

'What new test is this, Lord? You give me back this power to give life to a bloated dictator? You give me this power which I can only carry through my utter and unshakable faith in you, only to let me exercise it in a way that makes me lose all faith in you.'

'What you lookin' at me for, pal?' squawked Hamish.

'If you have a plan, Lord, I don't see it.'

'Which is what I've been saying all along.' There was no element of impatience in Messalina's voice.

Ramón began to look on his miracle as some kind of sick joke played on him by the Higher Power, but refused to lose his faith. Possibly it all showed Tony's incredible talent for destroying all that he came across.

'Maybe God is punishing me for marrying you.'

'Thanks a lot.'

'Well . . .'

'Maybe he's just telling you you have to decide between us.'

'OK, Messalina OK, let's quit trying to make sense of it already!'

'Now you're getting it. Come on, I'll take you home for a nice massage.' And she led him gently by the hand back to the cool adobe confines of the presbytery.

His congregation now resented him totally. They could not believe his power was random and outwith his control. They believed his failure to resurrect any of the loved ones they brought to him was a calculated insult. It was more than he could bear. Yankee John continued to insist that the solution was to go to Los Angeles and get rich.

Ramón remarked that he was seriously considering the idea.

Messalina was scathing. 'That's right: go to Los Angeles; make your fortune; desert your flock! Confirm their belief that you have abandoned them to serve the rich and power-ful. Or do you perhaps have the courage to battle with adversity, to stay here where you belong, and have faith that in time they will come to see that you are just as fallible as the rest of us, and that you have the strength to bear your cruel burden, that your suffering can help soothe theirs?'

The bar broke out in spontaneous applause. The priest was convinced, renewed in his struggle by the words of the woman who loved him. And who next day left him a note explaining she had gone to Los Angeles with Yankee John to make her fortune as California's first Cairn-of-Discarded-Cares Therapist.

Ramón was stoical.

'It is just another test from the Lord.' There was a calmness in his voice as he unconsciously tore the note into tiny pieces. 'I shall not lose my faith. I shall take solace from the Book of Job. He suffered far more than I, and at the last was received into the kingdom. Excuse me, I'm going for a walk up the mountain.'

Twelve hours later we found him, high up on the cold upper pastures just below the snow line, prostrate in the couch grass, unconscious, with a fractured skull. Beside him lay a large, bloodstained half-melted block of ice. When the ice had melted completely, we found inside it a Holy Bible.

The mystery was only solved when the local paper arrived ten days later. Conchita drew my attention to a small article on page eight.

'While blessing the bathroom on El Presidente's new luxury Lear Jet, Archbishop Mantilla inadvertently dropped his personal Bible down the revolutionary new lavatory bowl. It was custom-made for our mighty leader and is the largest-diameter toilet bowl ever installed on a civil aircraft anywhere in the world. Its size is a testament to the mightiness of our leader and our beloved homeland, for only a strong and mighty country could produce and sustain a leader with such princely buttocks of a size not seen since giants walked the earth. Indeed it surely proves that our beloved Presidente is a direct descendant of mighty Hercules. It is believed the Bible will have fallen to earth somwhere in the remote Mondongo region . . .'

'I don't know about you Señor García, but that's what I call bad luck,' said Conchita.

'I call it cruel, Conchita. What has the priest done to deserve such a fate? Ramón's creator has been having sadistic fun at his expense. Still, I suppose we must draw what good we can from the matter.'

'And what would that be?'

'Simply, to appreciate our own comparative good fortune and consider our own problems and regrets as relatively minor. We can never experience more sadness and misfortune than poor Father Ramón.'

I should have known my words would have flown straight to the ears of the Gods of Providence, for the very next day we suffered more disappointment than Ramón and Tony put together – and I do not exaggerate through self-pity. But judge for yourself.

There had been much discussion about whether we should club together to go on a village outing to watch The King performing in the Grimedale Weatherdome, and we were torn between the desire to seize an historic opportunity, and the distasteful prospect of betraying the memory of our dear departed Tony by swelling the coffers of his hateful and terrible family. Of course, in the end there was no contest. Imagine then our utter desolation, when we made further inquiries and could find no such place as Grimedale featured on the map. No travel agent had ever heard of it. We searched Tony's belongings for some clue, but there was nothing, apart from the notes in his personal organiser, and the photo of Emily. His passport gave his birthplace as Heckmondwike, Yorkshire. Which led us to wonder, what was true about Tony's story, apart from his love for Emily? Conchita was furious that she had been taken in for so long by a liar. Had he made it all up? What were the real circumstances of his tortured life? If his story had been less arresting, would we have listened to his outpourings of pain and despair? I recall a passage from Yankee John's doctoral thesis, which he forced me to read at gunpoint one drunken Christmas:

'A baby cries for attention and its cries are responded to because we know it is helpless. With age, with the onset of language and apparent autonomy, our cries for unconditional attention must become more artful in order to elicit the same imperative of sympathy from those around us.'

Personally I think a slap round the face and a simple exhortation to get on with it is more acceptable.

Whatever the true facts, Tony's grave is still worshipped by the Indians as a site sacred to their Torqnbllx, God of Diversion from the Prospect of the Void.

People will believe what they want to believe.

A few days later a gringo tourist came into the bar and ordered a beer. He wore a T-shirt with a terse two-word slogan emblazoned across it . . . And I thought to myself, after all the noble efforts man has made to explain and understand his world and his fate, perhaps it can all be reduced to that ostensibly asinine message.

The priest, who was sitting silently at the bar (he never speaks much these days), chuckled sardonically into his whisky as he read the words aloud:

'Shit Happens.'

And he chuckled again.

We all wonder of course, as good Christians, if Tony's and Emily's spirits live on beyond the grave, and whether they found happiness at last; if perhaps Tony had finally seen through his pointless and self-destructive addictions to gambling and philandering, and learnt to value what he already had. We wonder, if, like Tony's Elvis, their physical longings prompted them to possess the body of a living creature. It sounds preposterous, I know. However, in recent days, since the death of the two lovers, a pair of beautiful parakeets has been present in the trees around the bar and the town square. Initially timid, they now quite often perch close to the tables. (Hamish does not approve.) One of the pair has been known to accept a small sip of tequila, the other seems fascinated whenever Conchita is preparing fried fish. They seem devoted to one another, although the other day I thought I saw the male preening and displaying his plumage to another female, while his mate stood and watched from the next tree, squawking plaintively. The male parrot also enjoys hopping down on to a table and picking out lottery numbers with its beak, while its neglected mate watches from their nest and bangs her head against the branches in frustration . . . and I have recurrent nightmares in which the male parakeet learns how to talk . . .

ISLA DEWAR

Giving Up on Ordinary

When Megs became a cleaner, she didn't realise that if people looked at her a cleaner would be all they saw. Megs has as full a life as the people she does for, Mrs Terribly Clean Pearson or Mrs Oh-Just-Keep-It-Above-The Dysentery-Line McGhee. She's the mother of three children and still mourning the death of a son; she enjoys a constant sparring match with her mother; she drinks away her troubles with Lorraine, her friend since Primary One; and she sings the blues in a local club.

Megs has been getting by. But somehow that's not enough any more. It's time Megs gave up on being ordinary . . .

'Explosively funny and chokingly poignant . . . extraordinary' *Scotland on Sunday*

'Observant and needle sharp . . . entertainment with energy and attack' *The Times*

'A remarkably uplifting novel, sharp and funny' *Edinburgh Evening News*

0 7472 5550 4

review

BEN RICHARDS

Don't Step On The Lines

In a flat high above London Kerry can't stop re-membering Gary. Marco awaits the pleasures and temptations of summer in the city . . .

Kerry, finally taking control of her life, has returned to college to study English. Marco, friend and flat-mate, deeply obsessed with sharks, roams the bars and clubs of London. Drifting in and out of various jobs, relationships and drugs, he watches Kerry's progress with a mixture of love and envy.

Then Robin appears. For Kerry, Robin – rich, good-looking, a fellow student – represents new opportuni-ties and possibilities. For Marco, however, he is nothing but trouble.

'Scenes of London life sparkle within the narrative . . . It's all wonderfully recognisable and realistic, told with a laddish exuberance at once hilarious and touching' *Literary Review*

'Kerry is a proper nineties heroine: bright, lovely, struggling to define her life' *Mail on Sunday*

'Refreshingly unpretentious and very entertaining' *The Times*

'The London he sees is vivid and impressive' *TLS*

'A terrific book' *Time Out*

0 7472 5280 7

review